Leather, Lace and Lust

Putting It On to Get Off

Leather, Lace and Lust

Putting It On to Get Off

Edited by M. Christian
and Sage Vivant

HEAT
NEW YORK, NEW YORK

THE BERKLEY PUBLISHING GROUP
Published by the Penguin Group
Penguin Group (USA) Inc.
375 Hudson Street, New York, New York 10014, USA
Penguin Group (Canada), 90 Eglinton Avenue East, Suite 700, Toronto, Ontario M4P 2Y3, Canada
(a division of Pearson Penguin Canada Inc.)
Penguin Books Ltd., 80 Strand London WC2R 0RL, England
Penguin Group Ireland, 25 St. Stephen's Green, Dublin 2, Ireland (a division of Penguin Books Ltd.)
Penguin Group (Australia), 250 Camberwell Road, Camberwell, Victoria 3124, Australia
(a division of Pearson Australia Group Pty. Ltd.)
Penguin Books India Pvt. Ltd., 11 Community Centre, Panchsheel Park, New Delhi—110 017, India
Penguin Group (NZ), Cnr. Airborne and Rosedale Roads, Albany, Auckland 1310, New Zealand
(a division of Pearson New Zealand Ltd.)
Penguin Books (South Africa) (Pty.) Ltd., 24 Sturdee Avenue, Rosebank, Johannesburg 2196, South Africa

Penguin Books Ltd., Registered Offices: 80 Strand, London WC2R 0RL, England

These are works of fiction. Names, characters, places, and incidents either are the product of the authors' imagination or are used fictitiously, and any resemblance to actual persons, living or dead, business establishments, events, or locales is entirely coincidental. The publisher does not have any control over and does not assume any responsibility for author or third-party websites or their content.

PRINTING HISTORY
Venus Book Club trade paperback edition / 2003
Heat trade paperback edition / December 2005

Library of Congress Cataloging-in-Publication Data

Leather, lace and lust : putting it on to get off / edited by M. Christian and Sage Vivant.—
    Heat trade pbk. ed.
        p. cm.
    ISBN 0-425-20540-1
    1. Erotic stories, American. 2. Fetishism (Sexual behavior)—Fiction. 3. Clothing and dress—Fiction. I. Christian, M. II. Vivant, Sage.

PS648.E7L43 2005
813'.0108358—dc22   2005050464

PRINTED IN THE UNITED STATES OF AMERICA

10 9 8 7 6 5 4 3 2 1

Contents

Introduction

For writers, fantasy consumes an especially large part of our waking hours. We want to craft stories to suit our literary needs as well as the audience's desires. When we write about sexual situations, we don't begin with naked people.

That would just be crass.

Instead, we start with scenes where clothes are carefully chosen to entice, where the glimpse of shoulder, wrist, or belly button sets a heart to palpitating, and where one person goes to great lengths to convince another that the clothes simply must come off *now*.

For readers, fantasy consumes a commendably large part of your waking hours. When you read about sexual situations, you don't want your stories to begin with naked people.

That would just be boring.

Nudity is fine, nudity is great, but when it appears without preamble, it often makes people recoil. In fiction, as in life, you want to get to know a person first. You want to know why he's chosen to wear what he has. What does the attractive woman in the accounting department think about when she selects the ruffled blouse over the tailored one? How does her body move in what she wears and why are you even thinking about that?

When Victorian fashions covered nearly every inch of the body, any small patch of exposed skin—an ankle, a wrist, the nape of a neck—was an erotic opportunity. When Catwoman circled Batman in her eponymously named attire, it was what we couldn't see that left us curious and breathless. Why? Because the sex of our imaginations, the bodies we see in our dreams, is usually much hotter than anything in real life.

Clothing can be fun, mysterious, sexy, dangerous, expensive, flimsy, unwashed, billowy, stolen, understated, tight, or outrageous. We may be eager to see what's under it all, but we're also happy to hold off the revelation, to bask in anticipation. In that way, clothing can be seen as a prelude to sex or, in the case of strangers we see from afar, it's a replacement for or alternative to sex.

There's a reason why the fashion industry is a multimillion-dollar one. Clothing is our visual message to the world. It speaks for us and to us. It gives us the freedom to express moods, desires, needs, and peccadilloes. We can use it and we can hide behind it. Through our attire, we can become someone else or reveal aspects of ourselves that words cannot.

The stories in this book run the gamut of clothing's influence on our sexual personas, interactions, and minds. You'll read about Pavlovian responses to footwear, perfectly respectable undergarments that incite private riots, and dressing up to confuse or otherwise discombobulate. Here you'll learn about new venues for haute

Introduction

couture and how fabrics can be friend or foe. In short, you'll read about how effective an aphrodisiac clothing can really be.

All in all, we're a race of strangely modest life forms, so clothing is here to stay. Fortunately, we're also a race of inexhaustibly horny people who will always find ways to make clothing an erotic experience. So, covered or exposed, we're all in for a good time.

M. Christian
Sage Vivant
San Francisco, 2003

Killing the Marabou Slippers

BY MOLLY LASTER

They looked like any other innocent pair of bedroom slippers. But maybe they weren't quite so innocent. Maybe they knew what they were doing all along. You've seen the type—smug in their open-toedness. Willful in their daring high-heeled glory. Decadently trimmed with a bit of tender white marabou fluff on the front, just to get your attention.

I'd never owned shoes like these before. Sure, I'd seen versions of them in the Frederick's of Hollywood catalog, insolently positioned with toe toward the camera, daring the casual pursuer to purchase them. And I'd even drooled over such fantasy footwear when worn by my favorite forties screen stars: Myrna Loy. Claudette Colbert. Garbo. But those women had the clothes to go with the shoes—angel-sleeved nightgowns with three-foot trains, tight satin slips with plunging necklines. Such sexy slippers weren't meant for someone like me—a girl who owns plain white bra-and-panty sets, who wears

Gap sweats to bed, whose one experience with a pair of black fishnets was a comedic disaster. What purpose could a pair of wayward shoes like these possibly have?

Still, when I caught sight of the immoral mules at a panty sale in San Francisco, I bought them. Even though they were a size eight and I'm a size six. Even though I found the very sight of them fairly wicked. Even though my own bedroom slippers at home were made of plaid flannel and had been chewed on repeatedly by my golden retriever puppy.

I simply thought Lucas would like them.

He did.

"I'm gonna fuck those shoes," he said when I pulled them from the silver Mylar bag. "Sweetheart, those shoes are history."

I'd never seen him react like that to anything. My tall, handsome, green-eyed husband has a healthy libido. I definitely get my share of bedroom romping time. But as far as kinkiness goes, he has always appeared positively fetish-free. No requests for handcuffs. No need for teddies or "special" outfits to get him in the mood. No urgent trips to Safeway at midnight for whipped cream, chocolate sauce, and maraschino cherries.

"Put them on," Lucas hissed. "Now."

I kicked off my patent leather penny-loafers, pulled off my black stockings, and slid into the marabou mules. The white bit of fluff on the toes made the shoes look like some sort of pastry, a fantasy confection created just for feet. My red toenails peeked through the opening. Dirty, I thought. Indecent.

Lucas got on the floor and kissed my exposed toes, stroked the soft feathery tips of the shoes, then stood and quickly shed his outfit.

"They're bad," he said excitedly, positioning himself over my feet as if preparing to do push-ups. He's ex-military and has excellent formation for this activity—his body becomes stiff and board-like. The sleek muscles in his back shift becomingly under his tan skin. In this position, his straining cock went directly between the two mules.

"Oh, man," he whispered. "So bad they're good."

He went up and down over my shoes, digging his cock between them, dragging it over the marabou trim, sighing with delight when the feathers got between his legs. I could only imagine how those pale white feathers tickled his most sensitive organ.

"They're so soft," he murmured.

I'd been staring down at him, at his fine ass—clenching with each depraved push-up—at his strong back, the muscles rippling. Now, I looked straight ahead, into the full-length mirror across the room, taking in the total effect of our afternoon of debauchery.

I was fully dressed: long black skirt, black mock turtleneck, my dark hair in a refined ponytail, small spectacles in place. If you ended the reflection at my shins, you might have placed me for exactly what I am, an editor at an educational publishing company. Below my shins, however, was Lucas, doing ungodly push-ups over my brand-new shoes. My slim ankles were bare, feet sliding slightly in the too-big marabou-trimmed mules. If you disregarded the shoes, and imagined Lucas moving in stop-frame animation, he might have been culled from a series of Eadweard Muybridge pictures. But with the shoes in place, and with Lucas's body moving rigidly up and down, this picture looked more like something from a fantastic pornographic movie.

I stared at our images and felt myself growing more and more aroused. My plain white panties were suddenly too containing. My skirt and sweater needed to come off. Arousal rushed through me in a shuddering wave. But I kept my peace—this wasn't my fantasy, wasn't my moment. It was Lucas's. All his.

He began speaking louder, first lauding the shoes, "Sweet, so sweet." Then criticizing the slippers as he slammed between them, "Oh, you're bad . . . bad."

I stayed as still as possible, watching in awe as Lucas, approaching his limit, arched up and sat back on his heels, his hand working his cock in double-time. Small bits of pure white feathers were stuck to the sticky tip of his swollen penis. More feather fluffs floated in the air around us.

"Give me one of the shoes," he demanded, and I kicked off the right slipper. One hand still wrapped around his cock, he used the other to lift the discarded shoe and began rubbing the tip of it between his legs, moaning and sighing, his words no longer legible, no longer necessary. Then, suddenly, as if inspiration had hit him, he reached behind his body with the shoe, poking the heel of it between the cheeks of his ass, impaling himself with the slipper while he dragged the tip of his cock against the shoe I still wore.

I watched closely as his breathing caught, as he leaned back further still and then came, ejaculating on the slipper before him, coating those naughty feathers with semen, matting the feathers into a sticky mess. Showing them once and for all who was boss.

When he had relaxed enough to speak, he looked up at me, a sheepish expression on his face. "Told you those shoes were history," he said, red-cheeked. Embarrassed. "Told you, baby, didn't I?"

I just nodded, thinking to myself: The death of an innocent pair of marabou slippers. What'd the shoes ever do to Lucas? Nothing, but exist.

When Calls Ed Wood

BY TOM PICCIRILLI

The cats were up in the pomegranate trees again wailing their scrawny asses off next door. They did it at least twice a week, but by now I'd grown used to their prolonged screeching. It reminded me of ambulance sirens in New York and even made me a little homesick.

Monty's place had two main floors, an attic and a mother-in-law apartment around the rear. The landlord and his wife lived in the house proper, but they were always on the run in Mexico from drug dealers they'd burned in East L.A. Monty Stobbs stayed in the attic, and I lived out back directly below his window. He wouldn't waste time walking down all the stairways and would just call me on my cell phone.

I'd left New York after having a couple of shows presented off-off Broadway. They were both well-received by critics but didn't draw enough of an audience to stay afloat for long. Monty Stobbs had been hustling the same backers that the director had been hustling, and he'd invited me to come stay with him in Hollywood to write him a screenplay.

I wasn't naïve enough to believe it might amount to anything, but for the first time in my life I was desperate enough to fall into the starry-eyed Hollywood trap. I was being evicted and my wife had left the year before. She'd taken the kid, the dog, and the goldfish, but she'd left me with a case of crabs. The fuckers were so big I could identify them well enough to give them names, and after the cream started to work and they died off, I fell into sobbing fits. So there wasn't much holding me in New York.

The script had started off as a joke, which is bad in Hollywood. Nobody at the major studios has a sense of humor, and the small production companies are always looking for the next Ed Wood, something so awful it'll be a hot property in video units and when it shows up on late night cable. Manufactured cult films.

The script was called *Critter from Beyond the Edge of Space* and the pages smelled like beer. I'd drink myself into oblivion every night trying to figure out how I'd gone from writing my historical novel about the Trail of Tears to this piece of shit in front of me.

My phone rang and I picked it up. "What?"

"Listen, you need to rewrite a little."

"Monty, why don't you just shout out the window, you're using up minutes."

He said, "Put in some big-titted sorority girls."

"There's already four milkmaids and the Swedish Women's Volleyball Champions, for when the bus goes off the road outside the haunted house where the alien is residing."

"I know, but we need sorority girls too."

"How many?"

6

"Let's say three to be on the safe side. Can you do it?"

"Sure."

"We're going to start filming tomorrow."

It was the sort of thing I should've been expecting, but Monty slid one by every now and again. "The hell are you talking about now?"

"I found some backers and we're going to get enough footage to bring to a production company and get a budget. I've got our actors coming in tomorrow to film a few scenes."

"I'm holding the only copy of this unfinished screenplay, Monty. What kind of actors are these?"

"The best kind, they do whatever you tell them. One more thing, put in a bathtub scene."

"We've got two shower scenes already."

"Yeah, but Zypho the alien is gonna take a bath with one of the girls. Toss it in."

There was a time I would've shrieked louder than the cats next door about something like this, but I couldn't rouse myself enough to care much. I glanced over at the unfinished manuscript of my novel and fought back a sigh. "Sure."

When I was frustrated I usually went upstairs to the kitchen and baked. My grandmother had taught me how to cook before I hit my teens. I'd seriously thought about going to gourmet school and becoming a chef. On days like these I really regretted some of my life decisions.

Most screenwriters would've just drank half a bottle of JD down and been done with it. I made two apple pies and a lemon meringue with crust so light it nearly floated out the window.

My cell phone rang. "Hello?"

"Are you baking again? Knock that shit off, Betty Crocker, and get to work!"

I went back to my desk, sat at the keyboard, and in twenty-eight minutes I'd added three sorority sisters who were in a van coming back from feeding the homeless when they were sideswiped by the bus carrying the Swedish Women's Volleyball Champions, just outside of the haunted house where Zypho the man-eating alien had crash-landed.

One of the sorority girls has been going through dumpsters behind ritzy restaurants trying to feed a homeless family of five, and that's why she needs a bubble bath. Rich girl learns all about the harshness of poverty. Washes the street off her skin but not her soul. Further symbolism and morality lessons ensue before Zypho eats her brain.

Sleep was rough in coming. I was irritable, nervous, and the pies hadn't taken off the edge. Finally I drifted off. In the morning I got up early and ran downtown to make copies of the script. Who the hell knew how many people Monty had coming to the house. By the time I got back he'd rearranged the furniture, set up the lights and had the DAT and Sony VX-1000 digital video camera out and waiting.

I handed him the script. He took thirty seconds to flip through it and then said, "Perfect. You're a genius."

Working for Monty had completely shattered my self-esteem but he was somehow also good for my ego.

Monty said, "All right, these are just establishing shots we're doing today. Two of the sexy scenes to get the red-blooded assholes at the studios to kick in for a budget. We'll get the rich sorority girl in the bathtub scene done." He stopped and put a hand on my shoulder. "Very deep there, man, I like the social commentary. The underlying everyman feeling, the struggle of the masses, the clashing cultural order."

"Thank you."

"Maybe you can add a subplot, like at the end she goes back home and has a confrontation with her wealthy father, makes him start paying the migrant farmers more money."

"She gets her brain sucked out on page forty-three."

"Oh," Monty said, "right. Well, that's fine too."

"And we'll do the scene with the other two topless girls lost in the attic where the ghost of the insane eighteenth-century vicar is about to get them."

"They're not topless in that scene, Monty."

He grabbed the script from me, turned to the scene, pulled out a pen, and wrote in the words *naked bobs*.

"Naked bobs?"

He wrote in another "o" making it *naked boobs* "There, that ought to do it Anyway, the shoot shouldn't take more than the afternoon."

I hadn't been in Hollywood that long and still didn't know my way around the business much, but I had a feeling that Monty wasn't following so-called established channels.

I heard a car pull up in the driveway and Monty let out a giddy laugh that sort of scared me. I didn't mind him being sleazy, but when he got silly I feared that anything could happen.

"Here are our sorority babes," he said. "Don't worry—they're all over eighteen."

They sure were. Two women walked in. The youngest one was forty-two and kept showing everybody photos of her first grand-child. I recognized both of the women as models in men's magazines who'd been on the downslide for two decades. I had a nostalgic tug, remembering that I'd first beat off to layouts of these ladies twenty-five years earlier. I offered them some pie.

Monty handed out the scripts and the middle-aged sorority babes sat back and studied their roles.

Then Lauren St. John walked in and I nearly dropped my lemon meringue.

Lauren St. John had been one of the fantasy women of my youth—I'd seen her in *Doreen Does Newark* and *Indiana Bone and the Temple of Cum Sluts* and I'd flogged myself into a bloody little puddle. Over the past few years she'd worked her way into B thrillers and grade-Z horror flicks. She was closing in on fifty and looked barely a year or two older than when she'd taken on three foot-long schlongs in *Temple*. I was intimidated as hell, horny as fuck, and even sort of starstruck, wondering if I should ask for her autograph.

Her tits were 42DDs at least and she did this thing where she clapped them around a guy's face until he was almost unconscious. I remembered the protruding thumb-thick nipples and how men and women had suckled on her through her films. Her blouse had the top three buttons opened and I could see the beautiful curves of her tanned breasts and the beginning of a huge black lace bra. My breathing hitched and I started to hiss through my teeth.

The long fiery hair had dimmed to a smoky brown. There were lines in that lovely face but there were lines in everybody's face. I wasn't thirty yet and had more gray hair than my father did at sixty. Her body still looked wonderful beneath a pleated business suit. It was such a dichotomy to what I was used to seeing that I found it even sexier than if she'd showed up in a bikini. She turned a white smile on me that glowed with sincere affability. It was so beautiful that it nearly brushed me back a step. She held her hand out and said, "Hello, I'm Lauren."

"Hi, I'm Thomas."

Monty rushed over holding a diving suit and a mask covered in plastic tubes and elastic hoses. "The hell is this?" I asked.

"Your Zypho suit."

"*My* Zypho suit?"

"Well, somebody's got to wear it. I'm the cameraman so you get to be the monster. Get down to your skivvies and I'll help you on with it."

"Excuse me," I said to Lauren St. John. Monty ushered me into the bathroom. He'd been busy in here cleaning up, I noticed. The tiles had been scrubbed, the glass doors to the stall were sparkling and the tub shined. A large jar of bubble bath sat on the counter. A citrus scent pervaded the shower.

"Damn, Monty, I didn't know you could clean like this when you wanted to. And you break my ass for baking?"

"All right, so I was a little anxious, but the bathroom needs to be clean for Lauren's tub scene. Christ, man, those tits are gonna make us a million bucks!" He plugged the drain and let the water run.

I undressed and climbed into the alien outfit. It was a tight-fitting rubber getup that zipped up in the back and was way too tight. I could barely move at all and after Monty strapped the mask on me I couldn't see much either. I clunked around the bathroom waiting for Monty to help me out of there when I realized that he was gone and Lauren was in there with me.

"Are you okay, Thomas?" she asked.

"Uhm, well—actually—"

She took her skirt off, her blouse, and folded her clothes neatly and placed them on the counter beside her purse. My cock tried to spring to attention but the suit was so tight that it was like trying to get hard against a brick wall. It hurt like fuck, but I didn't mind much as Lauren slowly slid her bra off her shoulders. My Christ. Those beautiful tremendous tits fell free and I gulped so loudly it sounded like a gunshot. They were creamy and luscious and perfect to behold, with enough bounce that as she turned they swung low and rose again as she breathed, brushing us back.

She drifted over and stood in the tub and I was shocked at how beautiful she still was. Lauren grabbed the bath crystals and dumped half the jar into the bath. She got in and sat and began soaping her immense tits. They were still so firm that you could put a pencil under them and it wouldn't stick.

Monty ran back in with the DV camera in one hand, holding a arc lamp in the other. "You're Zypho, critter from beyond the edge of space!"

"Monty—"

"Now go on, get in the tub and feel her up with your tentacles of unholy love."

"Monty—I can barely see anything."

"What's to see? Wave your arms around . . . wait we have to set this up here . . . we've got to get your tentacles into her nostrils for the brain-sucking scene."

"Holy Jesus Christ."

I waved my arms wildly around and pretended to attack Lauren St. John and slurp her brain out of her head. I felt certain I was trapped in an Ed Wood movie—in a flick struggling to be as good as an Ed Wood movie—and that Tor Johnson was about to swing his bald, rounded body towards me any second. My legacy to the world was going to be Zypho from the planet Anianibr and it left a black depression gnawing in my chest. The only saving grace was that Lauren was so sexy I was starting to get a woody even through the rubber suit.

"Hey, what's the matter?" she asked.

"What?"

"You tensed up."

"Oh, sorry. I think I'm feeling a tad embarrassed."

"Perfect!" Monty shouted. "It's a print. A little editing and we're good to go. Great job, you two!" He rushed out and I slumped forward, too despondent to do much more than lie there.

She moved beneath me and my hard-on kicked up into high gear. Even if I didn't have a foot-long schlong it got her attention.

I couldn't help myself any longer. I put my hand on her left tit and hoped she wouldn't scream. Even ex-porno starlets can get offended. It was like reaching out and touching paradise. Huge and soft enough to hold up my weight. I prayed she wouldn't scream rape or grab a can of mace out of her purse. I kneaded the aureole and toyed with that nipple and grunted where I lay on top of her.

So my hand was on her tit and I couldn't stop thinking of the cops breaking in and sending me up to share ten years with a cell mate named Bubba Raul. It was a precarious situation.

"Uhm," I said.

"It's all right," she told me. "Just take these plastic things out of my nose."

"Oh, sorry."

I tried pulling the mask off but it was connected at the back of the neck to the bodysuit. "Can you get the zipper down?"

"No, it's stuck."

"Shit. There's no hole in the suit."

"You can't get it out?"

"Goddamn."

"Can you reach my purse?"

I lurched blindly, managed to find the purse, and handed it to her. She rummaged around for a second and came out with a box-cutter that I could see even through the pinhole-sized punctures I had to look through.

"Jesus Christ! What's that for?"

"Protection. I live in East Hollywood too." She drew out the blade and then kneeled in front of me.

"The fuck are you doing?"

"I'm going to make a slit in this rubber."

"For Christ's sake be careful!"

"I will."

Suddenly her hand snaked in. I was down to about a quarter-mast, but I thought that was pretty good considering the circumstances.

"It's all right," she said.

"Look, I'm not about to make the mistake of thinking that adult actresses are any more promiscuous than anybody else, so—"

"Are you really this cute and embarrassed or are you just pretending?"

I thought about it. "No, I'm really this cute. Well, under the suit anyway."

My breathing became ragged and I knew it wasn't just because of the ten pounds of rubber mask around my head.

Lauren hiked her knees up. I leaned into her, plunging inside so easily that it almost startled me. "That's it, Thomas," she whispered.

"God yes."

"Oh, Thomas."

I liked her using my name. It gave me a warm hitch under my heart.

"Can you see me at all?" she asked.

"I can feel you."

"This is the first time I've ever fucked a creature from outer space," she whispered.

It wasn't the truth. I'd seen her hump some guy in a costume almost as ridiculous as mine in *Alien Anal Attack* fifteen years ago. I didn't blame her for not remembering.

She kept our movements slow, rocking lightly as I pushed harder. She was wonderfully tight and had great muscular control. Her tits floated atop the suds and kept pointing at me. She reached beneath the water and raised them high, pointing those giant nipples at the eyeholes in the mask. She poked at me with them and then started doing the thing where she swung them hard and let them loose. I grunted and fucked her savagely, groaning with the heat and the fact that I was going at it with one of my ultimate fantasies. Her tits bounced wildly and slugged me in the forehead, the shoulder, the jaw, really letting me have it as she squealed and cried, "That's it, keep at it!"

Like I would stop. She gasped as I kept at her, finding the rhythm and enjoying how her tits bounced each time I rammed her. Soon she began trembling beneath my body. Lauren clung to me and drew her nails across Zypho's rubber chest. I reached under her ass, grabbed her hips and pulled her further onto me until I was embedded as deeply as I could go. She grunted at the force of my penetration and said, "That's it, Thomas." Whoever would've thought that hearing your own name would be such a turn on? Lauren climaxed again, shuddering so hard that I heard her elbows crack.

I felt my own climax coming on. She did too and urged me on, whispering, "That's it, that's it, like that, yes." She growled a little and it drove me nuts and she kept slapping me with her tits and I was every stud she'd ever fucked on film. She let me be the best and I was so thankful I tried kissing her through the mask. I held on to her nipples like two joysticks as I rode her until I creamed.

She froze for a moment and said, "What's that sound? That yowling."

I still had lights dancing along the edges of my vision. "What? Uh, those are the cats next door stuck in the pomegranate tree again."

I gave her three or four more shoves and then came, letting her milk me and I quivered and shook. I rested atop that chest and never wanted to leave. She held me for a while, worked at the zipper, and finally managed to get me out of it.

"What a workout," she said. "But I'm not done yet."

Already I was at half-mast again. "Neither am I."

"Where's your room?"

"Around back. Let me check on Monty first and then—"

"Then I want to look at your face when I fuck you until you pass out."

"Oh boy."

It sounded like a fine plan to me. We got dressed and left the bathroom and sat on the couch together, chatting about films and our lives and feeding each other slices of pie. We made out for a while until I realized Monty and the other sorority babes had been missing for a long time.

We went upstairs to find out what had happened on the rest of the shoot.

I'd been wrong. That yowling hadn't been the cats that time. Monty and the two actresses had been doing something pretty funky and unholy up in the attic. All three were in a daze and it looked like Monty's left shoulder had been tugged out of the socket. It was a good thing he was double-jointed. He popped it back in. His cell phone rang.

I said, "It's probably Ed Wood calling to tell us that we've bumped *Plan 9 from Outer Space* as the worst movie ever."

Monty got a faraway look in his eyes and said, "Wouldn't that be something?"

Underneath Your Clothes

BY ELIZABETH COLDWELL

I only noticed it because I dropped my pen. Otherwise I would have never known there was a secret life being lived so close to me. As I scribbled notes on the draft report that had been left in my in-tray for approval that morning, the red ballpoint slipped from my grasp and I had to go crawling under the desk to retrieve it. It was as I was beginning to shuffle out backward, knowing there was no dignity in the view this presented but not wishing to bang my head on the underside of the desk, that the pair of legs directly in my eye-line crossed at the ankles and I caught, for the briefest of moments, a flash of something utterly unexpected. Where I would have expected to see bare white skin above the top of the short charcoal grey sock, I saw instead a smooth expanse of sheer black nylon. The legs were under the desk opposite mine. Michael's desk.

I shook my head, convinced I must have bumped it without realizing. There was no way I could have seen what I thought I'd just seen. Michael played a lot of squash; he must have damaged his ankle and be wearing some kind of support bandage. Yeah, right, if they'd started making support bandages in ten-denier nylon. But not Michael Hodgson: not our project leader; the quietest, straightest man in the department. There were other men in the company who I could quite easily believe might indulge their feminine side at work, like Johnny in the marketing department, with his glossy, shoulder-length blond hair and pouting, almost girlish features, but not Michael.

But then, how much did we really know about him? After all, he had only joined the department a month or so earlier, to oversee and troubleshoot when the project had started running over budget. Janice, the departmental secretary, had subjected him to a prolonged bout of questioning when she had noticed the absence of framed family portraits on his desk, but all she had managed to find out was that he was in his early thirties, had joined the company five years earlier, and was single. It wasn't that Michael was unfriendly; he was happy enough to chat about something superficial during coffee breaks. He just seemed to feel that, as he was only going to be working with us for a matter of weeks, it was no basis for making permanent relationships.

I knew part of the reason Janice was being so nosy; I was single, too, and she was checking him out, none too subtly, on my behalf. She couldn't understand that I was quite happy being on my own—I needed time and space after Greg had walked out on me so suddenly—and she definitely didn't share my view that it was never a good idea to start an office romance. I had seen too many of those go sour in my time to want to make that mistake.

I had to admit, though, that the thought of Michael in tights intrigued me. He was certainly my type—I've always had a weakness for men with green eyes and toffee-colored hair—but it went deeper than that, tapping into fantasies I'd had for a very long time. Fantasies I had never dared to share with any of my boyfriends. If I had ever suggested to Greg that I might want to see him in my lingerie, that picturing him in stockings, his hard cock straining against a pair of silky panties, was enough to get me wet, he would have left me a damn sight sooner than he did. As far as I was concerned, dressing like that wouldn't have made him any less of a man; it would have made him more horny, more desirable. But he would never have understood that, and I would never have been able to explain.

I said nothing to indicate I had seen anything the least unusual under Michael's desk, but that night I lay in bed and gently frigged my pussy to the image of a handsome, green-eyed man with long, tights-clad legs and a hugely erect cock. A cock that I touched and licked through the thin film of nylon that covered it, till he groaned and his come oozed through the fine mesh, onto my greedy, sucking tongue . . .

And it would have stayed as nothing more than an image if Michael hadn't accepted an invitation to Janice's birthday drink. I'm sure he would have turned it down and quietly slipped away after work on Friday night like he usually did if it hadn't coincided with his last day in the department. We had finally put the project to bed, and even Michael was in the mood to celebrate.

The pool table was unoccupied when we walked into the White Lion, and that's when we knew it was going to be a good night. Eddie went straight over and placed a row of coins on the table's edge, making it ours for the next hour or so. Normally, it had already been claimed by the lads from the building site across the road—the White

Lion was the only establishment in the area that tolerated their work boots and site clothing—but tonight they were nowhere to be seen. We liked the pub for the same reasons they did; it was more relaxed, less of a yuppie pick-up joint than the wine bars and pavement cafés that catered to the after-work crowd who spilled out of the waterside office blocks. And even if we were still dressed in our double-breasted, skirt-suited corporate armor, at least we could take off our jackets, unbutton a few buttons, and have a good time, knowing we were unlikely to bump into any of the company's big bosses or, worse, their gossipy PAs.

While Eddie was racking up the pool balls, Michael took a contribution from the rest of us and went to the bar, returning with a couple of bottles of champagne and half a dozen glasses. Janice was slotting money into the jukebox, punching in the numbers of her favorite slow, raunchy rock songs. The look in her eye told me she was planning on drinking too much, flirting too much, and trying to entice one of the boys to go home with her. She usually succeeded; even though she was never looking for more than a one-night stand, there was no one who could resist the combination of her generous cleavage and sultry, smoky voice. Except perhaps Michael.

It was Janice's idea to divide the six of us into male/female teams: herself and Eddie, Louise and Tim, Michael and me. I couldn't decide whether she was still trying to set up the two of us, but I was happy enough with the plan, particularly when Michael, quickly realizing just how useless I was at pool, decided to give me an impromptu lesson. Standing so close behind me I could feel the warmth of his body pressed against my own, he took hold of my hands and directed them into place on the cue. But as he helped me line up my shot, all I could think of was that glimpse of sheer nylon. Was he dressed like that now? I wondered, barely managing to drag my attention back to the cue ball. With his help, I somehow sunk the shot, but we still lost the game quite easily, leaving the remaining two couples to take each other on.

I found myself studying Michael as he poured the remnants of the second bottle of champagne into all the glasses on the table. With his tie off and his normally neat hair ruffled up, he looked unbelievably gorgeous, and I knew that if I didn't do something, in a couple of hours he would walk out of this pub and, in all probability, out of my life. I couldn't let him go without telling him I knew about his little secret, and just how much it turned me on. Alcohol made me bold and loosened my tongue. The words spilled out of my mouth before I could stop them. "So tell me, Michael, are they stockings or tights?"

Any other man might have thought I was speculating about Janice as she bent over the pool table, her skirt riding so high that if she was wearing stockings, their tops were dangerously close to coming into view. But Michael knew immediately what I meant; his face went pale as he said, tight-lipped, "How did you find out?"

"I dropped my pen," I told him. "I had to go under the desk to get it back—and that's when I saw them."

"And what are you going to tell everyone when I go back to head office?" he said. "That I'm a pervert, a freak? Janice will love spreading that juicy little piece of scandal when she finds out." He broke off as Tim wandered over, clutching more champagne.

"Anyone for a refill?" he asked, sloshing more drink into our glasses without giving us a chance to refuse. Not that I would have refused; I needed as much Dutch courage as I could handle if I was going to get out of this situation without making a complete fool of myself.

I took a deep breath. "She's not going to find out, because I'm not going to tell anyone anything," I said. "And if you want the truth, I don't think what you do is freaky or perverted. If you must know, it makes me really horny."

There was a long moment's silence, compounded by the song on the jukebox coming to an end. Now I definitely had blown it. I reached for my handbag. "Maybe I should just wish Janice a happy birthday and go."

Michael put his hand on my arm. "Don't go, Lorna. Repeat what you just said."

Knowing I had nothing to lose, I said, "What, that the thought of you wearing stockings, tights, whatever they are, makes me horny?"

He drained the rest of his champagne in one gulp. "You can't know how long I've waited for someone to say that to me. It's always felt like this dirty little secret I've been carrying around, ever since the first time I tried on a pair of my sister's old tights. Don't get me wrong, Lorna, I don't go the whole hog. I don't wear dresses and I don't spend the weekends as Michelle, or anything like that. And I'm not gay. I just like the feel of nylon against my skin."

"You've got them on now, haven't you?" I said, praying I was right.

He nodded, and I felt a rush of liquid heat to my pussy.

"I want to see them," I told him.

"What, here?" he asked.

"No. Preferably at my place, and preferably with you wearing absolutely nothing else." This wasn't me talking, this was the champagne, but I still knew I meant every word of what I was saying.

"Okay, let's go," he said.

At that moment, Janice wandered over, slightly unsteadily. Her face was flushed and beaming, and her blouse was open far enough to reveal the tops of her plump, freckled breasts, cradled in a white lace push-up bra.

"Are you having a good time?" she asked. "Because I'm having a fucking fantastic time!" She lowered her head to mine, trying to be discreet, but the amount of alcohol she'd drunk had taken her way past discretion, and her voice was loud enough to carry across the room. "Do you think Eddie's fit, Lorna? I think he's really fit. He's got a great arse when he bends over to line up a shot."

I smiled indulgently at her, and then glanced across at Michael, wondering how we could best make our excuses and leave before one or both of us lost the courage to act on our erotic impulses.

Janice seemed oblivious to the looks that were passing between Michael and me. "You know, I've always had a fantasy about getting fucked on a pool table," she slurred.

Most women I knew had; it seemed almost compulsory, like fantasizing about being fucked by a fireman, or inviting your boyfriend's handsome best friend to join you in a threesome. I knew exactly how she pictured herself splayed over the table, her hands gripping the edges, skirt up and panties off, while Eddie ploughed into her from behind. Her imagination would no doubt add the cheering audience, the encouragement for her lover to get her big tits out on display, or slip his cock into her arse. It was a horny image, but it wasn't my idea of a good time. My fantasies took me to a darker, stranger place, and now I had found a man who shared them, I was eager to make them a reality.

"Well, why don't you ask Eddie nicely, and see what he says?" I suggested. I got to my feet and gave her a gentle peck on the cheek. "Enjoy the rest of your birthday, Jan. Michael and I have had a good evening, but we really should be off."

As we made our way to the door, I wondered how long it would take Janice to twig that we were leaving together, or whether she was too wrapped up in her own fantasies to realize. We stepped into the frosty night air just in time to see the friendliest sight in the world; a sleek black cab coming down the street with its "FOR HIRE" sign blazing. We hailed it, and when it slowed to a stop, the driver pulled down the window and I gave him my address.

The cab sped through the city streets, almost deserted now that the offices and the shops that relied on them for trade were shut for the weekend. Michael and I sat close together, his hand resting lightly on my stomach as I leaned into his body. There wasn't enough light for me to see the gap between the cuff of his trouser leg and the top of his sock, but I knew that if I could, I would have a glimpse of sheer nylon. The thought, combined with the feel of Michael's fingers stroking me almost absentmindedly was enough to keep me wet all the way to my flat.

The mechanics of paying the cab fare, stumbling up the stairs to the second floor, and turning the key in the lock seemed to happen without my being aware of them. I was on autopilot, heading for the bedroom and almost dragging Michael with me.

"Slow down, Lorna," he said in an amused tone, but I could tell he was just as impatient as I was.

I threw myself onto the bed, kicking off my shoes. Lust and hunger pulsed through my veins. "Strip for me," I ordered him, my voice steady and confident. As Michael shrugged off his jacket and then turned his attention to unbuttoning his shirt, I rucked up my skirt, spread my legs, and began to touch myself lazily through the gusset of my panties. His eyes seemed riveted at the sight as his shirt joined his jacket on the floor. Shoes and socks followed, and then he was reaching for the belt of his trousers. I wanted to slip my finger into my panties and stroke my clit directly, but that would take me too close, too soon, and I wanted to truly savor the sight with which I hoped Michael was about to present me.

As his trousers slithered to the floor, my breath caught in my throat. This was every hot, dirty fantasy I had ever had come to life. My eyes trailed upward from the crumpled garment pooled around his ankles. The fine, blond hairs on his legs were almost invisible beneath mesh of a denier much finer than I could usually wear without laddering, but that wasn't what drew my attention. Michael wore no underwear, and the tights, sheer to his waist, clung to his already erect penis and balls. His excitement was evident, dampening the nylon in a halo around the head of his cock. It was a beautiful, magnificent vision, more erotic than anything I had seen in my entire life.

Now that I had what I had dreamed of for so long, my self-assurance seemed to melt away. Need made me weak, robbed me of the ability to speak. In the end, I just opened my arms and beckoned Michael onto the bed with me.

Our mouths met, wet and hungry, and we kissed as our hands roamed over the other's body. Michael was tugging at the buttons on my blouse, almost popping them in his eagerness to undress me. I, in return, was stroking the long contours of his back before my hands settled on their real prize; his muscular buttocks, wrapped in their delicate second skin.

Stripped of my blouse and bra, I was aware of Michael's hands cupping my small breasts, thumbs rubbing my nipples till they peaked. But at that moment, my pleasure seemed like it could wait. Like an excited kid on Christmas morning, all that mattered to me was playing with the beautiful present, wrapped in tights, that knelt before me.

Kids, though, always want to tear the wrapper off in their haste to get to the goodies inside. Not me: As far as I was concerned, the wrapping was the present, just as much as the gorgeous, erect cock concealed beneath it. I touched Michael's cock through the nylon, skimming along its length with light, spidery strokes that made him moan. The soft hairs of his balls prickled through the fabric as I caressed those, too. And then I bent my head and did what I had done in my fantasies; I began to lick his thighs, my tongue moving ever closer to the hot, throbbing length of flesh that waited between them. I could taste salt on his skin, smell the muskiness of his genitals, trapped and magnified by the artificial fibers of his tights. I could have breathed in that scent forever.

The nylon was turning slick and wet as I mouthed it, my saliva mixing with the juice that leaked from the tip of his cock, but I would have happily kept licking him until he climaxed. Michael, however, had other ideas.

"Lorna, I want to come inside you," he said urgently. He reached for the waistband of the tights, about to pull them down, but I caught hold of his hands and shook my head.

Using a fingernail, I carefully poked a hole, close to the seam that ran between his legs. Grinning at a surprised Michael, I ripped downward until there was enough room to pull his cock through and out into my eager clutches.

I quickly removed my skirt and panties, leaving on only my hold-up stockings, and then I clambered over Michael, straddling him. Grasping his cock firmly, I placed it at the entrance to my pussy and lowered myself, taking him inside me inch by inch. My eyes never left his as I began to move, rising and falling slowly. He reached up and played with my nipples as I rode him. Our nylon-clad thighs slithered together, and I could feel the material at his crotch rubbing against my pussy lips every time our groins made contact.

It was all too much for both of us. He was groaning and bucking his hips frantically; I snaked a hand between our bodies and quickly rubbed my clit, feeling the spasms of orgasm starting to pulse through my sex. Michael cried out, and I knew he was coming. The tension that had been building within my body suddenly broke, and I followed him.

I slumped forward onto his heaving, sweaty chest. His hands stroked along my back as our breathing slowed.

"I'm sorry I ruined your tights," I murmured.

"That's okay," he replied. "You'll just have to buy me some more—as long as you promise to ruin those, too."

"Don't worry, I intend to," I said, feeling his cock begin to stir beneath me again. "In fact, if you're interested, there's a supermarket round the corner that stays open all night—and I do believe they sell their tights in packets of five . . ."

Cruising with Vickie and Marge

BY M. J. RENNIE

Although my family wasn't too pleased about it, I did the same thing Raymond Chandler did: I married a woman eighteen years my senior.

Still, I have no regrets. From the beginning my beautiful, raven-haired Vickie has made a far better wife than most of the babes my own age would have been.

Vickie makes me give her oral sex on a daily basis. I married her knowing that is exactly what would be expected.

Before marrying me, Vickie was a doctor's wife. But after ten years with him, she felt dead inside and divorced him. Her decision made two people happy: Vickie and me.

The good doctor refused to "go down" on Vickie. Though well-educated and financially successful, the fellow was an idiot.

I should start with our honeymoon. It was a two-week stay in a luxury hotel in an otherwise sleepy coastal town. We arrived dressed in our wedding clothes—Vickie in her beautiful white gown and me in formal tux. We kissed passionately as we crossed the threshold. Once inside, Vickie literally threw herself on the bed.

"I can't wait any longer, darling," she said, pulling up on her wedding gown. "Kiss me between my legs."

Drawing the ruffled white fabric up to her shoulders, Vickie revealed the most compelling sight I have ever seen. Beneath her silk wedding dress all she wore was a high-waisted white satin panty, so thin and sheer as to be almost gossamer.

Without even removing my jacket, I dropped to my knees, gazing in rapture at this vision of superlative beauty. Vickie opened her legs and spread herself apart.

My breathing became labored when I realized her panty was slit so expertly the divide was at first impossible to see.

Impossible, that is, until she spread herself. Kneeling closer to her soft center, I inhaled the delicious fragrance of her womanly musk. The panty material puckered along the edges, displaying skin so cleanly shaven not a single hair obscured her pouting outer lips.

I marveled at how the skillful stitching of the slit in Vickie's panty made a bend around her red clitoris while down below another showed off her small, pink anus.

Leaning forward, I was thrilled to see Vickie was already moist at her opening, so eager was she for my tongue.

Opening herself wider still, Vickie brought her legs up in the air. Her feet were on either side of my head, shod in white high-heeled pumps. Locking her ankles behind my neck, Vickie pulled me forward and down. My tongue shot out and plunged deep within her. I tasted pure honey.

Caught in Vickie's strong grasp, I hung on for dear life as she bucked through a series of shattering orgasms.

Then, with my face drenched from her liquor, Vickie bade me to climb upon her.

"Get undressed, Lawrence darling," she said, undoing the snaps down the front of her gown. "I want your cock in me."

I stripped and stood naked over my lovely wife, my cock hard and ready. Vickie threw off her gown, bra, and garters, showing me her lush body, nude, except for the slit panty. Holding her arms out, Vickie beckoned me toward her, her legs wide apart. I got in between them, feeling the delicious warmth of her bare skin.

My cock hesitated at the entrance to her juicy hole. Vickie guided me in, pressing my buttocks roughly to force me all the way. The feeling of being absorbed by her velvet soft vagina was a shock that briefly left me stunned. The moment we had so patiently awaited had at last arrived.

We looked into each other's eyes. Vickie's pupils were so widely dilated her brown eyes seemed black. We kissed and played with each other's tongues. I planted kisses on the sensitive lobes of her ears and let my tongue trace alongside her nose.

And then the thrusting began. Every push seemed to bring her another shuddering spasm. For me, it was nearly impossible to hold back. This first instance of sexual intercourse was pure sensory overload.

"I can't hold it . . ." I whimpered.

Vickie bit my ear and whispered: "Then let it come, darling. Go ahead and spurt it all in me."

My first ejaculation in Vickie's vagina was an experience I shall never forget. A mind-bending seizure struck me, followed by a long series of pulsating spasms. With each spasm a jet of semen shot out of my cock. Jet after jet after jet.

Then it was over and we relaxed, slowly, for a long while. We exchanged kisses until Vickie felt herself between her legs and said we should get up.

"That big thing really went off," Vickie said, "I'm soaked."

I nodded, being too weak to speak.

"Let's go in the bathroom so we can clean up."

Vickie hung up her wedding gown while I went directly into the bathroom. I was naked. She came in the bathroom still wearing the slit panty and high heels. Nothing else.

Vickie sat down on the toilet and urinated while I stood in front of her. She held my balls in one hand, using a washcloth to dab at my cock with the other. I listened intently as her urine splashed in the bowl.

"You couldn't help yourself, I suppose," she said. "But it's clear we'll have to work on your ejaculations. You're not allowed to ejaculate unless I say so, darling. You'll find I'm very strict about that. If you begin to feel too close, it's okay to withdraw."

"I'll remember that," I said.

"Good." Vickie stood up and kissed me on the cheek. "Now let's go do it again," she said. "I'm ready for more."

Vickie may be over fifty, but her shapely figure, radiant skin, and attractively styled brunette hair make her seem about half her age. A natural beauty, in her teens and twenties Vickie appeared on the covers of many national fashion magazines. Her robust vitality carries over into our sex life. On that score, Vickie's age has meant no reduction in her level of desire.

Instead, being married to a mature, sexually advanced woman like Vickie meant the opening of whole new vistas of experience and activity I might otherwise never have known. I quickly discovered that I loved taking *Sea Star* cruises to exotic locations with my older, but still lovely wife.

During cruises, Vickie requires oral sex on a nightly basis. Fortunately, there is nothing I love more than giving my beautiful Vickie dutiful head while a pale tropical moon rises outside our stateroom window.

"Come put your tongue in me, Lawrence," Vickie says, as she pulls back the sheets and spreads her legs, inviting me to suckle at length from her womanly fount.

"Yes, Aunt Vickie," I reply, kneeling beside the bed to wedge my noggin between her creamy thighs. Although she is not my aunt, Vickie likes me to call her "Aunt Vickie," especially during sex, in deference to her age and status.

Plus it's a little kinky, which she also likes. My tongue and lips have become so well developed from long, ardent sessions at Vickie's slit I am able to suck her for a full hour without so much as breaking a sweat.

After giving Vickie oral pleasure on a *Sea Star* cruise, I always have to give her a good bang as well, penetrating her either doggy-style or in the woman-on-top position. She really loves it doggy-style.

Our first cruise on the S.S. *Sea Star* took place in the early spring, just three months after our wedding. It set the tone for many later cruises we have taken since. Cruise rates are low that time of year and the ships are often filled with recent widows recovering from the death of a beloved husband.

The night we left port, Vickie had me tongue her for some fifty minutes before turning around and presenting her bottom to me.

I reached under her arms and played with her plump nipples,

while my cock poked between her legs, seeking her tight hole. When the moist target was located, I drove inside with a single thrust.

Marrying an older woman like Vickie was the best thing a guy like me could have done for himself. When Vickie accepted my marriage proposal, she noted that, among other things, her secure financial position could afford us many luxuries unavailable to a struggling young couple.

"Understand what you are doing, Lawrence," Vickie said. "Do you want to enjoy a wonderful marriage with a woman who knows how to give you exquisite pleasure or make babies with some ignorant girl?"

The answer, as far as I was concerned, was an obvious one. Gazing down at Vickie's ripe and still gorgeous body, my mouth practically watered.

For me, Vickie is the perfect wife. From her slender, long-nailed hands to the very slight thickening at her waist, she is ideal in every way. I especially admire her generous breasts with their fat brown nipples. I thank my lucky stars for making the right choice.

Once my cock was deep inside her, we did not move at all. Often we will remain that way, motionless after penile entry, for several minutes. Gradually our breathing becomes more labored as the sexual tension rises.

Finally Vickie squealed, forcing my rigid column back and nipping the head with her strong interior muscles. That was my cue to groan loudly.

Rapid and heavy thrusting commenced. I fell into a rhythm, loving the feel of my thighs slapping against the cheeks of her jiggly bottom. Down on her hands and knees, Vickie indulged herself in a veritable torrent of shrieks, cries, grunts, groans, yells, moans, sighs, barks, shouts, and screams. The more noise she made, the more frenzied she became.

"AAAEEEGGGHHH!" Vickie screamed. "UH UH UH!" It was wonderful to hear her.

The tropical moonlight threw the shadows of our bodies on the wall of the stateroom. Our elongated forms showed in such detail that I could make out the slanting shadow of my thrusting penis there, in sharp relief, on the wood-paneled wainscoting.

Vickie's vagina responds particularly well to the rear entry position, as it allows direct penile contact with her G-spot.

On our first cruise, I remembered how, a few months before our wedding ceremony, Vickie underwent the operation that tightened her vagina. She removed her panties and made me kneel in front of her, describing in detail how the surgeon was going to draw in, ever so delicately, the walls of her womanhood.

"See here, Lawrence?" Vickie pointed to the pinkish chamber within. "Just a minor adjustment on my box here and your penis will feel like it's in the grip of a twenty year old. Won't that be fun?"

"Goodness, Aunt Vickie," I said. "I can hardly wait."

Vickie sighed. "It's not easy for me either, Lawrence," she said. "But you won't be putting your cock in your Aunt Vickie until we are officially woman and husband!" True to her old-fashioned values, Vickie postponed intercourse until our wedding night.

However, Vickie did clearly indicate how active our sex life would be after the wedding.

"We will have one long honeymoon, Lawrence," Vickie said. "Just you and me. Intercourse and oral sex every day. We will enjoy cruises, travel, fun, leisure, and pleasure. That will be our life together."

On that first memorable cruise, while I banged her, I fondly looked down at Vickie from behind, delighting in the star shape of wet pubic hair closely circling her hot, tight hole. Soon she was going to drain me of everything in my balls. Oh, Aunt Vickie!

"Let yourself get carried away, Auntie," I told her as my cock went in and out. "Let yourself go completely."

Vickie panted and huffed, clutching her pillow and hanging on, it seemed, for dear life. I tilted my head back to look out the porthole, seeing the Goddess Luna floating silently above the dark ocean, as the *Sea Star* steamed serenely through the night.

I hung onto Vickie's beautiful bare hips and impaled her savagely, piling everything I had into every thrust. The sopping juices oozing from her slippery slit bathed my cock from stem to stern. We climaxed at the same time, our voices singing the harmony of physical release.

And that was just the beginning.

Therefore I knew, from personal experience, that Vickie was highly advanced sexually. But I had no idea how far she was willing to go until a bit later in the cruise.

Other than the intense sex Vickie and I indulged in, the trip at first was uneventful.

Then, about midway through the ten-day voyage, Vickie made friends with a widow named Marge. During hot, languid afternoons aboard the *Sea Star*, Vickie and Marge exercised together in the ship's gym and swam in the pool located on the poop deck.

For a woman in her early fifties, blonde-haired Marge was stunning in a jet black bikini. Still very trim and slender, Marge had exceptionally large breasts featuring sharply pointed nipples, a narrow waist, and a full, rounded ass that looked like it was carved from solid oak.

Cruising with Vickie and Marge

On the night before the *Sea Star* docked in Puerto Vallarta, Vickie invited Marge to dine with us in the Captain's Club. Following Vickie's instructions, I danced with Marge half a dozen times that evening—almost as many times as I danced with Vickie.

Marge wore a form-fitting black evening gown and the casual rubbing of her breasts on my chest was terribly exciting.

I could tell Marge sensed my excitement as well, because more than once she pressed her hip against my crotch, where I sported a massive erection.

"You dance beautifully, Lawrence," Marge said, her pale blue eyes fixed on mine. "I haven't had this much fun in ages."

"It's a pleasure for me also," I said. "Vickie has a way of making sure people have a good time."

At the Captain's Club, we feasted on an elegant entrée of grilled shark steaks, served with tender red beans and white rice. A spicy hot seasonal salad consisting of fresh spinach, endive, vinegar peppers, and thinly sliced cucumber accompanied the meal.

Vickie ordered champagne, a special brand guaranteed to sear away the inhibitions. We went through two full bottles and a carafe of California Chablis, served along with the food. The next thing I knew we were in Marge's cabin. Outside, a bright full moon hovered majestically over the dark waters of the Pacific.

"I'm a little tipsy," Marge confessed. "There's no way I can get this gown unzipped by myself. Could you please help me, Vickie?"

Entirely uninhibited, Vickie pulled the zipper down for Marge, exposing a broad expanse of smooth white flesh at Marge's back and shoulders. She wore no bra underneath.

Watching Marge undress, my cock grew hard as tempered steel.

"Should I leave the room?" I asked, looking around. I was unsure

37

of what I was supposed to do. "That's not necessary, Lawrence," Marge answered. "I know I'm among friends here."

Vickie tugged the slinky dress down so Marge could step out of it. She whirled around and faced me, wearing nothing except for a riveting black lace panty and a pair of black high-heeled pumps. She was the very picture of mature sexiness.

In truth, I have always adored older women. From my earliest recollections of myself as a male, I have always preferred older women to the ones my own age. They often seem to have a certain air of sophistication that is lacking in women of my generation.

Vickie fixed me with a familiar look, a look that said I better remember to obey her without question.

"Lawrence," Vickie said, "I want you to fuck my new friend Marge here. She's in need of a good fucking. Put your mind at ease because I've checked Marge out and she's clean and safe in every way. What do you say?"

"Uh . . . uh . . . ," I said, licking my lips. There was no way I could resist Marge's ripe, wonderfully maintained body. Her bare breasts and inviting curves struck me as succulent beyond words.

When Marge turned slightly to her left, I got an unobstructed view of her magnificent ass.

All my normal puritan resistance melted like wax in a fire.

Demurely, Marge stared down at the floor, folding her arms under her beautiful breasts. She did not meet my gaze. Clearing my throat, I said, "I wouldn't mind fucking Marge at all."

"Good," Vickie said. "Get out of your clothes."

Immediately I started unknotting my tie. In something like a flash I was completely nude.

After pushing Marge down on the enormous king-sized bed,

Vickie yanked off the lacy panty the widow wore. Vickie ordered me to get between Marge's legs and attend her pussy with my tongue. Marge's lovely pussy had an enticing fragrance and a sweet, syrupy taste. The downy hair surrounding her slit was silver blonde and neatly trimmed. I sniffed it deeply several times before applying my tongue to it.

Oh man! Excellent bouquet!

Marge's soft, hairy center was just right—wet, thick-lipped and elastic. I began lapping her vagina with a gentle, lifting motion, digging my tongue inside and dragging it upwards to her clitoris. Marge emitted a high-pitched shriek when I licked her erect clitoris and sucked it gently. Vickie was delighted when Marge orgasmed, juicing my face from forehead to chin with her feminine liquor.

Three gushes later, Vickie told me it was time to start banging her cock-starved friend.

Marge wrapped her legs around my waist as I drove inside her. I slid my hands under her solid rump while Marge whimpered and muttered unintelligible words. About the only thing I could make out from what Marge was saying was:

"Your cock is so big . . . so big . . . so big . . ."

Vickie stood behind me as I pumped Marge, cupping my balls in her strong, long-nailed hands.

"Ram it in her," Vickie urged me. "Bang her good." Like a machine, I pistoned the blubbering Marge.

Marge's sweetly lined face was damp with tears and she gave voice to only moans and gibberish. Multiple orgasms soon left her limp as a rag doll. Just as I was getting ready to fill her vagina with my semen, Vickie suddenly halted the action. "Not yet," Vickie said. "I want her to suck your cock."

I pulled out and waited while Vickie arranged Marge up on her hands and knees. Marge raised her head to show that she was ready. With a nod, Vickie had me stick my sex-slickened stiffy into Marge's open, eager mouth.

"Feed her your stuff," Vickie said. "She'll swallow it all. Every hot, gooey drop."

I didn't need to hear anything more. Marge's hungry mouth went down the length of my cock and back up again. She lingered over the head, teasing it and making little suck-suck noises. Then down again and up again. Down again and up again. Seconds later, a shower of jism erupted from my hugely swollen organ.

Marge happily gulped it down, as my milky bolts spewed down her throat. Truthfully, Marge's cocksucking was a bit amateurish, especially when compared to Vickie's expert lip service. But what Marge lacked in skill, she made up for in sheer enthusiasm.

Vickie also enjoyed it immensely. When she ordered me to go down on Marge again later, she was fingering her own pussy. Vickie made me touch the silken notch between her legs. I swear my adored wife was wetter than Lake Titicaca.

Together, the three of us had a most interesting cruise from that point forward.

But once we returned to the city, Vickie told me chances were zero that we would ever go on another cruise with Marge. I was disappointed, though I had expected as much. In keeping with her standard policy, Vickie quickly put the kibosh on any relationship that might threaten our marriage.

"I'm sorry to hear that," I answered. "I enjoyed doing it with Aunt Marge a lot."

"That is exactly the problem," Vickie said.

A Novel of Manners, Set Vaguely in the Heian Era

BY JASON RUBIS

The sash is called an *obi,* and to Susan it seems far more dramatic—somehow more purposeful—than either the narrow belt, called *shita-jime,* which is worn underneath, or the ornamental string *(obi-dome)* which serves to secure the *obi* and hold it in place. Susan has decided to dispense with the *obi-dome* and also the *obi-age,* which she has only read about and would have no idea how to describe; ditto for the little twin apron-cum-loincloths, *koshi-maki* and *suso-yoke,* which are to be worn underneath everything else. These all seem somehow superfluous, and, more to the point, her ensemble didn't come with them. For underwear, she's settled for a baby-doll tee and running shorts. But her *obi* is magnificent. It's pale green, and has a crane on it. With the little belt underneath, tightly hugging her middle, it makes her feel somehow anchored. Ready for anything.

The little white socks you wear are *tabi,* and Susan thinks they're delightful, even though hers aren't at all authentic. Real *tabi* are split at the toe, to allow for a firm grip on one's *geta*. Susan's aren't split, though they do have little red pompoms on the heels. But in the Japanese porn she's seen online, the kind that still shows girls in old-fashioned clothes, the *tabi* are a symbol of innocence. A girl getting fucked in *tabi* is understood to be a virgin, and that's very important.

Traditional *geta* are blocky and difficult to walk in, especially with unsplit *tabi*, but no more so, surely, than your standard six-inch spike-heeled pumps. Miraculously, Susan's outfit did come with a pair of *geta*, and forgoing them for a pair of, say, flip-flops would be unthinkable. Once she's made her entrance, teetering on the big wooden sandals and charmingly smiling *("Konichiwa!")*, no one will think anything of it if she sheds them and runs around in her mock-*tabi*, or even abandons them later in favor of bare feet. Lucas has clean floors.

"Who ever heard of a blonde geisha?"

Susan snaps her fan open (cherry blossoms on it, pale and pink) with a practiced hand, and poises it under her chin. "Fuck you."

Diane, on the bed, reading Barthes for her two o'clock Thursday seminar, says, "At least you should've done your hair right, yeah? Up in one of those big-ass buns with the ivory chopsticks sticking out. Total *In the Realm of the Senses* shit. Or you should've done the makeup. The real, real white stuff with the red lips. You know?"

"I'm pale enough." Diane's advice is, besides unwelcome, impractical. Susan knows no one who'd be able to do her hair that way, no surviving old-school courtesan with the know-how to apply that white makeup the proper way. Ancient knowledge, she reasons, not easily found today, and certainly not around here. It doesn't matter. The point is that WASPy little Susan is perfectly happy with her shoulder-length blonde hair and her not-entirely-authentic-or-complete costume. It feels right. And that *obi*, man. That *obi* is the thing. Hell yes.

"Don't you think I look good?" Tentative voice. Approval from one's friends—even *gaijin* friends—is important.

Diane—overweight but pretty in glasses, ponytail, sweatshirt—smirks. "Like sushi."

The guy in the cab smiled at her when she got in, and he does it again when they reach Lucas's building. Greasy and fat and broad-faced, he smiles and says nothing but "Have a good time" as he counts Susan's money and Susan clambers delicately out of the backseat. He doesn't leer or make remarks. A good omen, perhaps. Maybe he has daughters.

Outside the cab, it's the Village. Nobody notices Susan; if they do, their attention is negated with a jerk of the chin, and loud talk about Other Matters. So and so fucked so and so who's doing a show at such-and-such and this other one is *so* deluded you have to give her credit though she's been with Greg *how* long . . . ?

Lucas's apartment is three floors up but Susan can hear noise from the party; it drifts down to her in a cloud of laughter and shrieks and disjointed music. Floating up to the door, she smiles graciously at a trio of kids smoking on the building's stairs. Her fan is still tucked securely inside her sleeve; she doesn't feel the need to bring it out at this point. Even so, even with these three, she's made the right impression.

"Damn! Check out mama-san."

"Got some Suzy Wong shit goin' on."

"Madame *Butterfly.*"

As she is buzzed in, Susan wonders if there's any way she can use this image: three black guys playing a streetwise Greek chorus in a hip-hop dialect. Hasn't that been done before, though?

The party is very loud, wonderfully chaotic, thumping music, people standing shoulder-to-shoulder in crazy, *insane* costumes. Susan spots Lucas, mountain-tall in green eyeshadow and a heavy blue-black wig, drag cobbled together from his girlfriend's wardrobe and a few hasty visits to certain tacky stores in Soho. Said girlfriend (Angie?) is beside him, hugging onto his side like she's been grafted there. She's a whore. Neon red hair (dyed that afternoon, probably), ridiculously overdone makeup, a black corset, cherry-red, too-tight patent-leather shoes. Both Lucas and whatshername are laughing uproariously at no one and everyone. Susan stations herself a discreet three bodies away from Lucas and waits to be acknowledged.

Acknowledgment doesn't seem to be forthcoming. Vaguely offended, Susan sweeps toward the table of liquor at the room's opposite side, but a drink is thrust into her hand by someone who's gone before she can turn.

The drink is green, in a martini glass. It suits her. It goes with her *obi*. A chair opens up near a window and Susan decides to take it. Her *geta* are beginning to hurt, sooner than she had expected. The pressure of clutching the knobs with her unsplit socks is taking a toll; the overworked *tabi* have rebelled, the heels threatening to bunch up under her insteps. Susan doesn't feel like reaching down to pull them up every five minutes.

She recognizes a few people, trades nods with them. There's Magda, playing Wall Street in a charcoal three-piece, complete with a very nice maroon tie. David slumps by, apparently in one of his moods; he has elected not to come in costume and barely glances at her. Sean is Wonder Woman. Lucas's roommate Ben is a big hit in, of all things, a gorilla costume. He's over by the empty fireplace, pretending to sodomize a shrieking ballerina boy with a banana. A gallery owner Susan had been introduced to at Lucas's last party swoons by, seriously out of it in a standard-issue dominatrix getup. She props herself up on Susan's shoulder while she lights up a cigarette. When Susan smiles, Ms. Gallery Owner pats her shoulder and disappears.

Even while sitting, it's difficult keeping up with the flood of people. Everyone seems older than she is, or appallingly younger. Everyone is high or drunk together—except for Susan. No one has said a word about her costume. Her drink tastes like nothing but apple juice; once she's finished it there's nowhere to put the glass and no one offers to take it from her. She kicks her *geta* aside finally, and strips off her *tabi* with one hand, thrusts her bare feet out and glares defiantly into the air. If someone trips over her feet, she decides, it won't be her problem.

Out in the living room, something has caught everyone's attention. As one, the partiers back away from something on the floor, squealing and pointing. Susan, curious but unwilling to relinquish her seat, leans forward as far as she can.

It's a boy in a black T-shirt and shorts, wearing a pair of fuzzy cat ears. Greasepaint whiskers have been smeared on his face, and a long stuffed-stocking tail trails behind him on the floor. He's crawling over the floor, meowing plaintively, nuzzling hands and legs and shoes. Several people are crying Here kitty, kitty. Here pussy. Someone begins a off-key rendition of "Memories."

"Having a good time?" Susan starts and looks up. It's Lucas, leaning unsteadily against the wall, smiling down at her. His lipstick is badly smeared.

"I'm fine." She smiles demurely, remembers her fan, and tries to get it out of her sleeve. The empty glass gets in her way.

"So what are you up to these days?"

"Classes. Writing. You know." Susan gives up on the fan, settles for holding the glass out in a way meant to suggest it would be nice to be rid of it.

"You know Angie, right?" The girlfriend has emerged from the crowd gathered around the cat boy and stumbled over to reattach herself to Lucas. Susan says *Konichiwa,* careful to get the accent perfect. The effort is wasted on Angie, who, mumbling, begins sucking on Lucas's ear.

"Susan's a writer," Lucas tells Angie.

"What . . . writer? Wha's she write?"

"She's . . . she's a playwright. Studying to, to write plays. Right, Suze? *Ow . . .*" Angie has Lucas's earlobe in her teeth, worrying it with a playful growl.

"I'm working on a novel now, actually." Susan doesn't like being called Suze or Suzie or Sue. In fact, she hates it. Her name isn't Suze. "It's historical."

"Hysterical," Angie mutters, and giggles.

"It's set in Japan, during the Heian era," Susan tells her coldly. Apart from this little description, the novel does not, in fact, exist, but Susan's irritation brings it vividly to life inside her. She sees it, big and sprawling, an epic of love and passion and intrigue with so many characters they'll need to be listed between the table of contents and the first chapter. Whatever publisher she chooses will beg her to split it into five volumes, at least five. She'll make Lady Murasaki look like a minimalist. Susan's sudden vision of the book is righteous and burning; it drives away both jealousy and the treacherous little knot of heat growing inside her as she watches Lucas and Angie make out. Angie is trash, but she knows how to kiss a man, and Susan gets a nasty little voyeur's thrill watching her work.

She wonders if Lucas's cock is taped to his inner thigh, or tucked back under his balls or simply pulsing away in a huge, ridiculous erection that his dress discreetly hides. She wonders about his cock in general; does it curve to one side, the way she's heard some do? Is it unusually big, unusually small? Does it sport a tiny, fetching birthmark, perhaps right on the head? She had nourished faint hopes of satisfying her curiosity tonight, Angie or no Angie. She doesn't think that will happen now.

"We should introduce you to Mark," Lucas says, his words obscured by Angie's sudden application of her mouth to his. "He's with . . . Scribner? Harper . . . ? One of those. Is he around? Mark?"

"Over here. I saw him." Angie gets an arm around Lucas's ass, pulls him away.

Susan watches them move away, making for the hallway and, by implication, Lucas's bedroom, seriously considering throwing her glass at Angie's head. Then she jumps; something wet has been drawn over her bare toes.

The cat boy is crouched at her feet, licking them with delicate motions of his head and the occasional meow. Susan lifts one foot slightly and the cat boy tongues her sole, purring now. She turns her ankle this way and that; the boy follows the movements with his head, licking and nibbling at her arch and heel. It tickles, and Susan snorts back a giggle. It's difficult to say if he's an opportunistic fetishist or simply a little too into his role. Perhaps he's just out of his mind, but Susan is charmed nonetheless. No one has ever offered to lick her feet before. It seems an appropriate attention to pay a beautiful geisha, a dealer in unconventional desires.

"Oh, my *Neko!*" She can't remember the proper way to say "little cat" or better, "sweet little cat." Just plain *Neko* will have to do. She reaches down and scratches the boy's short black hair. Suddenly he's climbing into her lap. Susan squeals and drops her glass so she can get her hands around the boy's narrow shoulders. The glass hits the floor and rolls away unbroken.

The cat boy isn't much bigger or heavier than Susan herself. His body is warm and tight, beautifully compact against hers. He nuzzles her throat and lies sighing in her arms. His legs hang over her lap and his arms are thrust securely between her sides and the chair.

Susan glances around; the cat boy has already been forgotten by the party. Nobody is taking note of her conquest. Even so, she hugs him possessively. He makes a little chirping noise and she coos at him. Her kitty. Her *Neko*.

"What's your name?"

" . . . "

"What?"

"Milk. Gimme, 'kay?" He pulls away from her a little, plucks at her kimono, then nestles his head down with his mouth over one cotton-covered breast, sucking.

Susan inhales sharply. Her nipple is hard, suddenly, aching. The boy's breath on it is hot as he exhales, and freezing cold as he draws his breath inward. She digs her nails into his arms and shuffles her bare feet on the floor. Without the *tabi,* they look too big, ridiculous with their splayed, red-painted toes. But *Neko* licked them. He thought they were beautiful—or tasty, at any rate.

"Honey . . . hey . . . uhm, listen. . ." She can't think of anything else to say. *Neko* is still sucking energetically at her tit, twisting his shoulders with a slow rhythm. Susan's hips squirm in the chair. The sucking is like another tickle, almost unbearable; she doesn't want to push him away, but she can't stand it another minute.

She thrusts a hand down, manages to scoop it between *Neko*'s legs, flattens it against his crotch. She does it partly from desire, partly from a vague notion that she can slow down the torturous nipple-sucking this way. His dick is hard, but serenely hard. Unflappably, unapologetically hard. He moves his ass to accomodate her hand.

"Oh Jesus." Does anyone see them? Can anyone see them, has she somehow laid her own utter invisibility over *Neko* like a cloak? If she tore her *obi* away, undid the *shita-jime* and spread her legs, squirmed out of her shorts . . . could she fuck *Neko* right there in the chair? What would that be like? There with everyone to see them? At any rate, there's not much mystery about his cock, the way there is about Lucas's. Susan's fingers are free to measure it; it's got a nice length and thickness, with a firm, knobby head that makes *Neko* whimper on her tit when she plays with it. She can imagine it going inside her. He'd straddle her, push it in slow, mumbling kisses onto her throat. A perfectly beautiful fuck from a silent, tender (if not quite all there) lover.

"*Uuaoghhh!*" Something huge and hairy jumps in front of her, wildly waving plastic claws. Susan screams and hugs her *Neko* to her, but it's only Ben, chortling away inside his King Kong outfit. Susan glares, but it's too late to scold him; Ben is already shambling off, grunting and beating his chest, in pursuit of an oblivious girl in a rather limp pair of fairy wings.

The disturbance has taken *Neko*'s mouth from Susan's breast. He rolls onto his back in her arms, sighs, and pulls her hand back to his crotch.

Oh please, Susan thinks. But his long lashes flutter shut and his mouth moves.

Alright. This business on the chair isn't getting her anywhere. She knows she's not going to fuck *Neko* out here and not in Lucas's bedroom or Ben's, but she's going to fuck him somewhere. That much, at least, has been decided. The point is to get to that somewhere.

"Can someone please get me a cab?" she asks, sending the plea out into the roomful of floating heads. What she means to say is, "Can someone get *us* a cab," but why gloat? A passing girl sneers, making a point of the fact that *she's* not anyone's slave, but someone else, cell phone in hand, asks Susan where she's going. A tall guy in leather with a fussy little mustache. He glances at *Neko* as he relays Susan's destination to the dispatcher, and gives Susan a solemn wink.

"*Domo arogato.*" Susan gets a hand under *Neko's* shirt and finds his nipples. He smiles and they get stiff under her fingers.

Susan returns the smile. She'll leave the party barefoot, make Neko carry her *geta,* but leave her soiled, stretched-out *tabi* for Angie to discover the next morning, a sign that *she* wasn't the only one who got fucked last night. The cab ride will be blissful, a long trip through the Manhattan night, replete with kisses and covert strokes to various sensitive body parts. Susan will enter her dark apartment quietly, hand-in-hand with *Neko.* Diane will be in her room reading or sleeping. She'll hear all about it the next afternoon, and laugh and shake her head and say, "Boy oh boy, Susan, you're just too wild."

Neko's sweaty clothes and feline identity will be peeled from him slowly, luxuriantly. Susan will force him to be a boy for her, and nothing but. She can imagine exactly what he'll look like naked. She'll stretch him out on her futon and tease *him* for a change; half an hour or more of her nails and tongue and toes. Binding his wrists and ankles to the wooden frame isn't out of the question. Maybe she'll recite to him from her imaginary novel as she climbs on him and finally receives that tantalizing cock.

Of course (what is she thinking?), the novel is not imaginary. It's as real as either of them, a reality waiting to be introduced to the world: The epic story of a well-known and strikingly beautiful courtesan and her magical, shape-shifting lover who scandalize and delight the Heian court with their affair. A passion to outlive the centuries. A tale for the ages.

Susan can't wait to see how it all comes out.

I Am . . .

BY CHRISTINE MORGAN

I . . . I should warn you, Janet. Your Aunt Millie had . . . well . . . a bit of a wild side."

Janet had been about to say good-bye when her mother spoke. The tone of her voice was so strange, so different, that it gave Janet pause.

Moments before, it had been the usual patter of Mom's fretting. How she shouldn't have put this burden on Janet and Peter, but the real estate agent said that the new people wanted to move in by the fifteenth, and poor Millie, such a tragedy but thank God her pain was over, and was Janet really sure she didn't mind?

"A wild side?" Janet echoed.

She had been trying to reassure her mother that of course she didn't mind packing up Aunt Millie's things. While it might not have been the way she and Peter had planned on spending the first week of their summer break from the university, it was the least they could do. Aunt Millie had been very generous to them during their early, struggling years of marriage. And no, Janet didn't fault her mother at all for not taking care of it herself. Mom had a shop to run, and two of Janet's younger siblings still lived at home.

"I just don't want you to be startled by anything you might find."

"I'm sure I can handle Aunt Millie's deep, dark secrets," Janet said, smiling. "Good-bye, Mom. I'll talk to you later."

After hanging up the phone, she negotiated the cluttered kitchen where she had been working on boxing up dishware. Cardboard cartons and stacks of newspaper were piled haphazardly on chairs, while stacks of Aunt Millie's floral-patterned china waited on the countertops. Janet picked her way past to the door that led into the living room.

More china waited in here, delicate cups and saucers filling two armoires. Peter was up on a stool, gingerly taking down a collection of ceramic figurines. He glanced over his shoulder as Janet came in.

"How's your mother?"

"Still worried that she should have come out herself to take care of things." Janet laughed. "She told me that Aunt Millie had a wild side."

Peter snorted. "Her shelf of Harlequin romances, you mean? The ones that feature a lingering kiss and then a fade to black?"

"How do you know so much about those kinds of books?"

"I'm just saying, if that's your spinster aunt's wild side, I don't think we're in any danger of being corrupted."

"Spinster isn't a very flattering word. How come bachelor sounds so much more sophisticated?"

"How come promiscuous men are studs and promiscuous

women are tramps?" Peter returned with a shrug. "I teach math, not philosophy, and certainly not sex ed."

"I should have asked Mom what she meant," Janet said, placing a layer of foam padding over the row of fragile sculptures Peter had just finished loading into a box.

"Your family thinks it's radical to eat bacon and eggs for dinner."

"True. It's probably nothing more than Aunt Millie putting white chocolate chips into her Toll House recipe."

"Philistine!" Peter cried.

They had decided that it would be easier to stay in Millie's guest room rather than drive forty-five minutes back and forth from their apartment each day. With the kitchen in a state of disarray, and both of them worn out from their labors, Peter ordered out for dinner while Janet showered. After they ate, he showered and sat down in front of the television, while she opened a mystery novel. It was their routine, as predictable as sunrise and sunset.

Janet found that she couldn't concentrate on the story. Her mind kept wandering back to what her mother had said, and the peculiar, stiff way in which she'd said it.

Wild side. If anyone on her side of the family had ever possessed one, this was the first Janet had heard of it.

Her female relatives were all cast from the same mold. Short and slim of build, brown of hair and eye, birdlike in manner. They were good students and reliable babysitters who usually went on to marry a nice boy from the neighborhood and raise polite children. They played bridge and gardened, participated in school bake sales, and helped out with various charitable causes.

Those who worked held quiet, respectable jobs. Janet's mother ran a shop devoted to dollhouses and miniatures. Her cousin Tammy taught music. Aunt Millie had retired from forty years as a seam-stress.

No one in her family moved far from home. They chose the same vacation spots that their parents had taken them to, year in and year out. They developed nervous tics if some boat-rocking interloper suggested trying a new restaurant.

Janet knew she was just the same. In looks, in habits, in every-thing. Had her soul been suddenly transported back through time into the body of her grandmother, she could have picked up the rou-tine with barely a hitch.

She wondered what Aunt Millie had done that could have possibly made her mother say something like that. Had it been a deviation from a writ-in-stone family recipe, or something even more shocking?

"I think I'm going upstairs," Janet said, putting her book aside.

Peter tore his attention away from a documentary on one of the educational channels. "Need help?"

"No, thanks. I'm not working. I'm just going to poke around a little."

"If you find the secret room where your aunt kept the severed and frozen limbs of her victims, give a yell."

"Peter!"

"No severed limbs? How about a pentacle and bloodstained altar?"

"I don't think so." She gave him a stern look, and he gave back an impish grin. "You. Mom was right about you. She said all the Wheeler boys were smart alecks."

"So why'd you marry me?"

"Must have been my own wild side," Janet said. "Or maybe I thought I could reform you."

"Well, you've done that, at least. There used to be a time when I wanted to try skydiving. You cured me of that, as well as other bizarre notions."

His eyes twinkled to show he was teasing. Maybe he mostly was, but Janet wasn't fooled. The only arguments they'd had in eight years of marriage had come when he suggested doing something new, and she clung to tradition, familiarity, known factors.

She climbed the narrow staircase to the second floor. Aunt Millie's house was a charming little Victorian with all sorts of gables and nooks. It was in good condition and had fetched a tidy sum from the buyers. What bothered Janet the most was knowing that these strangers would come through and *change* everything. They'd tear down the wallpaper, repaint, do God-knew-what to the place.

If only she and Peter had been able to take the house. Aunt Millie had offered to leave it to Janet, but the medical bills had swiftly eaten up her savings and the money from the house would have to cover the cost of her funeral and other debts.

Aunt Millie's bedroom was at the end of the hall. Janet could hardly stand to go in there, too aware that Millie would never sleep in that bed again, or look out the window at her roses in the back garden. In that room, Janet truly knew her aunt was dead.

But it was that room, if anywhere, that might hold some clues to this mysterious wild side that had Janet's mother so distressed. What, exactly, did Mom think Janet might find?

When the house was new, the bedroom Millie used had probably belonged to a nanny. It was connected to a tiny nursery, which had been closed off for as long as Janet could remember. The master bedroom, at the front of the house, had always been reserved for guests.

Janet spent half an hour opening drawers and going through the closet. She found nothing out of the ordinary, only the skirts and slacks and cardigans that made up Aunt Millie's wardrobe. Everything was clean and still serviceable, and would have to be packed up and taken to a secondhand store. Someone would be glad to have them, old-fashioned though they were.

She tried the door to the nursery. It was locked, but the key was on a ribbon in the top dresser drawer. The door opened easily.

The room beyond was small, with a steeply pitched ceiling. Janet had irrationally been expecting to see bright wallpaper with cartoon characters, a crib, a changing table, a rocker, a box of toys. Instead, she was met by dark paneling and thick wine-colored drapes. The floor was hardwood, gleaming around the edges of a lush burgundy throw rug.

A full-length mirror dominated the wall opposite the door, giving Janet a start as she glimpsed her reflection. The other walls were lined in shelves full of the sort of cardboard containers Janet associated with under-bed storage. A small triangular vanity table sat in one corner, and the scent of perfume and cosmetics hung in the air like a whisper.

Perfume? Makeup? Janet remembered Aunt Millie as smelling of powder and baked goods, and never wearing so much as a hint of lipstick. Neither did she remember ever seeing her aunt's hair in anything other than a careless bun or ponytail, yet there was an array of combs, brushes, curlers, and other styling tools on the vanity. And above it, on another shelf, stood several wig stands sporting wigs in half a dozen colors and styles.

No wonder Mom had warned Janet about being startled by what she might find. She stood at the edge of the burgundy rug, turning slowly as she tried to make sense of what she was seeing.

Each of the cardboard boxes had a label pasted to the end. Janet read them off one by one, her incredulity growing.

"Claire . . . Agnes . . . Raven . . . Hippolyta . . . Catherine . . . Dominique . . ."

The names were written in her aunt's handwriting. Janet knew it well, from years of birthday cards and friendly letters, from inscriptions inside gift books. But she did not recognize any of the names. Except for Hippolyta, which she associated with Greek mythology. She certainly didn't know anyone belonging to those names.

She took down the box labeled "Claire" and opened it. The box held clothes, which Janet removed piece by piece. Black knee socks. Shiny patent-leather shoes. A pleated plaid skirt. A white blouse. A filmy white cotton bra and matching panties.

Underneath the articles of clothing was a sheet of stationery covered with her aunt's writing. Janet read it in silence, her eyes widening until she felt as though they might fall out of her head.

> I am . . . Claire. A demure young schoolgirl, but with a knowing look.
>
> Perhaps it's for you, Professor, and I will do anything for a top grade. Won't you keep me after class to discuss it? Here, by your desk? Won't you promise me an A if I get down on my knees and earn it? Won't you teach me something I can't learn from your lectures? I know you want to.
>
> Or perhaps, Headmaster, I've been a naughty girl and deserve a spanking. Summon me to your office and turn me over your knee. Raise my skirt and take down my panties, and paddle my bottom until it turns red. Let me lie across your lap and feel how my squirming excites you.

Janet read it again, her mouth hanging open, a hot flush rising in her cheeks. When she had confirmed that it did say what she thought it said, she dropped the paper onto the heap of clothes and scrubbed her hand against her leg.

"What in the world?" she murmured. "Aunt Millie? No, no, that's just wrong."

Peter had tried to spank her once. They had been making love, when without warning he'd started in asking her if she had been a bad girl. And then he had slapped her on the rump, a sharply stinging slap that made her leap out of bed in tears. He'd told her he only meant it in fun.

Why would anyone want to be hit? What kind of craziness was that? Fun, he called it. Fun. Well, she had set him straight about that.

She didn't want to, but curiosity compelled her to take down another box at random. This one's label read "Catherine," and it contained a gorgeous emerald silk gown with a plunging neckline. It was the kind of outfit that belonged on the cover of a torrid paperback, not the relatively innocent Harlequins but the ones with sex scenes that steamed on the page.

I am . . . Catherine. A chaste but fiery noblewoman with a proud beauty that begs to be conquered.

Can you tame me, oh daring Sir Knight? Our marriage might have been arranged, my body yours by decree, but will you win my heart as easily as you overpower and ravish my flesh? You may make me surrender my maidenhead, and my passion, to the lance of your manhood. But can you touch my soul?

What of you, oh roguish pirate lord? You've taken me from my ship, and spared me the crude attentions of your crew. Captive in your cabin, I am at your mercy. Will you take me and be done with it, or will you seek to make my humiliation whole by tormenting me with pleasure until I beg to be fucked?

The final word made Janet gasp. Her *aunt* had written this? She wouldn't have believed Aunt Millie to ever use words like that, ever! And what was the purpose of these outfits? The emerald-green gown was Aunt Millie's size. So was the schoolgirl uniform. Did she actually *wear* these things?

And why?

Janet held the silk gown to her shoulders and looked in the mirror. The folds of fabric draped her body. It would fit her, too. As if it had been made for her measure.

Grimacing, she shoved it back in the box as if she'd touched something nasty.

This couldn't mean what she was thinking it meant. She couldn't imagine Aunt Millie, of all people, dressing up to act out bizarre sex fantasies.

What was she going to tell Peter? He couldn't know what was in this room. No one could. But least of all, Peter. It wasn't just the spanking incident. Oh, no. There had been that other time . . .

Once, when they had been married for just a few months, he'd planned a surprise for her. He wouldn't tell her what it was, thinking she'd be happy, not fully understanding then how much Janet hated the unknown.

She'd come home to find a candlelit dinner, and that was all right. But then, Peter had excused himself to "slip into something more comfortable" and come back dressed like Captain James T. Kirk of *Star Trek* fame. When he'd also produced a miniskirted Starfleet uniform in her size, she had reacted with a mixture of disgust, out-rage, and hysterical laughter that sent Peter fleeing from the room.

Decent people, she had told him later, didn't *do* things like that. His mortified defense was that he'd only wanted to add a little ad-venture, that he knew she liked to watch old episodes of *Star Trek,* and he'd thought she might like it.

They had come closer to divorce that night than any time before or since. Peter had slept on the couch for a week, while Janet spent sleepless nights alone in the bedroom, unable to tell anyone else what was wrong.

How could she confide, even to her mother or closest friends, that her husband was a pervert, with weird kinky ideas? How could she tell anyone that the man she'd married wanted to play alien sex games in their marital bed?

It had blown over eventually, and he had never mentioned any-thing out of the ordinary again. No pretending. No dirty movies. No underwear ordered out of those filthy catalogs. No whipped cream, battery-operated appliances, or anything of such a vile nature. Their love life was fine. It didn't need "spicing up."

Except maybe it did.

The thought came out of nowhere, and Janet pounced on it fu-riously. There was nothing wrong with her and Peter's love life. It was perfectly normal. Perfectly predictable. Perfectly routine. Once a week, lights out, with an additional one on special occasions like his birthday or their anniversary.

This was wrong. This, Aunt Millie's secret habit, was abnormal and unnatural.

She was further proved right when she took the box marked "Hippolyta" from the shelf. Within was a getup that could have stepped straight out of a Boris Vallejo painting. Hammered gold brassiere, kilt-like skirt of leather straps, sandals that laced to the knee. Janet was drawn to the accompanying sheet of paper the way she was sometimes drawn to look at grisly accidents.

I am . . . Hippolyta. Queen of the Amazons, warrior-woman, wild and free.

You should be honored, my fine young stud. Of all my slaves, men first humbled by me in battle and then bent to my will, it is you I've chosen to share my couch this night. You are mine to command. I will have you rubbed with olive oil until your bronze skin is glistening and your spear standing erect.

See how you want me, even in your hatred? Oh, ancient enemy, man that you are, not even your animosity toward me can diminish your need. Your body betrays you, even as your mind resists. You ache to have me sink down upon your oiled length and ride you like the beast that you are.

Janet had to sit down. She staggered on legs that felt like stilts to the vanity table, to the stool. Her breath was quick, her heart hammering.

How could Aunt Millie have done this? And how had Janet's mother found out about it? She wished she hadn't hung up on Mom so soon. The warning hadn't been enough. No warning could have fully prepared her, but Mom could have been clearer.

Sick as it was, wrong as it was, the worst part of all was the horrible fascination. Janet was torn between wanting to run from the room, locking the door forever, and opening those last three boxes.

Could it be that this was . . . it couldn't possibly be arousing her!

The fevered flush, the slippery warmth, these had to be caused by nausea, not desire.

She chose the "Agnes" box next, and was initially relieved to see a heavy woolen dress. It had a high collar trimmed with lace, a bustle, and a built-in corset. Under the dress was a pair of shoes that shattered that initial relief. They fastened all down the front with myriad tiny buttons and hooks, with toes that came to a wicked point, heels to a wicked spike. Beside the shoes was a long, thin piece of wood. A switch. A supple birch switch.

> *I am . . . Agnes. Stern governess and schoolmistress.*
>
> *Look at you, you naughty little boy! Do you know what happens to little boys who play with their doodles? It's unhealthy. For shame. Have you been spying on the upstairs maids again, young master? Spying on them through a hole in the door, watching while they piddle and wash?*
>
> *Well, we'll have none of that around here! Down you go, on your stomach. I'll pull that nightshirt up to your waist and lash your bottom until it is striped and red. By the way you squeal and wiggle, I think you like it, you bad, bad little boy!*

Despite herself, Janet giggled. Wouldn't that serve Peter right? Wouldn't that teach him a lesson? Spank her, would he? Well, she should see how he liked it! Or the Hippolyta outfit . . . he wanted adventure, didn't he? She'd give him—

Her thoughts broke off with a snap. What had gotten into her that she would even be considering such a thing?

Still, it would be funny to see the look on his face if she strutted downstairs all strict and businesslike in those killer button-up shoes.

He'd be right where she had left him, feet propped on the ottoman. She could order him to take down his pants and bend over the cushioned footstool, and when his bare white backside was turned up and vulnerable, she could stripe it until he squealed.

Janet shuddered and hastily shoved the box back onto the shelf. She had to get out of this room, this awful room with its freight of depravity.

"There *are* only two boxes left," she said aloud, in a cajoling tone that surprised her. "Can't hurt to look. Just look."

So she opened the one labeled "Raven," and exclaimed at the rich black velvet that met her eyes. Elbow-length gloves, a domino mask, a ribbon meant to tie around the neck and clasp with a black opal cameo. Under these items was a sleeveless bodysuit made of stretchy black velvety material, and under that was a pair of thigh-high boots.

I am . . . Raven. Enemy spy, super-villain, sultry shadow of the night.

I'll think nothing of seducing you for your secrets, of writhing against you in the throes of passion though we both know that tomorrow may see us as deadly foes. It's that very darkness in me that so lures you, so tempts you into falling from grace.

Every hero has a weakness. She may be waiting for you, the sweet and virginal good girl heroine whom you must rescue from some diabolical plan. But it's the dark side you crave. I know things that she could never imagine. I'll do things you never dreamed. I am your nemesis, your Lilith, your downfall. And oh, hero, how you want me!

She stroked the soft, lush fabric. That bodysuit would cling like a coat of paint. It'd leave nothing to the imagination. She couldn't wear anything beneath it, either. A panty line or the strap of a bra would ruin its sleek lines.

And those gloves . . . was there anything more feminine and sexy than a pair of black elbow-length gloves? She slid the left one onto her arm, wriggling her fingers, smoothing the velvet until it encased her skin in a gentle embrace.

A shiver made Janet close her eyes. She saw herself slinking through a mansion, teasing open a safe filled with glittering diamonds, cat burglar surprised in the act by the handsome owner and offering him her body so that he wouldn't turn her in. And then, as he basked in the exhaustion of sexual acrobatics the likes of which Janet could barely believe, she'd escape with the jewels and leave him poverty-stricken, but with a smile.

Janet came back to herself with a start, realizing that she was languidly touching her lips and cheeks, running gloved fingers over her face. She peeled the glove off and threw it back in the box, and retreated to the stool by the vanity again to catch her breath.

These were no normal clothes, she told herself. They had some sort of power. Maybe they were treated with a drug, a hallucinogenic perfume, an aphrodisiac. It was the only explanation she could think of, though the idea of Aunt Millie dabbling in drugs was as absurd as Aunt Millie engaging in adult dress-up games.

The last box sat on the shelf, mocking her with its closed lid. "Dominique," whoever she was, dared Janet to let her out, sneered at Janet, taunted her and scoffed at her lack of nerve.

"Oh, yeah, is that what you think?" Janet muttered.

She removed the lid, and gaped at fishnets, stiletto heels, a scarlet miniskirt so short that Janet first mistook it for a belt, a red corset with black laces, and a satiny cape. She thought *she-devil*. She thought *Red Riding Hood gone bad*. But this box also held another, smaller box nested inside, and when she opened that, she came face to face with Dominique's tools of the trade.

A hood with zippers over the mouth and eyes, and straps that buckled tight beneath the chin. Handcuffs. A flat, padded-leather paddle. Cinching rings whose purpose eluded her. Tiny silvery thumbscrews. A coiled whip that made Agnes's birch switch look as threatening as an ostrich feather. Flasks of oils and lotions. Some sort of complicated affair of studded leather that turned out to be, after Janet examined it for several seconds, a harness. Other things so strange she couldn't hazard a guess.

She picked up the sheet of her aunt's stationery.

> *I am . . . Dominique. You will call me Mistress.*
>
> *So you like to be brought low, do you? The man of power and wealth craves humiliation, yearns to be controlled. I will make you wallow in filth. You will lick my shoes and beg for mercy, only to be met with more and inventive punishments.*
>
> *Down on your knees, worthless animal. Hear how you whimper as I lock the ring around the base of your stiff prick! What shall it be tonight? Hot wax to the nipples? These clamps applied to your most sensitive spots? No, you're not allowed to speak. You will do as I say, and you will love it.*

"Oh, my," Janet said.

The paper slipped from her nerveless fingers and seesawed to the floor. She sat down again, and for quite some time could only blink in amazement. Her stunned gaze roamed the room, taking in the names that seemed to call to her from the labels.

She could be any of them. Any of them at all.

It wouldn't be *Janet* doing those nasty things. Certainly not!

Janet would never enjoy being ravished or spanked. But if she were Catherine, or Claire? Janet would never, never treat a man like a brutish beast. But Hippolyta would, and so would Agnes, and Dominique. Janet wasn't a seductress. But Raven was.

Freedom. Absolution.

She repeated the words aloud, testing them. Freedom from inhibition. Absolution from guilt. That was what Aunt Millie's secret room offered her. No one would ever suspect Janet, not meek mousy Janet.

Well, and why not?

She rose from the stool, deliberated, and made her choice. When she had donned the outfit, she turned to Millie's vanity table and selected a wig to go with it. She applied the appropriate cosmetics with a sure and skillful hand, though she never usually wore more than a touch of lipstick.

Peter had just clicked off the television as she reached the bottom of the stairs. He yawned, stretched, turned, and saw her.

His expression erased the last of her lingering doubts. He stared, jaw hanging sprung, and then a light of amazed wonder dawned in his eyes.

"Janet?"

"No," she said. "I am . . ."

She paused, savoring his tantalized anticipation, and told him her name.

Contented Clients

BY KATE DOMINIC

Andre was more than a little miffed. I'd been quite specific letting him know that the matronly outfit he'd designed for me was about as sexy as a burlap sack.

"I want to show boobs, dear," I snapped, dumping the custom-made '50s style housedress on top of the naked mannequin's headless neck. "Mother's 'naughty little boys and girls' need to be squirming in anticipation of a nice, comforting nipple to suck on, even before I turn them over my knees."

"As Madame wishes," Andre sniffed, his beautiful green eyes flashing with righteous indignation as he tossed his short blond curls. In a flash of dramatic pique that only a former runway model could master, he turned and swept up the yards of atrocious yellow floral print. He froze in mid-pirouette when my hand snaked out and gripped his slender, denim-covered butt cheek. Hard. I wasn't sure what Andre's problem was today. His costumes were usually exquisite. But I was in no mood for an artistic temper tantrum when I had clients scheduled for that scene in less than a week.

"Madame damn well wishes," I said quietly. "And if Andre has a problem with that, perhaps Madame should call Andre's sweet, smiling lover over to give dear little Andre an attitude adjustment."

Andre looked nervously over his shoulder, his eyes locking on the large, bearded man hunched intently over the computer screen on the other side of the room. The only time I'd ever seen Bedford's lips so much as curve upward was when he was paddling the bejeezus out of Andre's ass. Bedford clicked onto a new screen, leaned back, and carefully stroked his chin. The latest design appeared on the web page he was updating, and Bedford nodded once, so slowly that the long, brown hair tied back at his neck barely moved over the flannel shirt covering his thickly muscled shoulders.

"That won't be necessary," Andre said primly, almost hiding a shiver as he carefully turned and set the discarded material onto a side table. He glanced once more in his bearish lover's direction. "Shall Madame and I sit down at the other work station and discuss alternative design options?"

"The operative word being 'sit,'" I snapped, releasing his asscheek. I managed to control my smile as Andre politely escorted me over to the computer, offering me a chair before he called up my profile with even more efficiency than usual. From the way his ass was twitching, I gathered that sweet, pouty little Andre's entire snit had been staged purely to let Bedford know that he was hungry for a good, old-fashioned ass-warming. Despite Bedford's apparent lack of attention, I had no doubt that he'd heard every word—and that a very sore and well-fucked Andre would be working standing up for the next couple of days.

It wasn't the first time I'd been an unwitting prop in one of my friends' private little scenes. I doubted it would be the last. I shook my head and bit back a grin as my voluptuous cyber model filled the screen and a nervous, eager-to-please Andre and I got back to designing the perfect costume for my stable of submissive little boys and girls.

Overall, I'd been quite pleased with PFA, Inc. Personal Fetish Attire had provided me with my first dominatrix outfits with almost off-the-rack speed—no mean feat, given my well-endowed size 2X proportions. As my clientele had grown, Andre and I had worked together to design some very chic leather teddies and harnesses that emphasized my Rubenesque curves for my hardcore "mistress" clients, as well as the flowing drapes of satin and lace that highlighted the ample padding so comforting to my naughty adult children. When I'd branched out into less traditional fetishes, PFA had quietly made some introductions—to other clients, for whom they then also supplied costumes. Several of my fantasy scenes had even been Bedford's idea.

"We got this guy who's really into horror flicks," Bedford had said one fall afternoon. He was lacing me into my new black corset as Andre put the finishing touches on my Halloween vampire costume. "Cleavage" didn't begin to describe the size of the valley developing between my boobs as Bedford cinched me into place. Andre had somehow managed to build in a truly comfortable support bra, without losing the sleek lines of the corset. "This dude would think he'd died and gone to heaven if you had your way with him in this costume, Ms. Amanda, especially if you bit his neck a of couple times. Hell, if you let him nurse on these mamas, he'd pay whatever you wanted. And honey," Bedford winked at me as he tucked the lacing ends under the intricately tied knots, "he can afford to pay whatever you want."

In short order, I'd found out that Timmy could indeed afford my services. Frequently. From there, it was a short step to a half-dozen men who wanted to be spanked and diapered and fed a cup of warm milk, then held on Mama's large, comforting lap to nurse contentedly on her huge ol' boobs while they went to sleep. That costume was easy, too. I set the scene to be one of "baby" waking up at night, so the seductive peignoirs that, along with leatherwear, were the mainstay of PDF, needed only a complimentary pair of feathered satin mules to have "baby's" hard, horny dick drooling into the neatly pinned cloth cotton diapers Andre had custom-made for them. At the end of the scene, I'd sit in the oversized rocker Bedford had built and unhook my specially made "nursing bra," one cup at a time, and let "baby" suckle my huge, dark red nipples until the heavenly stimulation—and the ben wa balls in my pussy—made me explode in orgasm. The sucking, along with my usual expert wrist action, usually had baby creaming into his diaper as soon as he'd sucked me through my climax. My submissive and infantilist clients were an excellent match for me, as my breasts were about the most sensitive part of my body. After a good session of nipple stimulation and roasting naked backsides, all it took was a few quick flicks to my clit or a well-placed toy to make my cunt gush.

Although my clients paid well enough that I only needed to have a few regulars, I was interested in branching out again. For the first time, I also had a couple of women clients. Both they and a couple of new "boys" that I'd taken on were hot to do a Teenager Gone Bad scene.

One of the girls, Cherise, had had serious problems with bulimia.

I'd had a long talk with her doctor before I accepted her as a client. Cherise, however, was not into infantilism. Spanking, yes. But at twenty-six, she saw herself more as a naughty high-schooler who needed someone to take her firmly in hand and teach her to be good and do right—and to help her gain a healthy dose of the self-esteem she was fighting so hard to achieve. After her last visit, I'd told her that next week "her mother" wanted to discuss her report card with her—most specifically, her citizenship grades. She was to be sure to wear her best school clothes and saddle shoes. Cherise had shivered, her face positively glowing as she kissed my hand and whispered, "Yes, ma'am. I'll be here right after school." Which meant 6:30 P.M. sharp, after she'd finished work and eaten exactly as the doctor's regimen directed.

Part of the success of our session, however, hinged on whether Andre got off his butt and got me a sexy enough "loving but stern 1950s middle-class Mom" costume. I knew Cherise's costume was done. Although Andre hadn't shown it to me, he told me I'd be pleased. He also assured me that my costume would most definitely not be lacking by Thursday evening when I picked it up. I assured him that it had better not be, or I'd be lending Bedford one wicked fucking Lucite paddle.

Of course, Bedford had heard the whole exchange, despite how engrossed he'd appeared to have been in the website updates. As I walked toward the door, I heard him growl, "Drop yer pants and get over my knees, boy!" followed by the sound of a chair being pushed back, the clink of a belt being unbuckled, and Andre's plaintive "I'm sorreeeee, Bedford!" I smiled and turned the "closed" sign to the window on my way out, locking the door behind me.

Whether it was the hiding Bedford gave him for "sassing the customers," for which Andre tearfully apologized into my answering machine, or just his usual desire to create gorgeously sexy attire, Andre outdid himself with the new and improved version of my happy housewife ensemble. The soft, full, autumn-colored skirt brushed just below my knees, a wide leather belt cinching Mother's ample waist in just enough to show her well-rounded hips. A simple beige silk button-down blouse tucked into the waist, veiling but definitely not hiding the cream-colored peek-a-boo satin and lace front-hook bra that was, again, wonderfully supportive and comfortable. Since it was a warm fall day, Mother wasn't wearing underwear per se, just a butterfly vibrator in a thin-strapped thong-type harness, a lacy garter belt that matched her brassiere and held the tiny control box for the vibrator, and thigh-high seamed nylons. Whether or not my errant daughter was going to discover what was beneath my skirt remained to be seen. I'd made plans for several contingencies. A pristine starched white cotton apron that tied at the waist rounded out my attire, along with low brown leather heels and a pearl necklace and earrings. By the time I took the hot rollers out of my hair and sprayed my period 'do into place, I had just enough time to spritz on some White Shoulders perfume before the front door quietly opened.

I walked to the stove and lifted the lid on the pot of thick hearty vegetable soup that was cooking, picked up the long-handled wooden spoon, and started to stir as I heard Cherise come into the kitchen. I looked up at her and smiled.

"Hello, dear. How was school?"

Andre had outdone himself again. Cherise wore a poodle skirt and a soft pink angora sweater that softened the angular planes that were slowly filling out as she grew healthier. When I nodded appreciatively, Cherise blushed and slowly turned around, the careful draping of the thick skirt flowing with her as she moved to show off how her pretty bottom was finally rounding out. Her legs were bare except for ankle socks and saddle shoes, and her fragile, usually pale face was suffused with a happy blush. The three textbooks she carried under her arm added more to her teenage look than her blond pony-tail held in place by a charming pink satin bow.

"School was fine, Mother." Cherise smiled, one of her truly happy smiles, even as she quickly lowered her gaze. I was surprised to realize how much I'd come to anticipate that quiet, shy look. "I got all my homework done, and I had lunch with my friends."

But Cherise was studiously concentrating on the pattern in the linoleum. Her deliberately averted eyes told my "mother's intuition" that something was up. I cleared my throat and set the spoon down on the counter.

"Cherise, are you wearing lipstick?!" I asked sharply, clucking a feigned disapproval. "Young lady, someone as naturally beautiful as you does not need artificial enhancements!"

The creamy, dark pink ribbon of color would have been impossible to miss. Andre had no doubt spent hours ensuring it would compliment the natural blush that slowly suffused Cherise's face. She obediently looked up at me, her blue eyes sparkling.

"I wanted to look pretty today, mother," she said shyly.

"Cherise," I said, shaking my head in mock exasperation. "You are always pretty. This," I pointed sternly at her lips, "is like adding lipstick to a rose. I am sorely tempted to turn you over my knee!"

"Oh, no, Mother." She reached back quickly to protect her bottom with her free hand. I wasn't sure how much of that was an act. Cherise loved the catharsis of a long, hard, tear-filled spanking; she wasn't satisfied until her backside was blazing sore and she was sob-bing like a baby. "I'm much too old to be spanked."

She moved to the table and set down her books. A bright yellow folded piece of paper fell out: REPORT CARD. Quickly she tucked it under her algebra book. I bit my lip and very deliberately wiped my hands on my apron.

"Nonsense, sweetheart. A pretty young lady like you is defi-nitely still of an age for a good, sound dose of Mother's hairbrush when you need it. I hope you're hiding that report card because you want to surprise me with your wonderful grades, and not be-cause of bad citizenship marks again." I carefully unfolded the card. A "B," three "C's," and a "D" were marked in heavy black let-ters in the academics columns—right across from five bright red "F's" in citizenship.

"Cherise!" I said sternly. "What is the meaning of this?!"

"Um, I don't know, Mother," she said nervously, shifting her weight from one foot to the other as she peered over my shoulder. "Maybe the teacher made a mistake?"

"Have you been doing your homework?" I demanded, giving her bottom a quick, sharp swat.

"Yes." She stepped quickly back, out of the line of fire, lowered her eyes again and stirred her foot in a nervous circle. "Well, most of the time. Sometimes I forgot."

"I see," I said icily, tapping the card on my fingers. "And the tar-diness, talking in class, and lack of participation were also caused by forgetfulness?"

"Um, sometimes." Cherise licked her lips nervously, highlighting the bright color of her lipstick.

"Yet you could still remember to put on your makeup."

Cherise clamped her hand over her mouth and stammered, "Just today!"

"Give me the lipstick." I held out my hand. "It had better be almost unused."

Andre knew me well. Cherise reached into her purse, and as she drew out the well-worn tube, I could see that the contents had been carefully honed down so that only half a stick was left.

"So, now you've started lying as well, young lady?"

Cherise hung her head in shame. Her pert little nipples were hard under her sweater. My labia started to tingle.

"I'm sorry, mother," she whispered. "I won't do it again."

"You certainly won't," I snapped, tossing the report card on the table and turning the soup down to simmer. "You've earned a good, sound bottom roasting, young lady."

"Mother!!" Cherise wailed, reaching back to cover her backside, this time in earnest. She backed up against the cupboard. I shook my head sternly at her.

"Not in here, Cherise." I took off my apron and carefully folded it over the back of the kitchen chair. "I'm going to be taking down your panties. If your crying draws the neighbors, we can't have them looking through the window and seeing your bare, red bottom wiggling all over my lap. We're going to your room."

"Mother!!!"

Ignoring the increasingly loud protests of innocence and the promises to do better in the future, I took my errant "daughter's" hand and marched her resolutely down the hall, hurrying her with a few well-placed swats when she dawdled. We entered "her" room, and I locked the door behind us.

For a moment, Cherise just stared at what was behind the door.

I'd taken the room that usually doubled as Mama's bedroom for the infantilists and changed it into a teenaged girl's dream, complete with delicately flowered chenille bedspread, turntable with rock and roll records, vintage movie posters, and a neat study desk, complete with dictionary, sharpened pencils, and a new, lined notebook. As Cherise looked around the room, I purposefully strode to the window and lowered the blinds.

"It's too hot to close the windows, Cherise. So don't even think to complain that the whole neighborhood is going to hear your spanking. You should have thought of that beforehand. Neighbors or not, I'm going to spank you until you're crying at the top of your lungs. Maybe it will do you some good to realize that everyone knows your mother loves you much too much to let a good girl like you get away with such nonsense."

"Mother!" Cherise seemed shocked, but I knew she could hear the air conditioning running, so she'd know this room was as sound-proofed as the rest of the house. But Cherise's low self-esteem in public was a big source of her problems. The instinctive shiver that ran up her spine told me how much she was enjoying the idea of "public" proof of her value to me. I walked over to the nightstand and moved the thick maple hairbrush to the front edge, within easy reach. Then I sat down on the bed and pointed in front of me.

"Come here, Cherise, and lift up your skirt and slip."

"Motherrrrrr," she wailed, stomping her foot and backing against the closed door. I'd learned on our first visit how much Cherise enjoyed losing the battle to avoid her spankings. "I'm too old to be spanked bare!"

"Right now, young lady," I snapped my fingers, "and for your insolence, you will now take your skirt and slip OFF!"

With a loud sniffle, she shuffled over to stand beside me and slowly unbuttoned and lowered her skirt. The delicate white satin slip that hugged her hips was a work of art. But when she removed that as well, I needed a moment of reprieve while she carefully folded her clothing onto the nightstand. Andre had outdone himself: pristine white satin tap pants, bordered with Irish lace and decorated with dainty pink butterflies, framed the softly swelling mound between Cherise's legs and clung to the new fullness of her bottom. I slipped my shaking fingers into the waistband and slowly lowered the exquisite panties, exposing the neatly trimmed soft blond tufts covering her vulva.

"I'm too big to be spanked bare," she sniffed, reluctantly lifting first one leg, then the other.

"Nonsense." I smoothed my skirt and patted my thigh. "Mother's lap is quite big enough to hold you." Cherise slowly lowered herself across my legs, reaching forward to grab a thick handful of the plush chenille bedspread as I pulled her into position. She stiffened as I situated her so that her angular bones were cushioned comfortably over my full thighs. I wanted all of Cherise's attention to be focused on her bottom.

"This is going to be a very serious spanking, Cherise." She whimpered as I slowly slid my hand over the smooth, creamy curve of her bare behind. "I'm going to paddle your bottom until it's so red and sore, you won't be able to sit down for the rest of the week." I caressed her until she was squirming. I wanted every inch of her backside awakened and hungry to be touched.

"You will give your best effort, Cherise, in everything you do." I brought my hand down sharply across her right cheek. She yelped, jerking, and I brought my hand down hard on the other side.

"Ow!" Cherise arched her bottom up to meet each slap. "Mother! That hurts! Ow! Ow! OWWW!!!"

A dozen sound hand spanks later, her bottom was pinkening nicely. After another dozen, she was sniffling loudly, though she didn't try to move out of the way. I knew that would change the moment I picked up the brush.

"By not doing your best, you're only hurting yourself, dear." I quietly lifted the cool-handled maple brush and, with no warning, smacked it loudly over her right bottom cheek. Cherise howled, and her hand came up to cover her behind. I firmly held her wrist against her waist and spanked her again.

"We'll have none of that, young lady."

"It hurts!" she wailed, her legs flailing on the bed as I began to paddle her in earnest. She twisted and bucked, yelling at the top of her lungs as I covered her entire bottom with sharp, hard swats, up one side and down the other, with the steady rhythm I knew she so enjoyed. "Ow, ow! It hurts!!!"

"Of course it hurts," I snapped, stopping just long enough to pull her tightly to me. "Mother is punishing you, dear. I want your bottom good and sore."

Cherise's ensuing howls told me she was really feeling each swat. She kicked her way through another half-dozen sound, hard cracks. Then I paused and set the brush down, cupping her heated bottom and sliding my fingers between her legs and over her labia. Cherise's whole cunt was drenched. She arched into my hand, crying out as my fingertip slid forward to caress her swollen clit. Cherise spread her legs, sniffling loudly. The smell of her arousal filled my nostrils. My own pussy clenched in response.

"Good girls always doing their best." I gently pinched her swollen nub, my nipples hardening as she cried out and pressed back into my hand. "They take care of themselves so they are strong and confident." I slid my hand back and squeezed her hot, red flesh, first one side, then the other. "You will remember to always do your best—for yourself, dear, but also because you know that mother will spank you if you don't."

I picked up the brush again. "Do you hear me, Cherise? You . . . will . . . always . . . do . . . your . . . best!" I punctuated each word with another blazing wallop.

"I will, Mommy! Ow! I will! I will! Mommy!!!!" After another ten scorching smacks, Cherise's screeches suddenly dissolved in great, heaving sobs. "I w-will, Mommy! I w-will!!!" Her body shook as the cleansing tears finally started flowing into the soft, fluffy threads of the bedspread.

I set the brush down and gently pulled Cherise into my arms.

"There, there, dear," I murmured, holding her tenderly to my breast. She clung to me, sobbing, as I unbuttoned my blouse. I'd barely finished when Cherise pulled the fabric aside and immediately began rubbing her tear-stained face against the soft, creamy lace. Without a word, I unhooked the front latch. My breasts fell forward and Cherise nuzzled her face against my nipple, taking deep, gulping breaths as she shook and licked. Sensations shuddered through me as her cat-rough tongue dragged over the first side, then the other, outlining and laying the areolas. My pussy throbbed. I lifted a shaking hand and gently stroked her cheek.

"My bottom hurts, Mommy," she whispered, her tongue never missing a beat.

"It's supposed to hurt, sweetie." I shivered as she tickled her tongue over the sensitive tip of my nipple. "That's how you learn. Suckle Mommy's breast if that will make you feel better."

Cherise opened her tear-filled blue eyes to meet mine. Then she smiled, and with a long low sigh, wrapped her lips around my areola and sucked the entire nipple into her mouth like a lonely, frightened child. She inhaled deeply and started to nurse.

I held her close, panting hard with pleasure. Each tug brought exquisite sensations. For a while we just sat there, the only sounds the hum of the air conditioner and Cherise's contented suckling, and my occasional moan. When Cherise's fingers slid down to her vulva, I moved my hand to her thigh.

"Would you like an orgasm, dear?"

When Cherise nodded, I eased her legs apart. She slid further down, spreading wider for me, and sucking hard. She winced as her full weight rested on her well-spanked bottom. My hand slid into her slick folds.

"Don't fight the pain, sweetheart." I stroked my fingers up and down her slit. She whimpered, her legs stiffening as she inadvertently leaned more heavily on her tender behind. "The soreness will remind you to listen to me, dear one."

Cherise wiggled uncomfortably a few more times, then looked at me and smiled tearfully. She kissed my nipple slowly. Carefully I slipped my middle finger into her quivering pussy and caressed her clit with the pad of my thumb.

"You are truly beautiful, Cherise, from the inside out." Her eyes filled again as I pressed my finger deep, curving up toward her belly. She trembled against me as I found the sensitive spot deep inside her vagina. "Only a healthy body can feel this intensely."

With my finger still inside her, I started massaging her juice-slicked clit with a slow, rolling motion. She cried out, sucking ferociously.

"Take care of your body, sweetie, so it can enjoy the pleasure of a healthy, happy climax." I kept up a steady rhythm, pressing deeply. Cherise's skin started to flush. "That's it, beautiful. Let your wonderful, young body come like the strong, lusty animal you are."

Cherise sucked so hard that my whole body quivered. Then with a loud cry, she arched into my hand, bucking and thrashing as her body convulsed with an orgasm that shook her from her toes to where her lips latched tightly onto me. She clutched me fiercely to her, sucking her way through a long, rolling climax.

She left me shaking with need.

Cherise slowly caught her breath, her lips falling free of my swollen breast. My nipple was a deep, bruised burgundy against her pale cheek as she lifted a shaking hand to my face. Her fingers traced the outline of my chin.

"Thank you, Ms. Amanda." Her face glowed with an almost luminescent blush. "I feel so good all over, even where my bottom's so sore." She stared at me, slowly brushing her hand over my cheek while another flush burned suddenly deeper and darker over her face. "Um, ma'am, I was just curious, but . . ." she took a deep breath, but this time, she didn't look away as she blurted out, "do you get turned on by my, um . . ."

Even the skin beneath her ponytail seemed to be blushing. I laughed and hugged her tightly.

"Yes, love," I kissed her hand. "Pleasuring you is intensely arousing to me."

"But you didn't . . . ?" Her eyes stayed intently on me as she stammered out her question.

"No, dear," I smiled. "I'll take care of it later."

Cherise nodded and snuggled back into my arms. Her breath was cool over my wet nipple as she sighed contentedly and whispered, "In two weeks, I get my report card from my Greek and Latin tutor. Do you want to see that, too, ma'am?"

The possibilities for those costumes were mind-boggling.

I kissed the top of her head and settled in for one final bit of cuddling. Andre was going to be very busy.

A Little Bit Like a Slut

BY THOMAS S. ROCHE

Sure, she looks great naked. But that's not what makes me crazy. What gets me hard, what gets me really, really hard, is getting just the faintest glimpse of what she has on under her clothes.

It's not that I don't like her body—she's incredible. Beautiful face, pale skin, bright green eyes. Full, kissable lips and a tongue that can work wonders. Teacup-sized tits with the most delicious nipples I've ever tasted. Slender waist and gently curving hips. Legs that spread like butterfly's wings, whether they're wrapped around my back or clamped around my face.

Naked, she's glorious. But it's nothing compared to when she's dressed.

She's got this taste in clothing, see. Something real, real special.

She dresses just a little bit—just a very, very little bit, mind you—like a slut.

A Little Bit Like a Slut

*   *   *

No, it's not one of those caricatured wardrobes you'd read about in a porn book—no spandex skirts, no halter tops, no lime-green platform sandals with fruit on the toes. No thick makeup, blue eyeliner, cocksucker-red lipstick. On the contrary, Jess rarely wears any makeup more than a hint of mascara, a touch of blush and a glaze of pearlescent-pink lip gloss. She doesn't walk around with a garter belt and no panties, six-inch fuck-me pumps, bleach-blonde hair ratted to all creation with that freshly-fucked "Motley Crue Just Shared Me With Their Roadies" Midwest white-trash charm. In Jessie's wardrobe, there are no push-up bras or skintight T-shirts that say "Just Do Me" or dog collars or black leather underwear with shiny silver studs in the shape of a target. She doesn't even own a pair of panties that say "Use Rear Entrance," though I can tell you, confidentially, that her rear entrance does, in fact, get used. And she doesn't have to remind me.

No, Jessica has impeccable taste. It's subtle. Fashionable, even. Almost to a fault. She reads *Vogue* and *Jane* and *Cosmo* and *Glamour* and *Vanity Fair, Vibe* and *Spin* and *Blender, Interview* and *Bust* and *The New York Times Magazine.* She's always on the cutting edge of fashion, or at least the teasing edge. She favors flared-leg pants— they're not even that tight. Just tight enough. And low—really, really low. I guess you'd call them hiphuggers, except that all the girls wear them now. But none of them, hip-hoppers or wannabe gang-bangers or glam-punks or ravers or sixteen-year-old club rats, look anywhere near as good in them as Jessie.

From March to October, she goes for the belly-baring baby-T

style that's become so de rigeur. Her tits always look magnificent, not least because they're small, so she doesn't always wear a bra.

From November through February, she's all about those tight fuzzy sweaters from high-class catalogs. In the craziest, subtlest colors you ever saw: Sunlight and Ecru, Faded Loden and Really Raspberry, Passion Peach and Sour Apple. High-necked, and tight.

Then there's the way those flared-leg pants hang down low on her hips. When she bends over you can see the top of her thong, because she never, ever wears panties with an ass in them. And she bends over a lot, because she knows exactly what kind of effect it has on me when she does.

I look at her with the kind of longing she doesn't have to see to feel. I look at her like my eyes are shooting laser beam. My gaze roves over her hips, tracing the string of her thong down into the crack of her ass until it almost feels like I'm biting, hard, driving my tongue between her cheeks and licking her tender, flirty little asshole. I start to get hard. And I want to fuck her right away, without fail.

I've had plenty of looks through Jessie's top drawer, and even more opportunities to see her underwear up close and personal. It's not that she wears slutty underwear—every girl I know wears thongs nowadays, except the ones who wear boxers. It's not that they're lacy, or see-through, or have little hearts or flowers or flying penises; they're not zebra-striped, leopard-print or tomato-red. Jessie's thongs are usually white, black, sometimes kind of Ecru or Really Raspberry. But it's the way she uses them. It's the way she pairs them with those low-slung waistlines, the ones that beg me to snug them down over her hips. No belt to unfasten, no need to unzip. Just squeeze my little girl out of her impossibly low-rise slutwear and next thing you know it's another day in Paradise.

Jessie's dressed like this since before I met her; she didn't start it for me. But she knows wearing clothes like that is exactly how to tease me. The truth be told, though, she's really not a very good tease. She's way, way too fucking horny for that. Jessie's "tease" usually lasts anywhere from ten seconds to ten minutes. Once she bends over and I start seeing her thong ride up, her pants nuzzle down, it's hopeless. She knows she's doing it, and if she pretends to be innocent about it, it's just her way of flirting with me. She knows she's torturing me; I know she wants me to do something about it. Even if she didn't, though, she'd let me, because she can't turn down the kind of need that pulses through my veins and into my cock. She'll even say "no" and I'll ignore her, so fucking hot for that luscious tight ass that I can't control myself. Jessie feels shy sometimes; all that showing off, teasing and flirting, makes her reluctant to really give in. She'll say "no" a thousand times, telling me we can't possibly do it in her best friend's bedroom during a party, claiming it would be wrong to do it in the bathroom on a one-hour flight, begging me not to make her do it here behind a bush in the park on Memorial Day while *Opera in the Park* serenades us with Rossini's lusty masterpieces.

She'll say *no, no, no, no, no,* even while she's putting her ass in the air and bending over, moaning as I enter her. *Especially* then, and the whole time. Until she comes the first time, and then "no" isn't in her vocabulary.

Luckily, she knows if she just says my name, first and last, I'll stop. So she gets to say "no" all she wants. And she does it a lot, because I've got absolutely no sense of decorum, responsibility or appropriateness.

Once I see the top of that thong, I'm an animal. That's why I told Jessie if she really needs me to stop she has to say my full name. I'll come to my senses. I'll let her go. Wherever we are—the car, her parents' house, an airplane, the street, her workplace, mine, a bar—she can put a stop to it any time she wants.

But she's never done it yet. She says my first name plenty of times—long, low moans from her parted lips as I unzip those pants and pull them down.

But she never, ever says my last name.

Last Sunday, we were in a cafe. Sunday morning, right? The most innocent time. Two blocks from church, three from our apartment. Kids frolicking outside, yuppies reading the pink section. Jessie and me sharing the Sunday *New York* fucking *Times,* intellectual as it gets.

Jess got tired of the *Times,* I guess. I'm sure 500+ pages wasn't enough for her. She went over to the recycling pile looking for a copy of something else to read. A big wicker basket placed by the door, it had a week's worth of newspapers piled there. Jessie bent over, way over, digging through the pile.

It was early October, warm. She was wearing russet slacks with flared legs. No belt, and a very short baby-T for a top. As she bent over, I could see the black string of her thong, riding up, teasing my eyes down toward the cleft of her ass. She didn't find what she wanted, I guess. She dug some more. And some more. And some more.

I tried to pretend I was still reading the *Times.* For the sake of the children. I shifted in the wooden café chair. Jessie's ass wriggled back and forth a little as she dug for last Tuesday's paper, an article on zoning regulations, probably. She bent over further, digging deeper into the pile. And further. I saw the very top of her crack. I cleared my throat.

Jessie looked back at me, playing hard-to-get. "They don't have the *Mercury News*," she said.

"Barbarians," I mumbled.

She came back over with a copy of the *Trib*, took her seat opposite me. She leafed through it for a while, looking bored.

"You ready to go?" she asked me.

"Oh yeah," I said.

"I'm going to use the restroom," she told me.

"All right," I said.

The café we were in was one of those old San Francisco brick buildings, probably a speakeasy at some point. The bathrooms were down a long narrow corridor and through the stockroom. I actually considered not following her back there. For about half a second.

Once she'd disappeared into the bowels of the café, I tossed the *Times* into the recycling pile and left my unfinished latte on the table. I hurried down the long corridor and saw the bathroom door closing. I heard the lock click.

I waited outside, letting her finish her business. Then, I intended to finish mine.

There was no line. I stood outside the single women's bathroom, even though the men's was unoccupied. Even though our apartment was only three blocks away. There was no way I was going to wait.

When the door opened and I saw Jessie's face, I put my hand flat on the door and shoved. She looked up, gasping, shocked. I hustled her into the bleach-smelling bathroom and slammed the door behind us. I reached back and shot the bolt as I pushed her over the sink.

"No," she said. "You can't—what if someone needs to use the bathroom?"

"They'll have to hold it," I said, going down onto my knees. "I've been holding it ever since you flashed that ass at me. *Mercury* fucking *News*, huh? I bet."

I popped the top button of her pants and didn't bother with the zipper. I snugged it down over her hips and slid it down her thighs, revealing her glorious ass with its string of jet-black dental floss masquerading as underwear.

"No," she said, "don't."

I grabbed her around the waist and pushed her over a stack of toilet-paper boxes. One leg of her flared slacks came easily over her open-toed pumps. I didn't bother with the other leg.

"Please," she breathed, leaning hard on the toilet paper. "Don't. Please," she moaned. "Stop."

I plucked the string of her thong out of the way and nudged her legs apart, pushing hard in the small of her back and forcing her to bend over further. Her slim buttocks parted easily and I saw the luscious pink rosebud of her asshole. My tongue drove into it and I heard her gasping. I licked deeper, my fingers wriggling between her parted thighs and teasing her swollen, full pussy lips. When I drew my fingertips up her slit, she grabbed handfuls of toilet-paper rolls and pushed back onto me.

Two fingers went in easy, three even easier. My tongue burrowed deep in her hole and when I teased her pierced clit she whispered "No, no, no, no, no!" Weakly. Hungrily.

I pushed up behind her, taking my cock out of my jeans. My thumb found the tight hole of her ass, moist with my spit. My other hand pulled the string of her tiny thong as far as I could to the side. I guided my cock into her pussy as my thumb penetrated her asshole.

"Oh God," she whimpered. "No, no, no, no, no."

I slid into her in one easy thrust, feeling her pussy suck me in as juice dribbled out over my balls. My thumb giving me leverage, I started to fuck her.

"No," she whispered as her hand slid down between her legs and began to violently rub her clit. "No, no, no, no, no!"

I fucked her smoothly, one thrust at a time to start with, then great, staccato pounding as I rammed deep into her. She rubbed faster and I worked my thumb deeper into her, fucking harder as I slammed her against the wall. The brushed-aluminum handicapped bar was right in front of her, and she grabbed it firmly as I fucked her against it. She kept whispering "No, no, no, no, no" until the moment when she went silent, dead silent, and I knew she was going to come.

She bit down on a wax-paper-wrapped roll of toilet paper to keep from screaming. I could feel her pussy clenching tight around my cock as I fucked her faster, feeling her come and listening to her muffled, desperate moans. I pulled up with my thumb to position her ass in exactly the right position, and then I fucked her rapidly in the rhythm I knew would make me come.

It did, seconds before her orgasm reached its peak; I emptied into her, my cock shooting hot and deep in her pussy. My free hand reached up and gripped her hair, pulling firmly as she whimpered.

When I tugged my cock out of her, a thin drizzle of come and pussy juice leaked out. I replaced the string of her thong, and she wriggled uncomfortably as she felt it soaking rapidly through. I plucked my thumb from her asshole, eliciting a gasp as her cheeks parted wide in surrender.

I helped her get her foot back through her slacks, wrestled them back up over her thighs and hips without unzipping them. I buttoned her pants closed and turned to wash my hands.

"Let's stop at the newsstand on the way home," I told her. "We can get you a copy of the *Mercury News.*"

"No," she told me, her voice hoarse as she gripped the stacks of toilet paper. "Let's go straight home."

Nacht Ruck

BY KAREN TAYLOR

I first saw her at an auction. I wasn't the only one who stared; she had brought a buggy alone.

She loosely wrapped the reins around the hitching post, next to a line of buggies and wagons, moving among the horses with an assurance I'd never seen in any woman. Then I saw the limp, and knew that no man would have married her.

She was greeted, and I saw her nod to a few of the women. I followed her into the barn, watched her settle in front of Mama, adjust her white prayer cap on her greying hair, and pull work out from the basket she was carrying. I moved closer to see her hands busily braiding strands of black horsehair. Mama bent forward from her seat, talking to her briefly. They chatted, and I saw her hands never stopped moving. She caught me staring, and when I started, she smiled. Mama beckoned to me, and I moved to her side, shyly. Mama introduced me, and she reached her hand out to shake mine. Her hands were calloused around the outside, from the base of the palm to the second joint of her little finger and on the inside of her index finger. To my surprise, her palms were no more calloused than my own. Her fingers were small and fine, the tendons prominent against the back of her hand, rising from the skin near the wrist to disappear above the knucklebone. I was sorry when she released me, and when I touched my hand to my face, it smelled of lanolin. My eyes followed her hand back to its work in her lap, and I noticed her index fingers bent slightly back toward her hand. I wondered if it was from work, her age, or some infirmity.

Mama said something about getting a basket of laundry from the woman's buggy, and I remained. She asked me about the book in my hand, and laughed when I showed her: *Mirror of the Martyrs.* I still preferred the inspirational book to any worldly literature I had tried. I told her I sometimes imagined my own body pressed to death by rocks, stretched on the rack, flogged with nettles, wanting to know if I, too, could bear the tortures our Amish heroes had done so many centuries ago. She nodded, knowingly, her fingers twisting the horse-hair in her lap.

I asked her if she missed not having a husband. She laughed merrily, her eyes dancing. I sometimes miss having children, she said. But not the other. I wanted to ask her why. But I thought I knew—and color flooded my face in a rush of heat. She saw it, and gently, her hand covered mine. We stood there silently, until Mama returned. The woman smiled at Mama, and asked that we meet at the market the following Saturday, asked if I could help her pack up and bring her work home. She can stay the night, the woman said, as she returned to the work in her lap, her hands busy plaiting the strands in her lap. I watched the tendons flex beneath the skin, and trembled.

Nacht Ruck

The rest of the auction was a blur. I didn't dare return to the barn, and joined my friends under the big elm outside. Nearby were a group of boys from our church, some of them smoking cigarettes. We ignored them and watched the grown-ups going in and out of the auction barn while we giggled and gossiped under the tree. It was summer, and all of us were trying our parents' patience. We were all the age of *rum springa*, the years between childhood and before baptism, enjoying our years of freedom before joining the church and giving up our worldly adventures. Sarah and Amy were going to a non-Amish friend's house that afternoon to watch a video. Hannah had cut some of the hair from around her face, and was daring me to do the same. Last week Josh had actually purchased a truck from a boy who had joined the Church, and took us all over to LaGrange, to play miniature golf. Katie whispered to us that after the miniature golf party, she and Grace and some of the boys stayed on to drink beer. One had gotten so drunk he passed out in his buggy and only got home because his horse knew the way. I gasped appropriately, but was privately relieved that Josh had dropped me off before the evening went too wild. Liquor was not my form of rebellion. My rebellion was much more secret, and only today had I ever met anyone else who even suspected. Even as I was thinking it, I saw the woman limp back to her buggy, free the horse from its post, and struggle in. The whip flicked across his flanks, and I flinched. Had she seen me? I thought I saw her smile as she drove past, but maybe it was just a wish.

I could think of nothing but her for the week. My chores were a mild distraction; watching the younger ones, walking them to the one-room schoolhouse I had attended until eighth grade, free after that to go about real world learning, as my Mama would say. The youngest children I would meet at noon and walk home to have the lunch I made for them. But the rest of the day's chores were different each day. Monday I helped Mama bake the pies and breads for the market. Tuesday morning I was up before dawn firing up the gasoline-powered washing machine for laundry, getting the clothes on the line that stretched from the house to the barn early enough so Mama and I could pack the baked goods in the buggy so Papa could drive us to town by nine. Wednesday my sisters and I weeded the garden, and plucked the sweet peas for shelling in the shade on the porch. That night I promised Mama that I'd get up early enough to do the extra laundry she had brought home, and I dreamt all night of lying in those sheets.

I was up before dawn on Thursday, washing *her* sheets, *her* quilts, caressing them as I hung them in a pleasing pattern on the line. I returned to the kitchen, helping Mama bake another batch of pies and bread for the weekend, and making several dozen cookies as well. Friday I stayed home while Papa took Mama to the market, because the baby was not feeling well. Fixed up a basket to hold the laundry I'd be taking with me on Saturday, filling it with sweet pea, rose petals, lemon balm, and other scents pulled from the flower garden. I packed a carefully folded black dress, black stockings, white apron and black prayer cap. And in the bottom of the basket, I placed my *nacht ruck,* my nightdress, for bundling.

Bundling started centuries ago when unheated houses led hosts to double up with their guests for warmth. The tradition evolved into a form of courting for those of us in our *rum springa* years, the only time boys and girls are allowed to be alone together before marriage. It is so fixed in Amish tradition that in my grandparents' day, a preacher who once spoke out about it in Shipshawana was silenced for nearly five years. It was because of this tradition that I was not yet ready to give up my *rum springa* years and join the Church. Truly, I suffered from the sin of vanity. I wanted to be seen in my *nacht ruck*, my bundling dress.

I had finished my *nacht ruck* over a year ago, when I turned sixteen, even though there was no boy I fancied, and none that fancied me enough to suggest calling after dark, to tiptoe into my room and spend the night with me, and come down for breakfast the next morning to meet my folks. By the time I was sixteen I was pretty sure there would never be a boy I fancied like that. But I had made a dress anyway. It was a ruffled, pale lavender color, its capped sleeves exposing my arms almost to the elbow. Pink ribbons at the sleeves, collar, and hem were unbelievably indulgent, the result of work secretly done over the past winter. The buttons on the bodice were an extravagance that only highlighted the worldly nature of the dress—something that would never be worn once I joined the Church. The *nacht ruck* represented my freedom, and I wanted more than anything to wear it for someone. I thought about her that night, and secretly touched myself after my sister fell asleep next to me, silencing myself in the down pillow so as not to wake the little ones.

I woke early on Saturday. The whole family went to the open market off County Road 12 where Mama and I met Aunt Fannie, who was already setting up her quilts to display to the tourists. I took the younger ones over to our cousins' wagon, where the chore of babysitting would be distributed among relatives, then helped Mama unpack her appliquéd pillow shams and her pies and cookies. *She* was already there, in a stall selling decorated saddlebags, horse brasses, fancy show bridles, and two or three riding saddles. She was talking with an English man, but her hands were busy, braiding strands of leather that were attached to a hook on her display table. I turned back to Mama and Aunt Fannie, helping to arrange the quilts and shams. When I turned back to her stall, the man had gone, as was one of the saddles. She was looking my way. I ducked my head, quickly sitting next to Mama.

It was nearly noon when Mama and Aunt Fannie sent me away, told me to make myself useful. I approached her stall with a picnic basket, told her I had made lunch. She smiled, and asked me to join her. I unpacked fried chicken, pickled eggs, homemade bread, and apple butter, and some Jell-O salad. We ate silently, but whenever I dared to look at her she was watching me, smiling that secret smile. After we finished, I packed up slowly, and watched her hands return to plaiting the leather, which she was gently pulling against the heavy brass hook, keeping her plaits under tension. I finally asked her what she was making, and she told me: a lash for the end of a buggy whip. I flushed, and nearly dropped a plate. She chuckled softly, and asked me to meet her at her stall in a few hours. She reminded me to bring the laundry. I picked up the picnic basket, and fled.

Late afternoon, Mama pointed the woman out to Aunt Fannie, told her that I was to be helping her that evening. They spoke of the polio epidemic in the 1940s, how it killed her brothers and sisters, how she was lucky to have survived. Mama admired her courage, her determination not to make herself a burden to our community. Aunt Fannie sympathized for her childless state but marveled at her skills with leatherwork and with the horses. They told me I was being a good Christian to spend time with her. But they didn't know that Christian duty was not my intent. They hadn't seen her hands work that leather.

She had sold another saddle; the horse brasses and fancy bridles fit neatly into the unsold saddlebags. I carried these, and she took the other saddle and my basket and limped to her buggy. I stepped up, sat next to her and we were off, down the county road. I kept my hands clasped in my lap, looking at her sideways. I'd never been in a buggy with a woman driving before. She was silent, calm, keeping the buggy on the gravel shoulder, finally turning off into a long dirt road. Twitching the reins, she turned the horse into a lane leading to a small house with a small barn at the back of a cornfield. She pulled the horse to a stop outside the barn, then stepped out of the buggy. Nodding to me to take the bags to the house, she began to unhitch the animal. I dropped the bags on the porch, and turned in time to see her lead the horse to a water trough inside a makeshift corral. I met her at the gate after she poured some grain into a feed box. When she turned and looked at me, I felt my knees turn to jelly. Her eyes were light blue, almost grey, and they pierced me through. She smiled again, and touched my cheek. I closed my eyes. When I opened them, she was limping toward the barn. Hastily, I followed.

The smell of leather and cut wood permeated the barn, and I stood in the doorway, inhaling the rich scent as my eyes grew used to the dim light. Aside from a stable near the front, the rest of the space was a workshop. Two long tables were covered with cut leather, half-formed into what would become more wares by the next week. Racks of tools I couldn't name were hung on one wall, the other long wall holding oak and hickory poles that I knew would be used for buggy and wagon hitches. Mysterious stands and arched wooden shapes stood further back in the dusty light and as I watched, she placed the unsold saddle on one of the forms. Beyond the forms was a smaller room, and I made out hides of leather on racks, some in bright, worldly colors. An odd bench with a piece of wood sticking through its center stood near one of the tables. Another small bench and a plain pine stool with castors seemed to be the only regular furniture. A sense of calm, decades old, permeated the room.

I stepped to a long counter filled with leather straps and carefully braided buggy whips. I picked up one of the straps and pressed it to my face, inhaling the scent of leather and lanolin. As I rubbed it against my lips, she walked toward me, smiling that deep, secret smile. I handed her the strap. Please, I thought, or perhaps I said it aloud. Either way, she accepted my offer, settled herself on the workbench and invited me to join her. I gathered my skirt, pulling it high behind me, and bent across her lap.

Her arm rose and I moaned even as the leather struck my buttocks. She slapped it against me again, harder, and my fists bunched the fabric of her dark green dress. She was as wonderful as I dared hope. The leather strap beat steadily across my buttocks and thighs, my cotton undergarments no protection, nor did I want any. The strap was surely leaving welts, and my face was streaked with tears. The pain grew intense, and my sobs more ragged, but she did not stop, and I did not struggle to avoid the leather's sting. It was all that I could have dreamed.

After a long while, she stopped, her strong hands caressing my reddened and sore buttocks, tracing the marks she had made. I thanked her through my sobs of pain and ecstasy. She said nothing, waiting for me to calm myself. Then she bid me stand before her. I refused, kneeling instead to look up into her eyes. I offered her more. Her eyes shone with pleasure, and I was overjoyed.

She reached out, and touched my face, dampening her fingers with my tears. She stroked my cheeks, brushed her lightly calloused fingertips across my eyelids. Her hand traced my hairline, and she chuckled at the cut strands peeking out from beneath my prayer cap. Last week I had played with my hair in front of the small hand mirror in my room, finally trimming some of the locks, wondering if the extravagance of cutting my hair would please her. Slowly, she worked the fingers of both hands under my cap, and gently pulled it from my head. No one, not even my mother, had seen me without my head covered since I was ten and old enough to dress myself. No Church-woman would ever be seen this naked. I trembled, closing my eyes as I felt her remove my hairpins, letting my pale blond hair loosen and fall around my shoulders. My nipples were pressed hard against my dress as her fingers carefully untangled the strands, and I remembered her plaiting the horsehair. I raised myself on my knees, and reached to the table. I retrieved a buggy whip, the lash newly repaired, and a fresh horsehair popper dancing on the end. Please, I asked again. Her eyes danced as she untangled her fingers from my hair, and stood.

I stood up as well, and pulled my navy blue dress over my head. With a deep breath, I removed my cotton undershirt, then bent to take off my black shoes and dark blue stockings. I folded my clothes carefully on the bench, and she set my prayer cap on top of them, the hairpins resting inside.

I could not see her face as clearly in the light filtering in from the afternoon sun, but I heard her sigh, and hoped that was a good sign. She reached out and traced my breasts, tickling the nipples with those strong fingers. She caressed my shoulders, running her hands down my back to my buttocks, and massaged them. A spark of pain reignited from the strapping, and I sighed, turned to kiss her, but she stopped me with a finger to my lips.

She pulled long leather reins from a hook in the wall, and wrapped first one, then the other around my wrists. My arms were pulled wide, and tied to two braces in the shed. She stood before me, her green dress slightly wrinkled, her grey hair carefully tucked into the white, pleated prayer cap. In her hand was the buggy whip. She kissed me on the lips, for a long time, her tongue tickling its way between my teeth, filling my mouth slowly until I hungrily sucked at it. She pulled away, and I gasped, feeling myself grow damp. I wanted to touch myself; I wanted her to touch me. But when she flexed the whip through the air, and the horsehair popper cracked, my desire changed again. I closed my eyes.

The whip touched lightly on my bare shoulders. I flinched, but it was more a reaction of surprise, the sting over almost as quickly as it had begun. I sighed, and heard her echo the sigh behind me. The whip touched my shoulders again, leaving nothing for a split second until the sting began. I gasped, surprised at the delay of pain. And I heard the whip whisper through the air. The ends flicked my shoulders, and I cried out. The whisper, the moment of nothing followed by the flood of shock and hurt. The lash whistled before landing on my already reddened buttocks, making me yelp in surprise and pain. Again the whip sang, and again the pain stung me deeply. She made it dance across my shoulders and back, tickling and biting, sometimes cracking the popper to surprise me, mostly letting the whisper of leather through the air be its only announcement. Yes, I thought. And maybe she heard me.

I opened my eyes, and looked into hers, but the light and my exhilaration were playing tricks and I couldn't focus. I wanted her to touch me, and I arched my body forward. Instead, she stepped a few feet away, then flicked her wrist. The whip caught my left nipple. I jerked back against the bonds, yelped. She flicked the whip against my right nipple, and I twisted in my restraints, trying to escape the stinging pain. The whip snaked across my bare thighs, leaving angry red marks. I twisted again as the lash whistled through the air, touching my breasts, my stomach, my thighs, making me dance. It was too difficult to think, and my face was hot, flushed, streaked with tears when she glided around me and once again brought the buggy whip down on my shoulders. I sobbed in agony, my voice breaking as I struggled to free my wrists from their leather bonds, hoping to shrink my body, to make it a smaller target. My legs were burning and I could hardly breathe, I was choking on my tears. The whip touched down on my body like an angry wasp, and I struggled like a beast until I was too exhausted to avoid its evil sting.

And then she was upon me, her hands caressing and exploring me, nimble fingers untying my wrists and helping me stumble to a low bench. Blinded by my tears, I groped for her hands, sobbing anew when I felt their cool touch. I caught them then, and pressed my lips to the palm of each. I was sniffling, and she kissed my eyes and forehead while I held her hands, worshipping them with my kisses and my tears. When I had quieted down, she picked up my clothes, and began to limp to the house, with me following behind.

She had a washtub half filled with cool water in her kitchen, and I stood in it while she brushed me down with a rough cloth, rubbing the sweat from my body and massaging a comfrey and herb ointment into my buttocks and shoulders. While I dried myself near the stove, she stepped back out to put the horse in the barn. I lit a kerosene lamp while I watched her brush hay off her skirt before coming back inside. In the lamp's soft light she pulled off her prayer cap and her green dress, and stepped into the tub. I watched her strong hands rub the cloth across her shriveled breasts, under her arms, between her legs. She threw a towel across her back and I saw the strong muscles flex as she pulled it back and forth vigorously, then, still naked, picked up the basket filled with fresh laundry, and limped into the small bedroom. I followed with the lamp, set it on a bedside table, and helped her pull the scented sheets across her bed and drew the heavily appliquéd quilts on top. I was smoothing the bed when she drew the *nacht ruck* from the basket, the fabric rustling in her hands. I stood frozen, as she examined it. Her fingers plucked at the pink ribbons, fondled the row of buttons at the bodice, traced the careful stitching I had done in blue. She reverently moved to my side, and helped me pull the soft fabric over my head.

She stared at me for a long time, her eyes seeming to shimmer with tears. She bade me turn this way and that for her, and I enjoyed the feeling of the fabric swirling about my ankles. She touched the sleeves, smoothed the fabric over the bodice, retied some of the ribbons, arranged my hair to fall softly over my shoulders to brush the collar line. I glowed under her attention. Finally, she nodded her approval. Together, we turned down the bed, and slid under the freshly laundered sheets, I covered in lavender silk and satin, she completely naked. She pulled me to her, her hands caressing the dress's silk, fingering the buttons. I kissed her lips, her neck. She shivered, then gathered my head to her breast and pressed my mouth to her nipples. I sucked eagerly, my tongue tickling the tiny nipples, feeling her move against me. Though she kept one hand pressing me to her breast, I felt her other hand move between her legs, and I suckled harder, using my tongue and teeth as she groaned, her body bucking against me. I tentatively reached to cover her hand as her fingers slowed. She clasped my tit, then pushed my mouth gently away from her nipple, rolling onto her side to slide her hands across my *nacht ruck*. She gathered the fabric in her fingers, pulling the dress up above my knees, then sliding one of her hands under, trailing her strong fingers across my thigh. We both gasped when she touched me between my legs, the wetness there a surprise to me and a delight to her. My dress was pushed gently to my waist, and she disappeared beneath the covers, where I felt her kissing my thighs higher and higher until her lips touched me where her hands had been. I cried out as she kissed and licked me, astonished at the strength of my response. I rocked against her, and felt a deep energy gather in my womb, expanding until it pushed me hard onto her mouth and I was crying out with pleasure, my hips thrusting against her. She rose from beneath the quilts, and I threw my arms around her, kissing her, tasting myself on her lips. She pulled the *nacht ruck* back down, covering my legs again, and was stroking the fabric when I fell asleep in her arms.

The smell of coffee woke me the next morning. I could see her in the kitchen, dressed in a black dress, a spotless white apron, her grey hair pulled up and tucked into a starched black cap. I joined her in the kitchen, still wearing my *nacht ruck,* and set the table. She pointed to a chair. When I sat down, she pulled out a beautiful silver-backed brush and drew it through my hair. Carefully she pulled the brush through, its soft bristles caressing my scalp, then pulling away as they glided down to my shoulders. I counted one hundred gentle strokes, my hair shining from the attention. It fell softly against my shoulders; she caressed my face, smiling as her fingers tangling through the cut locks around my face. She asked me to stand for her again, and pulled some of my hair forward so it fell softly against my shoulders and breasts, the blond strands glowing against the lavender material. She retied some of the ribbons at my throat and sleeves, and smoothed the silk down once more. Sighing, she told me I was beautiful. I told her I loved her and her eyes filled suddenly with tears and she turned away to rescue the eggs she was scrambling for breakfast. We ate breakfast in silence. I glanced at her while we ate; she was serene, her eyes as soft as a dove. She motioned for me to wash up while she went out to the corral and brought her horse around to the carriage. When I had finished the simple task, I returned to the bedroom and carefully made the bed, pulling the sheets tight and brushing out any wrinkles in the quilts. With a sigh, I pulled the silk gown over my head, and picked my clothes up from the rocking chair. I watched her out the window while I pulled my stockings on and pulled the clean black dress over my head, fastening the apron on with straight pins. She was buckling the harness onto the horse, and I watched her competent hands tighten and fasten the buckles. I turned to the bureau to peer at my hair as I pulled it into a tight bun, using the hairpins in my weekday prayer cap to fasten it into place. I pulled my Sunday black cap over the bun, tying its ribbons in a bow under my chin. I folded my dark blue dress carefully and put it in the basket that I had used to bring her fresh laundry. I began to fold my *nacht ruck* as well, but stopped. I looked again out the window; she was petting the horse and offering it something to eat. I watched the horse nuzzle her palm, heard it nicker. I turned away from the window, and back to the bed. I carefully laid my *nacht ruck* out on the quilt, spreading it on the side of the bed where I had slept. Then I gathered up the basket, and went out to join her.

Dress Pinks

BY M. CHRISTIAN

The funny thing was that the day—until about half an hour ago—
hadn't been half bad.

Rosy had gotten up at—for her—a respectable ten, and leapt
into getting showered and primped: good shampoo, excellent conditioner, moisturizer, gentle glides of the razor along her legs, practiced
sweeps of her brush to give her black hair just the right amount of
lift. After, she carefully crawled into what she called her dress
pinks—even though the whole outfit was just black and off-whites.
Most of the time she looked at the simple black, calf-high skirt, business high heels, taupe hose, satin blouse, and austere jacket with
more than a little distaste—but that morning she felt like she was
getting ready for inspection, and barely suppressed a snapped salute
when she checked herself out in the mirror before heading out.

That afternoon Mr. Perez had actually liked the cover and layout
treatments, going as far as to say "*Bueno*—exactly what I was looking

for!" What suggestions he'd made had even made a certain amount of sense, and wouldn't take more than an hour, maybe two, to tweak. After the meeting downtown at the offices of *Si!* magazine they'd all gone to dinner at Ploufs—a couple of glasses of a gentle white wine and the handsome Latino businessman had even hit them up for working on some designs for *Si!*'s sister mag in Argentina.

Heading back to her car, weaving just a little bit from the good wine and the heady success, she smiled, beamed, and congratulated herself on a job well done. Though, as usual, she couldn't help but wonder how much of her job well done had come from her talent as a graphic artist and how much had been the cool professionalism of her (metaphorically) three-piece business uniform.

Walking down the dark streets—click, click, click on her not too high, but high enough heels—Rosy smiled: the rule usually was to imagine the audience in their underwear, but for her she always seemed to bring a springy sense of humor to her presentations, relishing in the ridiculous facade of her hose, heels and silk blouse when she'd created what Mr. Perez had gushed over wearing an old Glamour Pussies T-shirt and threadbare, but comfortable, panties.

After all, she thought as she wandered down Dore Alley just after midnight, I'm in the business of images—I'm naturally a canvas for a particularly effective one.

It was about that time—turning from the narrow alley onto the larger river of Folsom—that she realized she couldn't find her car.

In a blush of anger and embarrassment, she stood on the empty street and ran quickly through what she'd left in the battered old Cougar. Right there. Definitely right there—she remembered the overflowing trash can, the *Guardian* news rack, the lighting store (which was still very well lit) across the street—it was definitely the corner. All that was missing was the car.

Luckily, Rosy's inventory didn't turn up a lot to be worried about, except for the car itself: an old coat, a five-year-old Thomas Bros. map, an ashtray still overflowing from Louise's pack-a-day habit. If anything, it was that damned disgusting ashtray that she suddenly longed for the most. Louise hadn't been the best girlfriend she'd had—far from it, in fact, her pack-a-day had been just one of her whole parade of self-centered and more than a little repulsive personal habits—but she'd been in Rosy's life for almost five years. Five years of toenail clippings in the bed, ancient dishes in the sink, moldy sandwiches in the fridge, and morning breath that could bring down light aircraft. But, still, Louise had been hers and she had been Louise's—it wasn't a fancy, three-piece relationship, but it had been a smoking, fuming one. They had melted together, flowed through many a long weekend—only crawling out of their heavily rolling orgasmic ocean when Rosy had been forced by 8:00 A.M. to crawl into her dress pinks and wander off into the real world to earn their living.

"Oh, fuck—" Rosy said, not for the car (because it was a piece of shit), not for the cigarette butts that were all that was left of Louise (because that was done for, and the wound was starting to really close up), not because she had to walk home (it was only eight blocks), or that she had to get up early (she didn't), but because there was just something profoundly lonely about that ten-block walk—without anything to look forward to in the morning, and without even the hollow reminder of a past love to keep her company.

"Well, that's a bitch," said a voice nearby. "Isn't it?"

Should have expected it, after all: Folsom and Dore, the leather paradise for a whole generation of gay men. "Damned straight," Rosy said, turning and smiling at the voice.

For someone who'd lived in the city as long as she had, Rosy didn't claim that many fag boys as friends. Maybe it was because she'd met Louise very shortly after moving to the city from her old home turf of Miami and they hadn't left their little Mission flat if they had to—but, more than that, Rosy suspected that after coming out to herself she just didn't see the attraction in them. It was as if after allowing herself to love women, she didn't have time for anything else.

"Yeah, a royal one—" she said, huffing out a good deep sigh as she looked again at where the car had been parked. "Not like the thing was worth stealing."

"Had it happen to me once. A piece of shit but it seemed everyone knew how to get in and take it for a spin. Had it ripped off half a dozen times the first two years I was here."

Looking at him, though, Rosy could feel a bit of the attraction—a gentle fluttering down in the pit of her stomach, and that bothered her. He was young—almost boyish in fact, something she knew was pretty rare for a hard-core leatherman. Ash-blond hair cut into a severe crew—showing off his very squared and elegantly shaped skull, and a very wispy mustache. He wore his own uniform well—a revelation that almost brought a giggle but did bring a smile to Rosy's lips as she realized it, that she was still in her own severe dress pinks. He wore tight, tight, tight leather chaps, thick-heeled calf-high motorcycle boots, a muscle-contouring similar black vest, and even a small cap. He looked like a recruitment poster for *Drummer*, a center spread for *Mach*, a living totem of the spirit of Mr. San Francisco Leather.

"Well," Rosy said, shaking herself slightly, "I'd better get to a phone—call it in."

"Who knows," he said, again in his deep but still remarkably musical voice, as he moved back—giving her space to step up onto the curb, "maybe it just got towed. Happens all the time."

"I can only hope," she said as she started to walk away.

Half a minute later she realized she had no idea where the nearest phone was, and turning around she was shocked—and again that fluttering deep in her belly—to see him smiling broadly. "There's one over this way," he said, gesturing back the other way. "Here, I'll show you."

It seemed so perfectly natural to take his arm when he offered—and together they walked off down the street. Even though she wouldn't have admitted it, on the arm of the leatherman her day had actually begun to look up.

"You don't seem freaked out—that's good!" he yelled into her ear.

Rosy shook her head, not wanting to bellow over the thumping disco. She definitely didn't feel . . . well, uncomfortable wasn't really the right word. She felt safe, certainly, but she definitely wasn't completely at ease, either. She was, at best, distracted.

Looking around, she smiled again to herself: only in San Francisco—a business afternoon, a towed car (thank goodness), a short walk, and then an evening spent in a leatherbar.

Rosy would have liked to think her leatherman charming, but the fact was she could barely hear him over the heavy-beating disco. It was hard, she discovered quickly, to be charming when your wit couldn't be heard.

But what Rosy was able to tell was that—deep breath, deep breath, deep breath—he was (ahem) kinda, well, sorta, um . . . damned sexy. It was very hard to accept, and in fact the first admission that she actually found him attractive had rushed over her like a kind of panic—like the same kind of panic that had grabbed her just a few hours before when she realized her car was gone. Rosy didn't have a indecisive past; she liked to say that she was a born lesbian: no clumsy proms trying to feel attracted to the boys, no waking up in the middle of a marriage to hunger for another woman's lips. None of that. Boys, to Rosy, were like some distant land—she knew where it was on the map, but didn't really care to visit.

Until her car got towed, and she found herself in the presence of the leatherman. Maybe that was it, she thought, smiling at him as she sipped her Coke. Was she really attracted to him or the leather? He was almost too perfect, a dead-cow icon, a Tom of Finland deity: gleaming leather chaps, vest with those merit badges of boy-sex S/M clubs, even the little leather cap. He was like a 32 cent stamp for hot leather-boy sex.

Seeing him made Rosy feel like she had a hot, hard leather fist up inside her. It was an unexpected and—yes, at first—shocking sensation, but the desire she felt rolling around inside her was strong enough to firmly shove that hesitation aside.

The only thing she really regretted, staring at her icon, was that her own dress pinks were so stiff and emotionless. She never wanted to before, but that night seemed a night for first times—she wished she had a collar on.

As she had been thoughtfully and—yes, she had to admit it— hungrily looking at him, he'd been looking at her. The leatherman had been looking at her.

He said something. Over the pounding of the music, she couldn't make out what he'd said. She leaned forward and yelled, "What?!" at him.

That's when he'd said it. Simple enough in an everyday context, but for Rosy in her power suit and him in his incredibly sexy leather, it meant a lot more—a lot that Rosy suddenly realized, fully, she was willing to go along with. "Do you want to go to the bathroom?"

That's how Rosy, who'd never even kissed a boy, ended up being led into the dinge and tile of a SOMA S/M bar by a leatherman.

"Did I say you could kiss me?"

No, he hadn't. He hadn't said anything actually. Dead silence had followed them, not a word, not a command, since the door had closed behind them. Surprisingly, the bathroom had been empty—a fact that she didn't puzzle till later, and ended up shelving as possibly his power as the Ideal Leatherman. He could clear a room by just wanting to use it.

Even though Rosy felt a kind of blooming of submission within her, she really didn't have the tools to deal with what was happening. She just had Louise and half a dozen girlfriends behind her. She knew the mechanics of boy-girl (what there was of it), and had a pretty good idea of what could happen to her in the tiny, moderately dirty bathroom but didn't know the first steps to the dance. It had seemed natural to just turn and try and kiss those strong- yet soft-looking lips.

Quicker than her own pounding heartbeat, he had her long brown hair in one knotted fist, pulling her head back. "Listen, slut, you're mine—you do nothing but what I tell you. Got that?"

She didn't know what to do. Fear bubbled up from down deep, and—even more shockingly—anger. A part of Rosy wanted to shake him loose, gut punch him, and walk proudly out. But another part of her . . . she was wet. That was it. But more than anything, what was getting to her? Was it his cock? Was it the possibility of a good, old-fashioned (aghast, "straight") fuck? Rosy, surprisingly, was able to look down at herself and answer, "no." So what was it, then—what was it that was making her simple, professional panties so damp?

Then it was there—simple and straightforward. In a little voice that sent shivers of delight and excitement through her body, she said, "Yes, Sir."

"Good, slut—very good. You're a good slut, aren't you? A hungry slut. You want it, don't you—you need it. You ache for it. Right, slut?"

"Yes, Sir—I do need it."

"Good, because you're going to get it."

One of his slender—yet very strong—hands reached up to her blouse, cupped her right breast. Before she could get ready, his fingers skillfully flicked over the swell of her breast till he found her—already hard—nipple. The squeeze was powerful, even though it was partially expected. With a gasp, Rosy gripped his strong arm and felt her knees quickly give way under the wave of pleasure spiced with pain. When her voice returned it was a high squeal: "Yes, Sir."

Again his hand found her hair, again her head was jerked back, but this time rather than his growled displeasure, his thin fingers traced the lines of her tight neck muscles. "Good. Very good. Sluts should always recognize themselves."

His other hand found her breasts again. The powerful squeeze brought tears to her eyes. Again strong fingers to her aching—and also throbbing—nipples. The pinch this time was even stronger but somehow controlled. It was a precise generation of pain pushing toward pleasure . . . or was it the other way around? Mixed up with endorphins of all kinds, Rosy couldn't tell anything, anything at all beyond the burst of sensation—except that she wanted more.

Distantly, she heard buttons hitting tile and metal partitions. Distantly, too, she regretted the loss of the blouse—but not the cause. She arched her body forward, offering him her breasts.

He took what she pushed at him, scooping first the right and then the left free of her business-style bra. Bare to the warm air, and the even hotter atmosphere of the bathroom, she groaned from their release and whatever else he was planning for their torment—and her pleasure.

His bite was quick, sudden, shocking, frightening—but like his fingers not the predatory tearing of a beast. Rather, it was like his perfect little teeth were being used as precise instruments for the delivery of agony. Just back from the plump nibs of her nipples, he gave her a quick stinging bite—before retreating just a little to then slowly, ponderously, grind his jaws together. The steady progress of his bite pushed Rosy even farther from the cool tile wall she was leaning against—and increased her grip on the side of the sink where her hand had grabbed. The hiss that escaped her lips was like a crack in a boiler—hot, shrill, and unstoppable.

She knew she was wet . . . no, Rosy absolutely was sure that the simple business panties under her dress pinks were soaking. She was always like that—a base, primal lover. Rosy was excited and so her cunt was hungry.

His fingers reached down and pushed up—hard—her no-nonsense black skirt. A firm pressure reached her through her taupe pantyhose and right through the pedestrian cotton of her panties.

The contact was a shiver that blasted up through her body, a ponderous skyrocket that straightened her spine and escalated the velocity and pitch of her hiss.

A part of her that had been resting just below the surface opened its eyes, growing from groggy to ravenous.

Something tore, parting under an unstoppable force—his fingers ripping through taupe pantyhose. Rosy took a breath, expecting the next, waiting for it, wanting it.

As the thin veil of nylon parted, he spoke: "Good, slut—very good. You want it, don't you, slut. You want it bad. You need it, you need it like you never needed anything else in the world. You need this slut—you need it now . . . don't you?"

She knew that the rules said that she should have said something, opened her mouth and played the role she was supposed to. But Rosy was excited and her cunt was wet—so all that emerged from between her tight lips and clenched teeth was another notch to the shrill hiss. But her heart was in the right place—and in her mind she was The Slut, his slut, his plaything, his toy. "Yes, Sir" might not have escaped her lips, but it certainly was loud and clear in her mind.

In the next moment he found out how wet she was—a discovery that changed the timbre of her sounds to a bass purr. She felt his fingers expertly part her damp underwear and find the slick folds of her cunt. Gentle at first, but then with more and more insistence, he explored her cunt: the plump lips, the tight, slick passage up inside her, the pucker of her asshole, and—deeper purr—the throbbing point of her clit.

There, he stopped—"That's you, slut, that's you right there. That's where you live. Right there: and now I've got you"—and right there he really started. He was more than a leatherman, more than her Master, he was a finger artist. The feelings rushed up through her. Not a skyrocket, no strange little metaphors this time: the simple fact was what kept ringing through her mind: "My Master's finger on my clit, my Master's finger on my clit." She was right in that magic spot she suspected but never realized was deep inside herself: Rosy the slut, Rosy the toy, Rosy the object of his powerful will.

It happened almost before she was aware it had started: a quivering, shaking body-rush of exultation that took even more strength from her legs as it brought brilliant flashes of light to her eyes and a thundering pulse to her ears. As orgasms went, it was good—not the best—but there was something else there, a kind of awakening. Not to him, but rather to Him—to her position and his power. It wasn't the sex that blasted through her but rather that she was the receiving end of his strength.

When her legs stopped shaking and she felt she wasn't going to drop down to the cool tiles in a quivering heap, she breathed in, deeply—one, two, three, four—and managed to focus on his smiling (slightly) face. "There was never a question," he said, "in my mind: good slut."

There was something missing, there was something she had to do. It was part of the act, part of the ceremony. She knew it was wrong to speak without being spoken to, but she had to complete the act—to place herself firmly in the world her leatherman belonged: "Can I suck your cock, Sir?"

"Yes, slut, you may," was his smiling response, pleased she sensed at some subterranean level by the eagerness and correctness of her desire.

Cool tiles this time under her knees, torn pantyhose riding up the warm, damp seam of her ass, breasts wobbling, tender nipples grazing the coarser material of her open jacket. There—in front of her, the altar of her leatherman, her leathergod: slick black chaps over too-tight jeans. A bulge of power just inches from her face. "You know what to do, slut," he said from above, thunder from on high.

Actually she hadn't a clue. Vibrators and toys, yes, but never to those other lips. But this was the new Rosy, and this was something she had to do for him—it was part of the rules. Slightly quaking fingers to his fly, a slow, steady inching down. She hoped that he'd help at some point, give her pointers or at least help free himself from the jail of his pants. No such luck, though—he stood, a leather statue, above her and didn't move, didn't say a word.

So she had to do it all. Hesitant fingers in through the metal-teethed opening, a gentle dig around. Ah, contact—not too soft, not as warm as she expected. A careful pull—not too insistent—feeling the fat head slide up and then, oh yes, out. Out, out, out—her first sight of her Master's dick, her leathergod's cock.

A moment of shocked silence.

A very long moment. Longer than any moment in Rosy's life. A record-setting movement.

It ended with a smile. "It's a wonderful cock, sir," Rosy said, kissing the tip of the long dildo—tasting a little cotton lint and much plastic. "It's fantastic, Sir," she said as she opened her mouth to take the tip in.

As Rosy licked, kissed, and sucked her plastic cock she absorbed the warmth of what she had discovered: not that she'd been ready, willing and able to suck a leatherman's cock; not even that she'd realized how much joy there could be in being a powerful figure's plaything; but that sometimes the wrapping, the uniform, is the best thing about what was inside.

*   *   *

Her name was Jackie. She lived in the Mission. She was a musician by choice (which was important), and a word processor out of necessity (which wasn't important). She was also Jack, and Jack was a leather . . . man, boy, person? Jack was leather, a gravely tone, and firm commands. Jack was a pair of chaps, a leather vest, a white T-shirt, and a little black leather cap.

Outside, in a light drizzle, they exchanged phone numbers. Before parting—Jack on a throbbing motorcycle and Rosy by cab— they kissed: soft lips and a hesitant but electric touch of tongues. "Another time?" said Rosy.

"For sure," said Jackie.

"Be sure and bring Jack," Rosy said.

"Oh, I will—you just bring the slut."

Debt of Honor

BY TULSA BROWN

At eleven P.M. that September Thursday, I was waiting inside my darkened shop, leaning on a rack of leather jackets, watching the street. My stomach was tight and my skin tingled, more anticipation than I usually felt over a "night job."

I'd had a lot of those, custom work for men who kept odd hours or a low profile. I was well known in biker circles because my shop, Leather Highway, specialized in chaps, gauntlets, and other road gear. But I'd never feared even the roughest customers. They treated me well and paid on time, in cash. They liked my work and being 6'2" and 242 pounds didn't hurt, either. That was considered "business acumen."

Tonight, though, I wasn't waiting for bikers.

"This is hot stuff, Brick," Del had said, his voice hushed with a greasy kind of glee. "And you can charge whatever you want. Perverts pay anything."

Great. I didn't want sickos, and I'd told him as much.

"No, no, I didn't mean it like that. It's just, you know discreet . . . Come on. The guy needs design work and I told him you were a fucking *artist*." He grinned. "It'll get your engine running."

That stung. My "engine" had been idling for over a year, while I'd worked seven days a week to build my new business.

"All right," I told Del.

Now I scanned the empty sidewalk intently, body humming with the vigilance of doubt. What had I set myself up for? Well, one thing was certain: I had a Loss Prevention Device under the counter. Anyone planning to rip off *my* shop was going to meet that Louisville Slugger in a profound and meaningful way.

Movement in the distance made me look. For an instant I was too surprised to be alarmed.

There were three of them, not one. The well-heeled man I'd been expecting was leading two others, each draped in a long, grey cloak with a hood. The capes fluttered in the evening wind but didn't open, a wavy lilt of fabric that looked ethereal under the neon. One of the pair was distinctly smaller and shorter, yet they were walking in step with haunting accuracy, two travelers marching from some distant time to this.

They stopped at my door. The man saw me through the glass but tapped his knuckle on it anyway, a courtesy he reinforced with a faint smile. I let them in, my heart running.

The only light I'd left on was in the cutting room behind me, and I regretted it now. With their heads bowed, the hooded pair easily kept their faces in shadow, a bad trait in people I hadn't been expecting at all.

"Mr. Arnason, thank you for seeing me on such short notice," the man said.

Shouldn't it be "us"? I wondered.

"Call me Brick," I said. "My mother did."

His face brightened at the quip, and he held out his hand. "Good to meet you, Brick. My mother called me Ken, among other things."

As we shook hands, the taller figure raised his head, stealing a glance at me. The face caught me like the ray of a strobe: a handsome young man in eyeliner so thick he looked like an Egyptian hieroglyph.

Then Ken started toward the lit room and the pair followed abruptly, as if pulled by a single tether. I waffled for a moment—what the hell was under those cloaks and should I take Loss Prevention with me? But curiosity had its deep hook in me now, and hunger always outran risk.

My cutting room was small, crowded, and warm. The walls were a beehive of diamond-shaped cubbies, the hides rolled up inside. There was one chair and a work counter of gleaming blades, but the room was dominated by the huge table I used for cutting patterns, its polished surface big enough to play snooker on. I'd eaten macaroni and cheese for a month to pay for that oak beauty.

My lighting was good, too. Under the 100-watt tracks, I saw that Ken was a trim man in his late fifties, with dark, close-cropped hair turning gunmetal grey. His rimless glasses were more severe than the blue eyes behind them, and his black car coat seemed to cover a bristling energy, the body of a man consciously holding himself still.

"I don't know what Del told you," he began.

"Nothing at all."

"All right. I'm attending a conference in a few weeks, and I need outfits for my slaves, to display them to their best advantage."

Slaves. The word lapped at me like a tongue. I'd half-suspected something like this from the moment I'd seen their long capes, but I wasn't prepared for the deep tremor I felt, hearing it out loud. Then reason thumped me in the chest.

"Listen, before we go on, I need—"

"To know these are adults, participating of their own free will?" Ken asked.

I was going to answer Yes, but the smaller cowl hood lifted, revealing a woman's heart-shaped face. Her brown eyes were ringed in kohl and full of dancing mischief. One fluttered in a wink: come play.

That was enough for me.

"I need you to define 'best advantage,' " I said.

Ken smiled at my turnabout, accepting it gracefully. "That which accents their submissive state, while enhancing their natural attributes."

"Did you have anything specific in mind?"

"Del said you were an artist, so I brought you blank canvases."

Ken turned, and an electric quiver of attention ran over the two figures. He swiftly unlatched hidden clasps in their robe fronts, first for one slave, then the other. At last he stepped behind them and pulled off both cloaks with a sweeping flourish.

"This is my Eric, and my little Kat—Katrina."

She *was* little, an inch or two over five feet, and the shock of her nakedness kicked my engine into second gear. She had long brown hair pulled up into a high ponytail, and nothing to hide the small, round breasts that thrust forward like an offering. Her nipples were spread even wider by the arch of her spine and position of her hands, which were clasped behind her back. She had soft, sloping hips and a pear-shaped ass, two servings of plump, perfect fruit. Her pubic hair was shaved into a demure stripe, accented by a postage stamp of a

G-string. Kat's eyes were lowered discreetly, but a smile lingered on her painted lips, as if she still tasted her saucy invitation.

Nothing was discreet about Eric. He was smaller boned than me, and beamed sleek animal health from his compact, well-formed muscles. His body had been shaved, except for a dark ribbon from his jutting pouch to his navel, and the brown hair on his head was bleached at the edges, bright frosting with dark shadows. Added to the whore's eyeliner, the result was unmistakable: a handsome man had been made pretty.

And he was fully aware of it. His hazel eyes held me boldly, mouth crumpled in a smirk, an insolent challenge simmering with sex and defiance.

Smack! Ken's hand caught Eric across the cheek, swift and certain redress. The young man blinked in surprise, then quickly dropped his eyes. But a whisper of the grin still held—he wasn't sorry, only chastened. I watched the pink mark come up on his skin, the distinctive ring of the slap still reverberating in the deep caverns of my body. I was perplexed and alarmed and excited.

Ken turned to me amiably. "All right, Brick, where do we start?"

There wasn't enough floor space to spread out, so I suggested Kat and Eric get onto the cutting table—without their boots, of course. They unlaced, then clambered up and waited obediently, hands clasped behind their heads. I gathered a few skins of black garment leather and a handful of cowhide straps, the kind I used for belts. I hoisted my big frame up, too, awkward and bearish, but left my shoes on. It was *my* table, damnit.

I don't know where the ideas came from. I'd seen things in magazines and on the Internet, but never thought about them after the page was turned. Yet something must have been brewing in my subconscious, because on that tabletop my imagination took an abrupt turn down a dark, sinuous road.

"I'm seeing a collar," I said, wrapping a band of leather around Eric's neck and securing it with masking tape. "Straps over the shoulders, connecting to a chest band, which connects with more straps down to the codpiece. Every length could be decorated with half-inch silver studs." Ken was relaxing in a chair below us. "Excellent. It reminds me of a harness."

I nodded. "I'll attach a steel ring to the chest piece, front and back, for a tether. And here's an idea." I turned the young man and laid a strip of black leather above the tight, round globes of his buttocks. "A flank brace. If I made leather cuffs with latch hooks, they could connect to a ring here, securing his wrists behind him."

It was very warm on that table. I had one hand on Eric's flat abdomen, holding him steady, and the other pinning the black strap above his ass, for effect. I handled him deftly, like a mason working mortar, yet I was completely aware of his hot, firm flesh under my touch.

So was he. I could hear his shallow breaths, saw the excitement swelling in his scanty G-string. He smelled of sweat and leather—my leather. The stirring below my own belt was so abrupt I turned away.

"For Kat, we only need to make a few alterations," I said. Trying not to tremble, I wrapped a strip of cabretta beneath her pert breasts, which pushed them up like a half-bra. She was so small under my big hands it was like dressing a doll. I dropped to one knee and draped another soft skin on the outside of her shapely leg. The gleam of the black hide, the closeness of her exquisite ass to my mouth, thrust my growing hard-on painfully against my zipper.

"And chaps for both of them, secured down the leg by buckled straps."

"Brick, you're a genius! I love it. Work up a quote for me."

I eased off the table, dizzy with my own heat, trying to hide my bulging crotch. As I scratched out numbers on a pad, I heard Ken snap his fingers. Eric and Kat shed their makeshift costumes and scrambled down to kneel on the floor, one on either side of his chair. From the corner of my eye, I saw him touch each of them affectionately, tugging Kat's silky ponytail, stroking Eric's cheek. The young man turned his head to kiss the palm that had struck him.

I felt seized, shot through with lust and longing. Until then we'd been four people playing a tantalizing game. Ken's tender possessiveness was beyond dress up, and so was their devotion. There was something real here, out of my reach, and I churned with unfamiliar envy.

On a surge of spite, I added a "1" in front of the total. Hadn't Del said this guy was rich?

Ken took the paper from me, and blinked. He turned a little pale. "Oh. Oh, damn. Would you consider payments?"

I was too surprised to speak.

"It's not unreasonable, really. I love your ideas and this is worth every penny to me, but I . . . we've had some expenses lately." He glanced down at Kat and touched her hair. "Wisdom teeth. We really need a dental plan."

I felt small in that room, lashed by regret. On impulse I bent over my sheet of calculations and circled another number, what I knew was my cost for materials.

"Here," I said. "I'll do it for this."

He blustered and argued, and so did I, insisting that he'd be good advertising for me at the conference. At last he agreed, but as they were buttoning up to leave, Ken clasped me in a warm handshake.

"This is very good of you, Brick. And these beauties might know a way to say Thank You."

"Oh, no, that's not—"

"Just think about it." He tilted his head and smiled. "It wouldn't be a hardship for them. You had my little Kat purring up on that table, and Eric, well, he likes the big boys."

I let them out and locked up. The path to my empty apartment was so familiar there should have been a rut in the concrete.

I wasn't a machine with an engine, I was a bear clawing out from a long hibernation, awake and ravenous. In the dark safety of my bed I lived it all again, the velvet heat of their bodies, the scent of aroused sweat, the thrilling shock of the slap. My cock was an urgent pole, an arm with its own fist. I stroked it and summoned the two slaves to my bed, fully outfitted in black leather and silver studs. I claimed them like a warrior king, rutted and rode them—his insolent mouth, her plump ripeness, bent each under my burning will . . .

I thought I'd have to clean the ceiling.

Friday morning Del showed up at my counter, leaning and leering.

"So? So? What happened?"

"Nothing. He didn't show."

"What!? That asshole." Del's disappointment flipped over abruptly. "Hey, don't get pissed at me. I don't even know the guy!"

I bit my cheek to keep from smiling.

The job had become a debt of honor to me. Regardless of the final price, I'd tried to cheat the man and that thought weighed on me. Each day I waited until the shop was closed, then laid out the hides and tools with the care of a ritual. I cut from the center of each skin—the best, most expensive strip—and tossed pieces away for so much as a misplaced needle mark. Eric and Kat would wear my finest work.

All the while my mind meandered down that sinuous path. How had Ken started such a life and how did he keep it? He wasn't a big man, and certainly not swimming in money. Yet his every movement held Kat and Eric in thrall. I wondered about his offer, and if he'd meant it. I wondered if both slaves slept in his bed.

It took ten days to finish the work. I dialed Ken's number, fingers damp on the receiver.

"Excellent," he said. "Do you want me to come to the shop, or would you like to bring the outfits to our house?" His voice shifted. "Eric and Kat could try them on."

My heart was thudding lightly above my collarbone. "I'll bring them by," I said.

I went home and showered. I trimmed my moustache but didn't shave, thinking of their smooth skin and liking the shadow on my own. Sandpaper. I dressed and pulled on the leather chaps and custom road jacket I hadn't worn in months and months. Then I went down into the parking garage, to greet an old and neglected love.

"Daddy's home," I whispered to my Harley-Davidson Softail Deuce.

I tucked my debt of honor into the two saddle bags and rode into the gathering dusk.

I hadn't spent much time in suburbia. It took me awhile to find the place, at the far end of a winding crescent, next to a park. The neighborhood was about thirty years old, like me, homes built at a time when land was cheaper and even the working Joe got a generous yard with his shingles. As I parked the Softail on the gravel drive, I was struck by the anonymous privacy of the place, a bungalow like any other.

Ken looked genuinely pleased to see me, but he resisted opening the Leather Highway bags I held out.

"Don't be offended. I just really want to see them on, for the full effect. And we'll have to wait a bit. Both Kat and Eric are late."

"Late?"

"Well, Kat's in class—community college. She went back as a mature student. We're both so proud of her. And Eric's still at work. He installs drywall for a contractor."

How strange it was to imagine those naked, painted slaves in class or taping drywall! Yet at the same time, it nailed the fantasy to the earth. This was real.

Ken ushered me into the living room. In a glance I saw that it had been decorated with good taste ten years ago. Now the functional, well-worn furnishings were the mark of a man who didn't entertain or who didn't give a shit, or who put his money into what truly mattered. I admired all three possibilities.

"Can I get you a drink?" he asked.

"Sure. Whiskey, if you have it."

Ken's voice had a wry twist to it. "By a stroke of luck and poverty, that's *all* I have."

I liked him. He was at ease in his own skin, a comfort that swept aside the decades between us. Yet this time he also seemed older. Out of the black car coat, he was smaller than I'd thought, not frail but . . . distilled.

Ken was back with my drink, luminous amber in a short glass. He looked my leather garb up and down, then grinned.

"My God, Brick. You were already a hit. This time I'll have to use the crop to keep them off you."

"Does that happen . . . much?"

He hesitated, the canny silence of a man who saw me through my clothes.

"It happens as often as it needs to. You have to remember that physical discipline isn't punishment with us, it's attention. I use it to stimulate, to draw a slave's awareness to his body, and my dominance over it. I use it to define boundaries, and yes, for my own arousal. But mainly it's attention, because that's where a slave is truly alive—in the master's concentrated gaze. If I wanted to 'punish' Kat, I'd send her out shopping or to the movies, while I spent time with Eric."

I was leaning forward in my chair, fascinated, a low hum vibrating up from the base of my spine.

"Also, each slave is different," Ken continued. "With Kat, the arena will always be emotional. That's partly because of her nature and partly because of her physiology. She's just so small, it would be easy to brutalize her. And brutality isn't discipline, any more than strength is power." He grinned. "And don't think she doesn't know it! Her size is her beauty, and her weapon."

"And Eric?"

"A different creature altogether. He's a much more physical slave, and more advanced. That's a challenge because the master has to be three steps ahead. What did I do yesterday? How can I surprise him today, and still answer his needs?" Ken's voice softened. "At the table of pleasure, the master serves the slave first."

The words rang inside me. "That's . . . a responsibility," I said.

"More than you know," he murmured. His gaze drifted to the

darkened window, as if watching for them to come up the drive. But there was only the reflection of his own face, thoughtful and drawn.

In a moment he turned. "Does this mean you're accepting my offer?"

My heart leapt. "Yes."

"Well, let's go down to the playroom and wait for them there."

Ken left a note with the bags and I followed him to the basement. The playroom was simple, carpeted open space and a few accessories. Two large rings hung from the ceiling, set at different heights. There was a king-size bed, and a rack of crops on the wall. Without thinking, I reached out to touch one of the stiff braided handles and Ken appeared at my side, cordial but alert.

"It takes practice," he began, then laid out the ground rules. For safety's sake, he would handle the crops, then leave us to privacy at my signal.

Kat and Eric came home within minutes of each other. I listened to their footsteps and the seductive murmur of their voices above me, my body awake, palms growing damp. At last they came down.

I'd been imagining this for ten days, yet I was unprepared for the raw current of desire that rushed through me. They were harnessed like horses, a diminutive mare and a fine stallion, bare skin fettered and glorified by the combination of studs, straps, and chaps. My handiwork.

"My God, Brick," Ken's voice was hushed with an awe. "They're . . . a vision. Absolutely perfect." He caught himself and the cool detachment returned. "Why don't you display them for me?"

"My pleasure."

I shrugged off my leather jacket, the tight grey T-shirt underneath revealing my broad torso and powerful arms, an upper body that could bench-press 300 pounds. Dark hair swirled in flat patterns on my forearms, and crept out at the collar of my shirt, not shaggy, but definitely bearish.

I heard Kat inhale at the sight. It made me bold.

"Eric, wait on the ring."

I motioned Kat toward me and she came, trembling faintly. With a firm grip on her pony tail, I tilted her head back until she connected with my gaze, beaming down a full foot above her. Her brown eyes were liquid and I drank them, heat igniting in my belly and balls. I could have taken her to bed at that moment, but I remembered: serve the slave first. I turned her around and swiftly snapped the latch-hooks of her cuffs to her flank ring, which secured her hands and thrust her breasts forward.

"My goal," I said to Ken, "was accessibility. These garments shouldn't impede you in any way. The bra is a perfect example."

I reached into the right cup and nudged up her nipple, which had been hidden beneath the leather. I rolled it between my strong fingers, gently, then with increasing pressure, until it was a hard bud. I tweaked it abruptly and she gasped, a breath of surprise and pleasure and pain. Ken nodded his approval.

Dropping to one knee, I bent Kat's little body over my jutting thigh. I reached under her collarbone with my right arm, a loose embrace that gave her something to lean forward on.

"You'll notice how the chaps follow the curve of her ass," I said, tracing the heart-shaped line around the swell of her cheeks.

Snap! Snap! His crop flicked out with the skill of a marksman and Kat twisted suddenly against my leg. That movement and the pink stripe on each plump curve thrust me to full erection.

I unhooked the single thong of her G-string, baring the cleft between her legs.

"Complete convenience," I murmured, my breath thickening. "She is always available." My fingers opened her sex lips, which were rapidly becoming slick. I nudged one finger forward to her clit, teasing the firm head with feathery caresses. She moaned in her throat, breath hot against my hairy arm, and spread her legs wide, trying to thrust her hips higher.

Still coaxing her clit, I eased my wide thumb into her wet cunt. She began to rock back and forth, as much movement as her bound arms would allow, a slow, strained finger fuck. Ken was flicking her lightly with the crop again, on the buttocks and the bare spaces of her inner thighs. Occasionally he caught my wrist or forearm and the light, tantalizing sting enflamed me. Love bites.

But I could hardly bear it, this moist, moaning woman bent over my knee. I withdrew from her wetness and eased her swaying body upright. I stood abruptly, thrusting her over my big shoulder, and Kat let go a startled cry. I carried her to the bed like a choice prize of war.

"Wait," I said, as if she could have done anything else.

"Yes, lord."

The words stroked my deep, silent self. I stripped off my T-shirt, and unzipped to relieve the pressure on my throbbing cock. The white of my underwear pushed through the opening as I strode over to the more physical slave.

Ken was already waiting, eyes shining, a new crop in his hand. Eric clung to the ceiling ring with both hands, face trapped between his own biceps. His smoky eyes ran over my dark, naked chest and bulging crotch, excitement wiping away any trace of insolence. I trailed my fingers in a tease over his bare skin, following the lines of his harness, reminding him of every strap. His erection strained against the soft leather of his codpiece. On a whim, I help up my palm and he kissed it, his reverent lips sending a shivering thrill down to my balls.

"Hang on tight," I said.

I moved to the side of him, placed one hand firmly on his abdomen, and hooked two strong fingers through the steel circle on his flank brace. With a powerful pull I swung his lower body back and up, lifting his feet right off the floor. The veins in my arms bulged as I held him, suspended between the ceiling ring and my powerful grip, while Ken delivered nine stripes to his tight buttocks. Even in my trembling effort, I was fascinated by the process and Ken's skill—how much and how hard. When I set Eric down again, he was panting, and so was I.

Ken caught my eye and I nodded. Yes, I wanted to be alone with them. Now.

"Strip, and come to bed," I said to Eric. I unhooked Kat's cuffs and told her to do the same. With a swift tug, I released the belt of my chaps and peeled off the jeans and leather as one. There was a breath of stunned silence as both slaves paused to stare. My cock rose up from its swarthy nest like a brute, an animal with its own urgent life, as thick as Kat's wrist. The engorged head had swollen to a taut bell, pre-cum glistening on the hungry, darkened flesh.

"Holy shit," Kat whispered, forgetting herself.

"Bed," was all I said.

At that table of pleasure, they ate me alive. Whatever command I thought I'd had of my body vanished under their hot mouths and eager hands. They'd been trained to serve together and I was overtaken by the double force, strength, and softness stroking me to blind, furious need. More than once I had to pause, gasping, afraid I'd shoot my load all over the sheets. They grinned at each other. They were the masters here.

I finally came, Kat's legs clamped tightly around my hips while Eric cupped my balls and gnawed at the back of my neck. The deep, shuddering pleasure shook me in waves, pulled bass moans from the center of my belly as I jetted what seemed like the whole hungry year into their tight embrace.

And then it was terrible. I lay in languid bliss, one arm cradling each of them, Eric sucking dreamily on a nipple while Kat played with the hair on my chest. In that moment I knew exactly how big the hole in my life was now, the tiny darkness they'd stretched into a gaping chasm.

I tore myself away like a Band-Aid, dressed with my back to them, and felt their surprised, hurt silence follow me to the stairs.

"We tried," Eric blurted.

I paused, my hand on the doorframe. "That was the best," I said softly. I slipped out of the house like a thief.

Ken was waiting outside, leaning against a tree by my motorcycle, smoking a cigarillo. I was a man with my soul blown open. What the hell could I say?

"Thank you."

"We're the ones who should be grateful. You did amazing work and you were more than fair—"

"No," I cut him off. "I wasn't."

Ken listened silently as I told him the truth, how I'd bumped the price and why. Jealousy is a hard thing to admit, but finally I felt the debt lift from my shoulders.

He was smiling faintly. "How about that. There's an honorable man left in this country." Then, "You don't envy me, Brick."

I felt the quiet words register, not sad but resigned, and the revelation opened up inside me. In my mind's eye, I saw his tired reflection in the window again.

"What . . . is it?"

"Oh," he took a breath, "the big C. My stomach's half gone. Bowels, intestine, spleen; they're on their way." His smile was bitter. "It's a race now."

Words and images were clicking into place. I tried to blurt out how sorry I was, but Ken held up his hand.

"Please. Old Doms are maudlin enough." That was his reason for attending the conference, he explained. "I'm a sentimental SOB. I was going to . . . shop for them. Someone who would keep them together, and be what they need. Strong, sexy. Honorable."

The word hung in the air like his cigar smoke.

"How long?" I asked.

"Nine months, a year, maybe longer. I'm pretty obstinate." His voice shifted. "You could be ready in six. You're a natural, and I'm a good teacher."

I deliberated for a full three seconds, then seized his hand in a warm grasp. "I don't know what to say."

He grinned. "That you can start tomorrow."

"I won't be late."

The night was a new thing and I roared into it like a rich man, a warrior king on a Softail Deuce.

Cashmeres Must Die

BY O. Z. EVANGELINE

Stuart Metzler sat in his 1959 Pontiac Chieftain on his Maple Street driveway. Mmmm . . . that new car smell. *One day they'll bottle and sell it,* he thought. He pulled a small memo pad and pen from a suit pocket and made a note. "New car smell—replicate and market!" He took in the car's interior. "Dashboard needs more knobs! Bigger!" he jotted. As a Strategy Formulation consultant, he had diverse information and ideas but felt occasionally envious as he watched clients succeed in their projects. He experienced random, uncontrollable urges to lie, and enjoyed gauging reaction. Stuart anticipated the day's work, and wondered what his secretary Vicky would be wearing.

Donna Metzler stood in her bedroom staring into a lingerie drawer. In a jumble were the panties: the one hundred percent white cotton high waist, the pastel nylon, the killer girdles, the Days-of-the-Week undies. She consulted a calendar: Tuesday! She sometimes

wore Sunday's undies during the week. Cotton felt best, softly clinging in her curves and nooks and crannies. Nylon felt strange, and
smelled stranger when dirty. Girdles could be a bitch, but on occa-
sion they helped achieve the ever-popular iron belly effect. Brassieres
with evil-eyed tips looked up at her: silk, cotton, nylon; underwire,
torpedo, push-up. "The Breasts! The breasts must be controlled!
CONTROL the breasts! Mmmm ha ha ha ha HA!" She imagined a
mad designer at Playtex.

Donna finished dressing in a pink and white checked cotton
blouse with a peter pan collar, black Capezio pants, and flats. She
grabbed her keys, purse, and sunglasses, and was out the door. She
commandeered her Chevy Bel Air and drove the Springfield streets.
The homes and lawns seemed quiet and perfect. A little too quiet. A
little too perfect. She imagined chaos and pain behind closed doors:
little pastel houses, like gaudy wedding cakes, poison under layers of
froufrou and frosting. The whites were dingy. The soufflés were flat.
The decanters were tapped. The one-eyed god droned, selling soap,
lies & subliminalism . . . Snap out of it! Donna told herself.

She pulled into the Texaco station on North Main. Donna smiled
as Tony appeared at her driver-side door. He broadly grinned. Was it
her imagination, or did his eyes and teeth project sparkles of light?
His uniform was always suspiciously spotless. His chronic perkiness
was a turn-on. Men in service were a turn-on.

"Check your fluids, Mrs. Metzler?"

"Please, Tony."

In his office Stuart pulled a magazine from his desk drawer. *Secre-
taries* boasted photographs of smiling women answering telephones,
typing, serving coffee, bending over to pick up dropped pencils, and

more. A young woman sat behind an open-front desk in a grassy field. Her hair draped her face and heavy-lidded eyes as she chewed a No. 2 pencil and dreamily stared. She wore a sweater and skirt, but no stockings. Her legs were parted. She wore white cotton underpants, the whitest imaginable white, which contrasted with her freckled tanned thighs. *Debbie is a secretary who dreams of an acting career. In her spare time she volunteers at her local senior center, and as a Big Sister.*

Vicky Miller sat outside Stuart's office at her desk in a small reception area. She wore a twin sweater set, form-fitting skirt, nylon stockings, and heels. Her desk neatly displayed a front strike Remington typewriter, telephone, and intercom. She opened a desk drawer: it boasted nail files, polish, small cosmetic bag, perfume, hairbrush, extra pair of nylons, almost everything a young woman might need to look and feel her best.

Stuart buzzed. "Miss Miller, please come into my office."

"Be right there, Mr. Metzler." Vicky grabbed a steno pad and pencil, and entered the sacred chamber of dark, rich woods, shades of forest-green, wall trophies, and Men in Suits.

"Miss Miller, may I ask, what is that sweater you're wearing?"

"Why, it's cashmere. It's very soft. Feel?"

"But of course. Cashmere . . ." He hesitantly reached and slowly ran his hand over Vicky's left sweater sleeve. "It's amazingly soft."

"It's heavenly. But I've often wondered. What does a cashmere look like? They don't have to kill them, do they?"

"Vicky, I'm sorry. Cashmeres must die."

Her eyes slightly widened and her moist lower lip trembled. Stuart patted and rubbed her left shoulder. Warm sensation filled his palms and sent nervous vibration through his arms, shoulders, chest, belly, and cock. His cock! The world seemed full of teasing textures. His cotton pajamas, his cotton flannel bedsheets, his starched boxer shorts. As he imagined being surrounded by its texture, his prick swelled against his cotton boxers and slacks. Memo: "Create and market cashmere bed sheets. Slash cost!"

At Wilson's Tailors, two men discussed a transaction.

"The styles, items and material we discussed . . . how very un-usual."

"Can you do it or not?"

"Yes, we can. But it will not be inexpensive."

"Very well."

"It will require fittings."

"Just do them in sizes 8, 38B, and medium. And make it snappy."

Stuart let himself in and marveled at his surroundings. "Honey, I'm home!" Minimalist Deco furnishings rested upon shag carpet. White tailored polyester drapes were drawn against the sun. Dark wood paneling and a faux stone fireplace helped to complete the decor.

After a dinner of hot dog casserole, iceberg lettuce, and cherry Jell-O, Stuart and Donna sat on the plastic-covered couch. Donna wore yellow baby-doll pajamas. Stuart wore a T-shirt and boxers. As he clicked the television remote, a dark, intense man came on. "Portrait of a little woman with big dreams, one Annie T. Zimmer by name. A housewife cursed to wander a physical universe where there is no end to dirt and drudgery. A woman for whom perfection is an impossible dream and who feels criticism like knives. A bitter woman who's never been able to capture realities more intangible than herself—respect, success, acceptance and love. Up ahead, an intersection of her desires, an entrance that leads to opportunity and . . . The Twilight Zone . . ."

BRRRVVVUP! As Stuart and Donna moved toward one another, their legs made moist suction noises as they peeled from the plastic. His hands fondled her cotton-covered breasts, as his mouth explored hers. Her lipstick was messy and waxy and smeared. She smelled of Ivory Soap. He was scented with Old Spice. His nipples rubbed his T-shirt as his chest buffed hers. He moved his knee from between her legs. Her transparent cotton pajama bottoms clung in her splayed pussy lips, a thin sheath of soft yellow, bisecting moist pink underneath.

She gripped his tented cock through his shorts, pulling the cloth firmly over it. She could feel its unique shape as she squeezed and ran her hand up and down its covered expanse.

He left on her soft pajama top. As she laid on her back her breasts slightly drooped toward her prone arms. He put his fingers under her pajama shorts waistband and pulled them down, peeling them from her and slipping them down her legs, and off. He cupped her and stroked her and slid his middle finger inside her. If not for the flange of his spread hand he felt he might be consumed by quivering monstrous wetness. She ground herself around him, hips rocking and heels digging into plastic. He guided his cock in and out of her, shallow to deep, shallow to deep, shallow to deep! As she arched her back, engulfing him, her moist backside slid forth then back. Her head against the arm of the sofa, they slid towards orgasm. *There! Yes!* Stuart's face froze as he pumped and stopped; Donna briefly cried out, before they lay in tiny pools of moisture. BRRRVVVUP! Donna rose and went to the kitchen. Returning, she leaned over the sofa and cleaned it with a damp sponge.

Donna walked out her front door, onto the walk and lawn. Cars gleamed in driveways. Sprinklers hissed in the dark. Plastic flamingos wetly shone. Drops of water splashed on her naked skin. As streetlights sent their shafts, her form glimmered, face and breasts and belly and legs. A spotless sidewalk led her past her neighbors' houses, which seemed to be breathing, their surfaces slightly rising and falling, rising and falling.

"Check your FLUIDS, Mrs. Metzler?" Tony the Texaco man was suddenly in her path, eyes and teeth sparkling, maniacally grinning. He had something draped over his left shoulder.

"What?"

Tony quickly unrolled a large tarp and threw it over her, lifted her, and slung her over his shoulder. Donna struggled as Tony marched the sidewalk, whistling "I Get a Kick out of You." Physically subdued and verbally stifled, she noticed that the material smelled of motor oil and auto mechanical chemistry. It draped and rubbed and chafed her skin, as her waist bent over the jut of Tony's shoulder, breasts flattening against his back.

"Mmmmmpppph . . . Mmmmmmppphhh!"

Wake up! Lucidity ruled; she awoke in her twin bed.

Stuart and Donna sat across from one another at the kitchen table. Stuart gobbled meat: sausage, bacon, and, to insure adequate protein consumption, eggs. Toast, juice, and coffee rounded out his menu. Donna nibbled boiled eggs and fruit.

"Need more butter, sweetie?"

"I'm fine, thanks." Stuart said, his mouth and chin greasily shining.

"Busy day today? Lots of clients scheduled?"

"Fairly busy. How about yours?"

"Cleaning. Shopping. Gassing the car. Nothing special." She smiled.

Stuart drove west on Oak. He loved his large formidable Pontiac, a veritable tank of a vehicle. He imagined almost effortlessly driving through fences and walls. The interior needed additional features, he thought: beverage holders. A small built-in television. A minuscule broiler oven. A tiny barbeque grill.

"Good morning, Vicky." He strode past Vicky's desk and into his office, sat down at his desk and opened his briefcase. He pulled a magazine from it. He laid the issue of *Goat World* in front of him and flipped it open. *The Himalayan Cashmere ruminant mammal of the cattle family, with hollow horns, coarse hair, and a characteristic beard. It is closely related to the sheep. It has been bred for centuries for its highly valuable hair and wool. It can exist only in mountain regions of the Himalayan Mountains and in Tibet and Mongolia, at altitudes of l5,000 feet or more. Himalayan cashmere goats live in herds and feed on grass and shrubs.*

Its long, straight, coarse outer hair has little value; however, the small quantity of the underhair, or down, is made into luxuriously soft wool-like yarns with a characteristic highly napped finish. This fine cashmere fiber is not sheared from the goat but acquired through frequent combings during the shedding season. Cashmere is a much finer fiber than mohair or any wool fiber. It is soft and lighter in weight than wool, and quite warm; however, because it is a soft, delicate fiber, fabrics produced from cashmere are not as durable as wool.

The intercom buzzed. "Mr. Metzler? Mr. Johnson is here."

"Fine. Send him in."

"Good morning, Mr. Johnson. Please have a seat."

"Thank you. Mr. Metzler, I understand that you suggest that Corp Inc. not proceed with—"

"The fast-food idea?"

Stuart smiled. His eyes gleamed. "I do. In my opinion, the fast-food business is a flash in the pan. It will never last. I'd recommend going into Specialty Retailing. It's all in the report."

"Specialty Retailing?"

"Yes. Specialty Retailing. Choose a single type of merchandise. Scotch tape, for example. Sell only that item. Ka Ching! See?"

Donna sat at the cluttered kitchen table and read over coffee. She had a magazine jones. The paper was glossy. The colors were bright. The text was perky. Their pages called to her from newsstands and checkout stands. Their energy could be exciting. Comforting. Some of the information was practical. *Woman Today* offered advice. *A housewife should run her house the way an executive runs his business: with goals, schedules, and plans. Plan for dinner, or at least shop early. Take time to rest and relax during the day as to avoid exhaustion and depletion. With proper planning, one can have all home duties finished before noon. When he arrives home, greet him with a warm smile. Don't voice problems or complaints. Don't complain if he's late for dinner. Just count this as minor compared to his potentially rough day. Make him comfortable. Suggest he lean back in a comfortable chair or lie down in the bedroom. Have a cool or warm drink ready for him. Fluff his pillow and offer to remove his shoes. Speak in a low, soft, soothing and pleasant voice.* The last part made Donna warm and tingly.

She took a brush to her laundry after applying *Stain Be Gone!* White was the worst. Blood and food stains were tough. She held the cotton fabric in her left hand and agitated the brush with her right. White . . . whiter . . . whitest goddamnit! Housewife. Housewife! What was she, married to a house? She might as well make love to it . . . embrace it . . . roll naked in its piles of silky laundry . . . straddle her vacuum cleaner and ride its vibration as she cleaned Cleaned CLEANED, her physical orgasm melding with a psychic one, her rocking grasp satisfied, her sanitary standards met—before slipping falling dripping into soft fragrant fabric folds, pulling their texture around her mounds and curves; around her neck and under her arms and between her legs . . .

BBBBBRRRIIIIIIIIGGG! The doorbell brought a flushed Donna to reality. Her friend Susie was at the door, sporting magazines, chocolate cake, and brandy. Donna loved their occasional mornings together.

"Catch you at a bad time?"

"No, not at all. I'm ready for a break. Come into the kitchen." They took a seat opposite one another at the table and spread the goodies on red Formica.

"Fork for that? Or do you just want to use your hands?"

Susie smiled and sloshed St. Regis into two jelly jar glasses. They sipped and gulped, and dug into chocolate cake.

Susie thumbed *Women's World* magazine. "So, I was reading this article. The Yesnik Report says that sixty-two percent of women masturbate, and that clitoral orgasm is natural and superior to vaginal orgasm."

"Really?"

"S'true, the article says. Donna, do you ever masturbate? Have you ever seen your clitoris?"

Donna laughed and swilled her slightly fiery brew. "I've touched myself, sure. But I've never really seen that part of me. My clitoris."

"Get a mirror."

"Susie!"

Donna leaned back on a vinyl chair. Through her parted robe blue silk panties shone.

"S'okay. Go ahead and slip them off." She refreshed Donna's drink.

Donna lifted her hips and rolled her panties down, pulled them off, and tossed them aside. She leaned back on the chair and parted her legs. Susie held the angled mirror inches away. With her right index and middle finger Donna slightly spread her labia and saw the mirrored reflection, a steamy pink jungle of curves and folds and bumps staring back at her, from the small round mirror frame.

"The clitoris is at top center. S' hidden, like. Now, put your finger there and rub . . ."

Donna pressed a fingertip into herself and watched it slightly disappear.

"Hic! Oh shit. HIC! Now I've got the hiccups! I hate it when this happens!"

"Donna, first you need to take a teaspoon of sugar. Then hold your breath and drink twelve ounces of water. Hold your nose as I plug your ears. Always works for me."

"HIC!" She ate the sugar and gulped water—held her breath and held her nose. Susie stood closely behind and plugged Donna's ears.

Donna began to laugh as the doorbell rang. Probably another salesman, she thought. She choked on laughter and spat water across the kitchen. "HIC!"

"Just a MINUTE! Be right there!"

The garment bag hung in Donna's closet. She took it from the rod and laid it on the bed, unzipping it and flinging it open. Padded hangers were stacked between layers of hot pink softness. In front of the mirror she adorned her body with black pearls; bra and panties; shirtwaist dress; apron; gloves. She slipped on black high heels and walked to the kitchen. Her heels clicked and clacked on the black-and-white-squared linoleum; her calves curved and bulged and protested at the assault of three-inch heels; spinal alignment threw her head and pelvis forward. Layers of cashmere trapped warmth; her kitchen trapped warmth.

Stuart entered the kitchen. Donna stood at the stove with her back to him. He was hit with a wall of odor: cooking browning bird, raw white onion, pungent spice, sulfurous vegetables; of moist rising yeasty bread dough in a cotton cloth-covered bowl; of Youth Dew perfume and coconut shampoo. Had the scene been depicted in a cartoon, a cloud might have enveloped him.

He watched her cook. He smelled chicken juices steamily drenching sage stuffing in her hot Amana. She made gravy. In a skillet bubbled seasoned browned drippings. She added half-and-half, poultry seasoning, and coarse ground pepper. As it began to boil she added a flour and water paste and turned down the heat. Fat, starch, moisture, and heat chemically colluded, combined, and expanded, its mass getting thicker and creamier and larger.

He approached and stood behind her, the molecular essence of her skin and clothing mingling in his nose and brain. His bare skin brushed the back of her dress; he stroked her breasts. His erection pushed against her buttocks, moving in soft cashmere folds; she loved the feeling of its stiffness against her; she yearned to envelop it. He untied her apron and let it fall. He lifted her clingy dress up and over her head; static electricity sizzled between it and her lingerie, between it and her hair. In a synergism of warm skin and fibrous fluff, she faced him and gripped his cock with a gloved hand. He watched her vivid, pink-fluffed fingers stroke his peachy-pink blue-veined cock. She gently, firmly grasped its head, then quickly slammed her hand down its shaft—slowly gently up! Quickly firmly down! She moved to the table and sat on its edge, leaning slightly back, legs apart, black high-heeled feet askew. The pink cashmere panties were to spec: bikinis with a slit in the crotch. Her pussy looked a study in color, a surreal blossom, flesh pink surrounded by hot pink fibrous softness, upon red Formica. He stood at the edge of the table and stroked the panty; he stroked her exposed pussy. She guided his hand. "Here . . ." His finger parted her and angled upward, flesh-hook rubbing her clit. He more deeply explored; he felt an odd texture. He seized slick round hardness and pulled. Out slid glistening black pearls. "Cashmere Cunt with Pearls, On Red" the painting might be named. He pushed his cock into her as she melted over the edge; she wetly slammed herself against him, around him. As she straightened her back, the angle of his cock more forcefully pounded her. Her clit was electric white-hot; he prodded her higher and deeper as forms of sensation merged and released in her screams. He faster stroked her cashmere-covered cunt as he tensed and came, shooting pearly white into pink, on red. White bodies sprawled on red. On the stove, rich brown gravy bubbled over edges of stainless steel and splattered onto a white surface, as it made its way to a drip pan.

Sheer Excitement

BY DEBRA HYDE

Lovers have their ways. The romantic among us send flowers to the workplace while those risqué leave breathless little voice-mail messages that stop just shy of phone sex. The sentimental ones leave lipstick endearments on the bathroom mirror or little love notes in a brown-bagged lunch. But perverts have their own language of love and it's usually spoken in some dialect of fetish.

Eric and Tanya were no exception to this rule. Although they started out as the flowers and love-notes type, they quickly grew bored with the standard "Love You" methodology. After all, roses were fine when you liked gazing into each other's eyes across a candlelit dinner, but they preferred to ogle each other's naked bodies. They preferred unconventional sex to great romance.

It didn't happen all at once, though. They discovered their language of love in bits and pieces, in a nipple pinched here, man on the bottom there, and in the worshipfulness that comes with prolonged cunnilingus.

But when Eric copped a certain feel a certain way, everything changed.

Readying for a black-tie event, Eric spotted his wife in the undergarment stage of dress. Rather than do the usual guy thing of grabbing her round, plush ass or slipping his hand into her cleavage-enhancing bra, he knelt behind her as she bent over to pick up a pair of heels. He ran a fingertip up her thigh-high stockings, lightly, with just enough touch to sense its luxurious weave. An audible sigh escaped his lips. Hearing its tenor, Tanya knew he had the start of a stiffy in his pants.

That he copped a feel didn't annoy Tanya, but it did surprise her. When she turned and peered down at him, Eric looked up, meek and innocent. But it was the kind of innocence that comes only once, like getting caught with your hand in the cookie jar for the first time.

Tanya knew Eric well enough to suspect some kind of cat was about to slip from the bag, and she already knew that the game would best play out if she seized the moment. She furrowed her eyebrows and questioned what, exactly, had tempted Eric to caress her.

"You have a thing for my legs or my stockings?" She raised her hands to her waist and stood strong. Just like an Amazon. A big, majestic, all-powerful Amazon.

Eric had never seen anything like it. He gulped, visibly. He glanced at her legs, briefly, furtively, the way most men glance at women's breasts, before rising to meet her haughty stare, a stare that he'd only ever met in his wildest fantasies.

"Your legs are beautiful, but the stockings are . . . are . . ." He sputtered for words, and then fumbled, "I—I—couldn't help myself."

And so Tanya discovered that Eric had a thing for stockings.

All evening long, as she watched Eric work the room, Tanya wondered exactly what new door of eroticism he had just opened for them. Perhaps it was one in which she could make it a priority to discover his every little weakness—and then play it for all it was worth. Granted, she had toyed and teased before—a powerful woman on top wasn't entirely new to them—but would she discover new erotic territory in interrogating him further about this? Would he dwindle from normal guy mode into something smaller, meeker, and mouse-like?

Her mind raced with speculation and when it finally settled on the thought of riding his face until he was breathless and ready to admit to anything, she flushed, excited.

For his part, Eric looked across the room and saw Tanya drain the last sip of drink from her glass. He extricated himself from polite conversation and, without hesitation, moved to the bar to fetch her a fresh drink. Watching him go to work at her behest while she stood in the middle of a crowded room and considered topping him made Tanya wet.

Sex is going to be thrilling when we get home, she thought.

In fact, they didn't even make it past their living room couch before she pounced. She hiked up her skirt and rode his face until he was breathless. Then she grilled him about what exactly this stocking thing was all about.

"How did you develop this stocking fetish?"

The troubled look on Eric's face told Tanya that she had hit pay dirt.

"When I was a teen, we came home from a family vacation and the boy we hired to care for our cats had gone through my parents' drawers. Maybe he was looking for my dad's porn, I dunno, but the idiot left all my mother's underthingies out on her bed! I knew what he'd done was awful—I mean, just seeing her stuff tossed on the bed like that was . . . was . . . icky. Then, I saw the disgust in my mom's face. It was unbearable. Later that night, when I had to take a leak, I saw all her pantyhose and underwear in the bathroom trash. That's when I knew for sure just how sick the whole thing was."

He sighed, this time poignantly. Tanya knew his sighs and this one told her that there was more to this embarrassing story.

"And?"

"And that night I had a wet dream."

Tanya screwed up her face in mock disgust. "That's sick!"

She rode his face until his tongue went numb.

At Tanya's insistence, he had revealed everything about his little quirk, and it had destroyed a barrier that he could've never crossed on his own. It was one thing to harbor a desire, but another thing to lay yourself bare and admit to a fetish. But admit it, he did, through lips made slick with his wife's sweet juices.

After that evening, Tanya planned to become an explorer and chart a course into new erotic territory. Eric, on the other hand, thought he'd died and gone to heaven. He was amazed how a simple brush of his fingers against the seam of her hosiery had taken them further from the mundane than they'd ever gone before.

Now, every time he thought about it, he shivered, thrilled by the possibilities. Finally, he might be able to appease this odd little indulgence without becoming the proverbial furtive pervert all those old sexology books claimed would be his legacy. He wouldn't be condemned to anonymously watching women on the street, always longing and lusting.

And the possibilities seemed endless. Maybe he could even look up at Tanya from the floor, caress her legs, and adore her towering presence. Maybe he could shrink at the sight of her, pretending to be the little boy who cowered in his mother's perilous stature, and even if it felt like a weird, pseudo-Freudian mother/son thing, it would be couched safely within the boundaries of adult erotic expression.

Eric could barely wait for another taste. Eager, he left a note in his wife's checkbook, inviting her next move. "You know my deepest secret now. You can do anything you want with it." Then, he sat back and wondered where this would take them. The lump in his throat was so large that it hurt.

Tanya's next move showed up on Eric's voice mail at work. "The hosiery fairy left you a little something under your pillow. When I get home, I better find you naked, flat on your back in our bed with your little presents heaped around that little cock of yours."

Tanya planned to test the boundaries of Eric's fetish. Did he like all things hosiery or was he particular and fussy, strictly the garters and heels type? And what about panties? She heard that Japanese men had a big thing for panties, so big that their comic books often employed a dirty old man who skulked after a flash of panty as a comedic device. And Eric was, without a doubt, stacking up to be a dirty man, despite his youth.

When she arrived home and found Eric sprawled on their bed with her pantyhose heaped around his throbbing, hard cock (which, incidentally, ran counter to her jab of "little"), she promptly asked him, "Did you notice how many pairs of pantyhose I gave you?"

"Five," he answered.

"Yes, that's right. How astute of you. Now you're going to learn how I intend to use them."

Tanya tied him hand and foot to their bed, one set of pantyhose for each appendage. Eric groaned at the soft feel of silky fabric holding him in place. He flexed his arms and legs to get a fuller feel for the bondage.

"Don't thrash around," she warned him. "These'll tighten up on you if you do. If your hands turn blue, fun's over." She took the fifth pair of pantyhose and wrapped it around his cock and balls, tightly, and tied it off. "This one, however, can be good and tight. Let's keep that cock of yours nice and hard." She patted it smartly and then slid off the bed.

Slowly, Tanya undressed. She stripped herself of her suit, her shoes, and her blouse. She shed her workday identity—Fortune 500 existence be damned. She shimmied from her half-slip, her bra, and panties. However, she left her black, thigh-high hosiery in place. *The perfect accent,* she thought, as she climbed onto Eric and lowered herself onto his face.

As the smell and warmth of Tanya's cunt overtook him, as the captivating feel of her strong thighs met his cheeks, Eric moaned, amazed and aroused and full of anticipation. He greeted Tanya's cunt lips with a gentle, grateful kiss, a worshipful kiss. *Sweet of him,* Tanya thought, *but not what I want.*

"Forget the niceties, Eric. I've had a long day and I need a damn good release. Put that tongue of yours to work."

Eric groaned at her order and put his tongue into motion. He licked the length of her slit from back to front several times and then focused on her clit. He thought of a hummingbird's wings as he worked it, hoping his attempts would be as swift and beautiful.

Tanya, however, didn't appreciate Eric's busy attention to her clit. "Hold your tongue still," she told him. Eric groaned, disappointed, but he complied. He made his tongue rigid.

Tanya sank onto him, and Eric's world changed as the folds of her labia surrounded his tongue, as her cunt engulfed him. As her wet warmth rose and fell on his tongue, her hosiery rubbed along his jawline. Divine, it was divine! Eric prayed they'd chafe him enough to leave friction burns. His eyes flickered shut in blissful submission and he felt himself begin to drool. He felt Tanya seep as well. Her heavenly hosiery grew damp against his face.

Their efforts weren't enough to make Tanya come, however. Frustrated, she pulled herself away from Eric. "This isn't working," she complained. She went to her dresser, opened a drawer—the sock and pantyhose drawer—and rummaged around.

Eric watched her, admiring her round ass, the way her hair draped down her back, and, especially, the hint of skin that showed through her hosiery. His cock throbbed at the sight of his lover and he licked his lips as he waited and watched, eager to savor Tanya's generous juices. If he ever doubted the wisdom of admitting his fetish to his wife, he never would again. Every time she fucked him, she made another one of his dreams come true.

But Tanya had her own dreams, too. She had begun to realize that in ruling Eric, she could use erotic drama to subvert or enact any number of real-life or fantasy elements. With her prowess undressed and unmasked, she was like the comic book superheroines of her childhood, minus the spandex garb and special powers. Through bedroom assertiveness, she could transgress against the demure deference of her grandmother's era and she could stomp on the soft femininity of her mother's generation. By taking charge, she could pretend that the men who might complain about the she-bitch in the boardroom would be too much in awe to do so in the bedroom. But mostly she realized that her cunning—her *sexual* cunning—made her powerful, and power, in turn, made her attractive. And Tanya enjoyed being desirable.

Rummaging complete, she returned to Eric with a dildo in her hand.

"Open your mouth."

They were simple words but they were demanding. Eric did as commanded and found himself biting down on the flange end of the dildo.

"No fault of your own, but your tongue isn't big enough. I need something meatier to satisfy me."

This time, when she lowered herself onto Eric's face, she took the entire dildo into her cunt. It felt incredible, filling. Her cunt hugged its thickness and every stroke rippled within as she fucked it.

When she looked down at her husband, she saw struggle written across Eric's face—struggle and erotic bliss. His teeth gripped the dildo in a determined bite, as if to secure it against the pummeling she gave it. As she watched him, she felt the first rumbles of orgasm. Keeping her eyes on him, she placed her finger on her clit. Fever pitched, she came in one long, deep orgasm. Fierce throbs clutched at the toy in Eric's mouth and they seemed to go on forever.

Soon enough, her orgasm faded and she pulled herself off Eric's face. As if to signal a finale, one stray contraction coursed through her as the tip of the dildo left her slit, making her shiver and moan.

Satisfied, Tanya took the dildo from Eric's mouth and, casting it aside, turned her attentions to his captured cock. She fondled it and caressed its length. She admired its reddening color, its bulging veins, both barely discernable through the wraps of pantyhose that covered Eric's erection.

"You know," she mused, "I've never jerked you off." She looked from Eric's cock to his face and smiled at him. "Maybe it's time to change that."

Tanya ran her hand up and down Eric's cock. A shiver shot through him as she did.

"Oh, you like that, do you?"

He answered her with a breathy and urgent "yes."

"I thought so." Tanya began stroking Eric. Her hand caressed the pantyhose, sending sensations right through the fabric to his dick. It was pure indulgence and it made his dick strain against the fabric.

But he also noticed that Tanya looked distant, almost preoccupied. Had he displeased her? Was she bored? Or worse, was she about to change her mind? Uncertainty—all part of abandoning his male pretense and privilege, part of giving himself over to Tanya's imperious power. He longed to be her vassal, her servant, someone who existed only to appease her every whim and her every lust.

Eric had hoped Tanya would reveal herself as stern, implacable, maybe even cruel, but she'd turned out to be far more imaginative than the idiotic stereotype that ran through his head. She'd proved herself wily; she knew how to toy with him, and her teasing had proven far more effective than her scorn. All of which made his undoing truly amazing. Stunned by her brilliance, he was only as smart as his hard dick was dumb. And he knew that that would make him a slave to her every command.

As he trembled under her touch, Tanya spoke.

"You know, I've debated for days about telling you this, but now that I've got your dick in my hand, I can confess something to you."

She looked briefly at his dick, this length of meat that she now stroked, then back to Eric. She smiled, slyly, wickedly.

"Once, I saw you masturbating. Months ago. I came home from work a little early and found our bedroom door ajar. I heard you moaning and when I peeked in, I saw you naked, sitting in the corner chair. You were masturbating, really working it. It was embarrassing, me finding you like that, so I stole away downstairs. Just as I turned to leave, I heard you come."

Tanya leaned into his ear and whispered, "Don't believe me? This is how you stroke yourself."

She worked him faster, squeezing and twisting his shaft. Eric's cock bulged suddenly under her manipulation. Tanya laughed. *At my expense*, Eric thought, yet he relished it so much his cock reddened, it was so aroused.

"You're so predictable," Tanya shrewdly observed. "And when you get *that* hard, you do this."

She stopped the squeezing and twisting. She focused her strokes on the head of his cock, and, deliciously, she hit that one spot that made orgasm imminent. It was proof perfect that she had indeed watched him. Eric blushed painfully as he felt himself moving toward orgasm.

"It doesn't take long, does it?" Tanya asked. "That's what I noticed when I caught you in the act. Between that and your pantyhose fetish, I've developed a whole slew of naughty ideas."

Tanya kept her eyes on her work as she spoke. "I figure that if you like pantyhose, maybe you like panties, too. So I'm going to wear my panties for days and nights on end. Get them nice and stinky. Then you'll sleep with them over your head, the crotch as near to your nose as I can get it."

Eric couldn't believe how raunchy her ideas were—and that she was jerking him off to them. He had never seen her like this and his cock lurched at her ideas.

"Oh, you like where I'm going with this," she observed facetiously. "Then I bet you'd like a urine-soaked panty gag to keep you quiet the next time I need to fuck this cock of yours."

Eric's breathing deepened. He was close, Tanya realized.

"I'll keep it in place with a pantyhose hood over your head."

That did it—that made Eric explode. He groaned once, loudly, and pushed his cock hard into her hand as a jet of jism spurt from him. Tanya slowed her hand and milked him, pulling three more spurts of come from his cock. It pooled on his belly.

Tanya didn't waste any time removing the pantyhose from his cock. She placed it square onto his wet belly. She untied him and pointed to his belly. "Don't get up until that has soaked up your mess." It was an order, Eric would discover, that required him to lie in place for a good twenty minutes beyond the end of their scene.

Eric would make another discovery days later when he opened his briefcase at work. There, atop several files, he found the come-caked pantyhose inside a plastic sandwich bag. There, too, he found a note. *From now on, you'll masturbate with and into these, without exception. And you'll present them to me whenever I demand to see them. I plan to examine them tonight. Which means you must jerk off once today before you leave work.*

Eric gulped. He blushed. Hands shaking, he pocketed the plastic bag inside his suit jacket. But as stunned and overwhelmed as he was by Tanya's order, he still made his way to the men's room later that day. He did what she demanded of him, and he loved her all the more for it.

As he jerked off, he imagined himself on his knees, offering up the evidence of his often-repeated efforts, caked in crusty nylon fabric, while his luscious wife stood over him. No longer the work-a-day woman, she would tower there, an exquisite and unyielding Amazon. She would inspect his offering. She would judge his efforts and deem them worthy or lacking, all the while making Eric's devotion to her surer and unbreakable.

And they would love every minute of it. That was, of course, to be expected. After all, lovers have their ways.

Prêt-à-Porter

BY STACY REED

Claire walks into her first closet and makes her way toward the dresses. She walks past her Miu Miu pants and Diesel jeans, blouses from Prada and Christian Dior hanging behind them. In the fall, she will unpack her sweaters from the cedar boxes lining the southern wall and hang them behind the slacks and jeans: the wool cardigans, the light cashmere sets, and then the fine gauge angora pullovers. She pushes past her skirts: pencil straight linen skirts that cling to her well-muscled thighs; tiny pleated minis in which bending over is not an option; yards of taffeta-like liquid that frolic around her heals with each step. At the back of the room, facing floor-to-ceiling rows of Dolce & Gabbana crocodile pumps, Manolo Blahnik Carolyne slingbacks, and Chanel ankle-strap spectators, hang the dresses; shimmering or demure as a crocus, they progress from the shortest to the longest, divided by season. Claire has banished from her vocabulary the legendary complaint: *I have nothing to wear.*

The dress dictates the sort of experience she will have, so she gives her selection thought. Something navy and fitted, but not tight, something she could wear with pearls, would probably land her a serious young man, the type of guy who jogs before work and checks on his finances every night. Easy to provoke this type to fuck with all the aggression he's been channeling into "productivity." This vintage Halston or this limited-edition Yves Saint Laurent? Claire rubs the raw silk of a red sari that has been folded and fashioned into sweeping, trembling tiers. This could win her some kind of artist, or maybe a cute but vacuous boy who fancies himself a bohemian because he can't hold a job. She lets it drop. You always look sexy in Versace, but . . . *Ah! the floral print from Dior.* She bought it the moment she saw it on the runway. Folds of billowing organza hover slightly above her surprisingly dark nipples. Magnolias floating in stem-green silk cling to her waist and hug her hips. Were it not for a slit to the thigh, she could not walk. At the knee, pebbly freshwater pearls are sewn into the hem. Surely this will entice a man who prefers high feminine to efficient contemporary. Then a minimalist architect might fall for it precisely because it defies his aesthetic. But of course all speculation is useless; like almost all of her dresses, this has never been worn, and will be worn only once.

Since her calves are toned and her skin is as pale and opaque as cream, Claire rarely bothers with hose. No way this dress could accommodate even the tiniest strapless bra, so she skips it, and the panties as well; the dress is cut too close to camouflage a panty line, and even if Claire felt like putting up with a violating thong, the dress is cut so low in back that she would sport the "butt floss" look. She only needs to select a pair of shoes.

Claire steps into a pair of sea glass marine Choo stilettos, and turns to face the wide floor-to-ceiling mirror. Her generous cleavage looks accidental, but can't be missed. Her thighs are as sturdy as a colt's. The dress displays her ass to its firm finest. Any number of men might like this one. She licks her fingers and meticulously pulls a few choice strands of her black bob toward her chin. She hurries to check her bag: perfume, mouthwash, condoms, Astroglide. She cuts off the lights and takes the elevator to ground level.

She hands the doorman a ten as he ushers her into the night with a stiff bow.

"Thank you, Ms. Vitello."

Claire sweeps past him and hurries down Royal, past the Monteleone and the antique stores, each with doors open, pouring the shockingly cold breath of air-conditioned excess into the southern evening, each specializing in its particular taste for Victorian mourning jewelry, antebellum chandeliers, Russian alexandrite broaches, jade lamps, or Oriental urns and rugs. She doesn't frequent these opulent stores glittering along her street; emerald pendants and Sheffield samovars are of no more use to Claire than makeup.

Walking in the French Quarter is faster than taking a taxi, and infinitely more entertaining. Her heals clatter against the pavement as she pushes through the thick clots of tourists throwing dollar bills into the upturned hat of a kid who looks about eight. He's glued steel plates onto the bottoms of his Nikes and has taught himself to imitate tap dancing well enough to charm inebriated sightseers hell-bent on experiencing "the local color." A guy in shades stomps on a wooden board and belts out "Sweet Home Chicago" over an ill-tuned guitar while a skinny girl dances barefoot beside him. An old man in a shiny polyester suit plays saxophone on the corner, and whores in spandex twirl on the wrought iron lampposts. Claire zigzags among the knots of spectators, reaches Bourbon, and places a fifty in the sax player's case. He doesn't pause.

She turns the corner and sees the ideal spot: The Maiden Voyage. This place is filled with horny men. It is filled with women without clothes. A win-win situation.

The air is cold, colder than the antique shops, as cold as the air in the sleepless, flashing interior of Las Vegas. The men lounge in overstuffed swivel chairs, many of them in sweaters. The women jiggle and bounce on the stages with feigned but boundless enthusiasm, and very tight nipples. The smell of ashtrays and dime-store perfume assails Claire. She'll never get the stink out of her dress. Already it is defiled.

As if the naked nymphs strutting in tacky five-inch heels try his patience with silicone and peroxide, a redheaded kid, by the looks of him not far over drinking age, turns away from the stage and stares at Claire. She is the only woman in the club who is not an employee, and her presence carries the thrill of even greater transgression. The dancers are obliged to cater to the clientele. It is their job. But this woman, this is clearly a woman of wealth and the power to deny. Corrupting her, now that would be fun. The redheaded boy scatters some bills on his table, excuses himself across the club, and climbs onto a barstool next to Claire. She pointedly ignores him and studies the concave stomach and overdeveloped calves of the vixen on center stage.

Without glancing at him, Claire asks "Like her ass?"

This startles him. She's already outmaneuvered him, placing him in a position to seem either crass or prude. "*I* like it," she goes on, and places his square, freckled hand emphatically inside her bare left thigh.

He motions to the bartender, another beautiful young thing swaying about in fantastically high heels and little else. He orders two mint juleps and says to Claire, "My name's—"

Claire places a finger over his lips. "Your name doesn't concern me."

He looks confused, then asks brightly, "Do you come to New Orleans often?" as if they could ever meet again.

"Some of us live here," she says and plucks a sprig of mint from her drink. She'll let the other leaves marinate in bourbon and rum, but she always starts a julep by balancing the sweet, cold alcohol with the slightly bitter herb.

"Really? I'm from Houston. I fix cars." He is quick to explain, "Nothing but custom jobs. People who want a faster engine, a lower, more streamlined body, or maybe heavy speakers rigged up from the trunk. That sort of thing." The redhead makes a presentation of buffing a heavy gold pinky ring inset with a sizeable diamond against his starched broadcloth oxford. "It's good money."

"Yes, I see."

"How about you?"

"I buy clothes."

"Like for one of those fancy shops on Magazine?"

"Something like that," Claire says, then takes a long drink of the watered-down julep. "Let me see your hands." Without asking why, he offers the one for inspection while keeping the other on her thigh. His fingernails are clipped brutally short, or maybe just worn down, and they are stained with grime. Thick calluses have formed at the base, mid-joint, and on the tip of each finger. Good. She is in no mood for some prissy CEO who pays someone twice a week to file and buff his nails. Not tonight.

Claire tosses back her drink and says, "This place is for tourists. Let me show you around."

The man doesn't argue, simply settles the tab and escorts Claire into the teeming quarter. He seems at ease being led, freed from the tedium of consulting his map every two blocks.

"Are we going to a cemetery?"

Claire rolls her eyes. "Do you have a vampire fetish?" Christ, he no doubt does. But this is Claire's fantasy. Plenty of prostitutes specialize in the penchant for vampires, and for a little extra they'll take it to a graveyard. Claire has a different agenda.

She heads toward the river and the crowds thin as they approach Tchoupitoulas Street and disappear altogether as they wander into the steel bowels of the Warehouse District. She scans the shadows. The pitiless yellow glare of the sodium lamps renders the stretches in between all the more inviting. Then she sees an alley no more than three feet wide wedged between a garage and an art gallery. Perfect. Claire leads the redhead toward the alley and, after walking just a few paces, they are ensconced in merciful darkness. Only peripheral grays and the winking glint of scrap metal permeates the gloom. She can barely see his face, which is perfectly fine with her.

He politely, if ineptly, reaches for her zipper, but Claire bats his hand away. "Never mind that. Just shove it up," she says, already tugging at the hem herself.

He tries to ease the skirt of her dress up her thighs, but it's no use. The seam rips and the glistening freshwater pearls go bouncing across the filthy cement and roll into puddles faintly shimmering iridescent with oil. He mutters an apology, but pushes the tattered hem to Claire's slender waist anyway. He shoves his roughened fingers between her shaved labia and hones in on her swollen and slippery clit.

"That's a good boy," she breathes. "But I know you can do better. Suck my nipples too."

Without taking his fingers from her clit, the man fumbles a breast from her bodice with his free hand. He inclines his head and takes her hard nipple in his mouth, staining the organza with his saliva. Claire places his coarse fingers on her other nipple and whimpers. The man rolls her clit between his thumb and forefinger until her shudders gradually subside. She unzips his pants and takes his eager cock in her tiny, smooth hands.

"Tell me what you want," she demands.

"Whatever you want." He wraps his hand around hers and says, "That feels good."

"What if I want something else?" she asks.

"Sure. Anything."

Claire keeps pumping his dick with one hand and moves her other along the elastic of his underwear until she finds the side seam. The elastic breaks easily and she extricates the briefs from between his thighs. "Thanks. Now tell me what you want."

"Let me fuck you."

"Is that all?" she asks and sinks to her knees.

His cock is weeping semen, and Claire antagonizes him further by avoiding the shaft and gingerly licking and sucking his taut balls. He tugs at her thick, straight hair and she lets him. Obligingly she suckles the head of his prick, then allows him to push the rest of it into her full-lipped mouth. He thrusts for several minutes, then begs, "Now will you let me fuck you?"

"As long as you promise me one thing," she says as she stands and rolls a condom down his cock. "Don't come inside me."

He gestures to the empty foil wrapper. "How come?"

"I want something to remember you by," she says and guides his dick into her gushing pussy. He pushes her up against the wall of the narrow alley and within a few strokes Claire is stifling her moans against the redhead's powerful shoulder. Relieved that she's come again so easily, he clutches her ass and starts banging into her more vehemently, but she grabs his hips and pushes him from her.

"You promised," Claire says, and peels the rubber from his engorged cock. She wraps his underwear through her strong, tapered fingers, and within a dozen or so masterful tugs of her practiced hand she feels his warm semen splatter against her silk Dior, rain down on her Choo stilettos, and then ooze in an exhausted trickle through the cotton shorts and into her waiting palm.

In the gray moments before dawn, Claire hails a taxi; she's too tired to walk, and besides, these shoes pinch her toes.

She steps into the cab, and is greeted with the usual "Are you okay, lady?" They always think she got mugged.

"Corner of Royal and Bienville."

She gets out half a block from her apartment. Garbage men are doing what they can to tidy up the ill-used streets. "Hey, baby! Nice dress! See some action last night? Hey cunt, I'd love to eat *your* pussy! Bitch, think you're too good for me?"

Claire turns and glares at the "waste management" employee. He wears a tight wife-beater that's yellowed under the armholes. His biceps are covered in tattoos clearly not executed by a professional, the sort of "body art" you get only in prison. *Johnny* is penned high on his right pectoral. "No way, sweet thing. I think you'll do just fine."

The garbage man goes slack in the jaw and ogles her speechlessly. *What the—?*

"Come on." Claire turns on her heel and strides down Royal, not bothering to look behind her. She knows he's there.

The few tourists still swerving around with absurd fuchsia drinks adorned with miniature umbrellas stare. She's taken her Choos off and has stepped on some glass; a trickle of bright red blood is drying between her pedicured toes. Her dress, which even a drunk can see is expensive, is torn and soiled. Her knees are chafed raw and her bare back is covered in scrapes and pocked with flakes of brick—or is it cement? Yet no one asks her if she needs help; she's too *happy*.

Claire breezes past the doorman who smiles at her indulgently. He's seen it before. But when the garbage man tries to get past him, he says "Sir, I don't believe you reside here."

Johnny throws back his massive shoulders and puffs out his chest. "Fuck no! But this is where I've come."

"Sir, we do not care to invite foul-smelling men without proper shirts onto these premises."

"I don't need no invitation from you, buddy," says Johnny. "I'm here with *her*."

The doorman turns to Claire in confusion. "Ms. Vitello—?"

"He's with me," Claire interrupts and leads the garbage man into a mirrored elevator while the doorman looks on in awe.

The doors open at the eleventh floor and Claire leads the sanitation worker to a closet at the end of the hall marked "Housekeeping." She knows the maids won't start vacuuming the carpets and polishing the mirrors for another hour, and that is all the time she needs.

The door is not locked and they walk into the flowery ammonia stench of the small broom closet. Surrounding them are mildewed plastic buckets, dry-rotting sponges, coarse brown paper towels, toilet plungers, and mops left standing in puddles of gray water.

Claire heaves herself onto the rim of the cold metal utility sink. "So do it."

Johnny just shrugs and cocks his head to one side. "Do what?"

"You said you'd love to eat my pussy. Go ahead."

The garbage man cups her heart-shaped face in his hands. They smell like fish. "Sure thing." He pinches her cheek playfully, and she immediately feels the bruise start to form. He pushes her knees apart and she groans when she hears the back seam of her dress splitting even wider. As he kneels on the floor of the broom closet, one knee over the drain in the floor, he shoves her dress around her waist and says, "Good. I love a shaved cunt."

Claire looks down at his head bobbing frenetically between her legs. His hands, stained black as a coal miner's, clutch her thighs. She moves them up against her silk-swathed tummy and rubs them up and down her torso. The effect is breathtaking: streaks of filth smudge the creamy magnolias and washed-out green of the bodice. Johnny's hands stretch to stroke her tits, and the plunging silk neckline rips clean off the organza yoke. Her breasts spill out and he tugs and pinches her nipples as his tongue darts furiously across her straining clitoris. Claire bites down on her lip hard enough to draw blood and prays that some of the other tenants hear.

Johnny lifts his head and smiles like a kid who's just won a spelling bee. "You ready for my big dick now?"

"I'm ready for bed."

Claire takes a five-hundred-dollar bill from her purse. She holds it in front of her pussy. "Which one will it be?" she asks around an irrepressible yawn.

"You think I'm some kind of whore?" he demands.

"Quite the contrary. I would never pay you to fuck; you'll get the money if you leave." She takes another five-hundred-dollar bill from her purse. "Your choice."

He takes the cash.

"Mind if I keep this?" she asks and yanks his ribbed shirt over his head.

"You paid for it, lady."

Claire first buries her head in the shirt and inhales deeply, then wipes the cream from between her legs.

Claire unlocks her door, turns on a light, and unzips her dress. She walks with the remains of her Dior in her right hand and her ruined heels in the left to her second closet. She tugs a string connected to a bare bulb and blinks blearily at her extensive trophy collection. An Alexander McQueen skirt stiff with semen; Yohji Yamamoto wool pinstriped trousers with the zipper and a back pocket ripped off; a badly lacerated bowling shirt with *Bill* embroidered on the breast pocket; white Hermès gloves blackened at the palms and fingertips; an Emanuel Ungaro dress with grass stains at the shoulders and seat; velvet Farhi pants torn at both knees; a silk Hugo Boss tie still knotted at either end; Fendis with one of the kitten heels broken off. Claire lays the underwear and wife-beater out to dry. When she wakes up around noon she will fold them and stack them in a chest with her other prized acquisitions. She hangs her soiled and tattered dress lovingly on a satin hanger and arranges the shoes carefully on a shelf beside the others.

Now what will she wear tomorrow?

Red Nails in the Sunset

BY JAMES WILLIAMS

It is all unconscious, he knows, unintended, yet it sometimes seems
to be deliberate: the way she hides any bit of information, no matter
how irrelevant or innocuous: speaking of individuals in the plural so
no person's sex or gender can be discerned; lunching with "a friend"
as if there is mystery afoot although if he inquires it turns out to be
always the same friend; going "shopping" but never saying where or
for what.

   She does not mean to be secretive, or so he thinks: she is just hidden. Maybe it's a female function, like keeping nearly all her arousal
and release within herself, so very unlike him and other men who
stain their underwear, their pants, their worlds with even unfulfilled
excitement—it's enough to make a preacher howl.

   She comes home late again, according to his lights, some hours
after he'd said that he'd arrive. Out the living room window the sun
is just about to dip into the last layer of horizon-bound clouds, and

light is already spreading up and down and out in Deco rays and shafts. Of course she'd be befuddled, even miffed, and rightly, if he should mention this, since she'd not said a word about her own arrival time and he'd neglected to ask, as he always did, assuming she'd be home about the same time he was if she didn't tell him otherwise. He believes that he will never learn to ask, any more than it will ever occur to her to volunteer. He knows this discrepancy does not bode well for them, but he also knows it will take awhile for one of them to wear down—probably himself. She swings the door open and doesn't even see him, sitting in the living room in his cozy easy chair, his stockinged feet up on the dog that wags its tail and strains to bark and run and greet her but knows better than to move just now, a dark hardback book without a jacket and stained with a jumble of rings where drinks have been set down on it shut over his long slender fingers. He peers at her in the foyer over the dwindling ice cubes in his lowball glass. She puts a couple of parcels on the floor and fingers her key from the loose, once-jimmied lock, puts it in her purse, shuts the door, shuts the purse, picks up the bags and boxes, and is on her way.

"Good evening, Love," he says softly, so as not to startle her.

"Oh!" she says deliberately, like a matron auditioning for the ingénue part in a B-movie that will never be made. She turns her head toward him at exactly the same pace that she opens her small mouth into a single, lonely, perfect vowel. He sees her red lips pucker, how the dark skin crinkles and purses, moist beneath the bright red lipstick she likes to wear. He thinks of her other dark skin, crinkled and pursed, moist and puckered, and sets his book down underneath his glass so the condensation will not stain rings on the dark mahogany piano. He moves his feet and the dog, released, bounds forward, prancing and yipping around the woman who feeds and walks her. He comes forward and relieves her of her packages, all but the one she clutches to her bosom. He sees how the pale box presses the black silk jacket back into the red silk blouse, back into the red lace lingerie, back into the warm flesh he knows is yielding when she lets him touch it with his thankful fingers, his smooth, inquisitive palm. He thinks of the dark skin there, crinkled, pursed, and puckered but not moist unless she lets him touch it with his lips, his tongue. All of a sudden he wants to cry: to give up hope, and with it all the tension in his body, not just the tension of the stressors in his life the doctor warned about, but even the tension that holds his body up, the tension that holds the parcels in his hand, that holds his hand in its peculiar shape, that holds his arm up, that holds his head up on his neck. He wants to cry and fall down in a puddle, melting like the wicked witch of the west, like a sno-cone, like a fancy candle, like a cube of butter worshipping the sun. He is the east, and Juliet is the sun.

The sun has disappeared in the living room window. It throws its light upward from beneath the horizon leaving golden clouds magenta mauve and rose backlit with orange and fiery red. He falls down on his knees. He lets himself go and slides to the floor, her parcels splayed around him like the legs of a spine-shot fawn. His knees don't hold him either, and he slides the rest of the way. He feels his fingers twitch as if they want to reach for her but do not have the strength and only brush lightly over the tops of her black suede pumps as he completes his fall in space and lies prostrate just where her next step would have been.

"Oh!" she says, turning her head downward at exactly the same pace that he falls.

The dog looks up at her, snuffles around his face, looks up at her again, balances from paw to paw in unmistakable uncertainty.

Is he all right? Can he get up? Does it matter? What would happen if he stayed right here? What would happen if he had to stay right here? Her foot is merely inches from his mouth and so he kisses it, a delicate brushing of his lips across the bones that show above the vamp, and then another kiss neither delicate nor slow but firm and lingering. He lets his tongue out, licks the weave of nylon, wishes for her skin. Her foot smells distantly of the lavender she wears all over, he can also smell the very expensive suede. He lets his tongue get underneath her arch and she says, "Oh!" and grasps the stairway balustrade, lowers herself discreetly, without looking, into the hallway chair.

He has never noticed before how inefficient their housekeeper is. Dustballs have gathered against the floorboard molding like families of cowering mice knit together with doghair shirts. Spider families no doubt extinct have ceased to feed on carcasses of flies and moths that fell with Carthage. The dog is lying in the doorway that is the path to kitchen and kibble, the doorway she would walk through next, if she were walking. The dog is resting her head on her paws but her brows are knit like long-lost relatives that met only recently, and her eyes switch back and forth like windshield washers keeping her vision clear from the master on the floor to the mistress in the chair and back again and back again.

Why not? What's to stop him? He removes one shoe and sets it carefully aside. He kisses all the stockinged toes at once. He removes the other shoe and does the same with it and with the toes on the other foot. He considers his position; then, since nothing seems to happen unless he makes it so, he takes the sole of one foot in each hand and wraps the foot in his long fingers from the longitudinal arch to the instep. Has he ever noticed how very much smaller she is than he? The whole of her frame is a scaled-down model of what he has always thought was human. He sees her as a different sort of animal and wonders if his bulk offends her, or if she simply sees him as she'd see a horse, an ox: a fairly domesticated larger animal, clumsy but not intentionally dangerous, best handled circumspectly, fit for heavier labors than she likes to undertake.

Still, everything waits. He sets her far foot down again and raises both his hands along her closer foot and leg, exploring the curves of ankle and metatarsal, heel and Achilles tendon, pinch of shank, swelling calf, and shin. In front the knee is rounded at the cap, in the back not even nylon can disguise the skittishness of skin as tentative as scrotum, labia, eyelid. Now he has reached her thigh, and as the volume of her leg expands he feels the sticking rubberized lace that announces to his fingertips the top of her dark stocking. There is skin beyond, warm, beckoning if you asked him, and he could ride his fingers forward he expects, up the skin to the next lacy station—but.

The dog emits a single whine, not even a whimper, then, sighing, settles more completely on the floor, eyes largely closed as if nothing is happening but still you never can tell. He pulls down slowly with his eight fingers, two thumbs poised for tasks that are not certain yet, and the top of the stocking rolls down into a round rubber band, a circular cuff descending that thickens as he lets his fingers do a little spider dance extruding smooth bare skin where once there was only nylon.

The stocking is low enough now to grow loose on the conical cylinder of her thigh, and he grips it with thumbs and fingers to pull it more swiftly down. Below her knee there is no longer any secret, and he takes it to her foot when he unexpectedly—hits a snag? No: he feels her fingers on his head, stops, looks up at her. Her eyes are wide: this is not the greeting she expected, if she expected any greeting at all. But her lips are moist and her bosom moves. It is pleasure he descries and, "Use your mouth," she says.

Use your mouth, she says. Use your mouth, she says. This is not the greeting he expected, if he expected any greeting at all. He lowers his face from hers again and brings his lips down to her toes. No. He bends his neck so his lips can get a grip on the roll of nylon above her heel, at her Achilles tendon. He tugs it down behind her heel, over the back of her foot, and then the rest is easy, he pulls forward from the back and feels it slide right off. He leans back so he can look up at her and sees she has extended her hand. He nods forward and deposits the ball of stocking in her open palm. It is the most natural movement to settle back, and as his body falls face forward toward the floor again to encounter and encompass with his lips, his tongue, his entire mouth, the foot he has made naked. "Oh!" she says, and her arch flexes, her toes extend and spread, he licks where there is room between them for his tongue and "Oh!" she says, her foot gives a little kick against his soft palate, his head turns up and down and around at exactly the same pace that her toes twitch.

The western sky has gone all pearl grey blue and lilac except one scalloped high fringe of pink. He slants his eyes in her direction so he can look up at her and sees she has extended her hand, a small red object in it. He lets her foot go free from his mouth, surprised when she wipes it thoroughly dry in his hair, front and top and bottom and back. He looks more closely at the thing she holds out to him and sees it is not red but contains red: nail polish. He looks into her eyes and she nods forward and deposits the little bottle in his open palm. He closes his hand around it, such a small hard thing, and thinks back to what he knows. He shakes the bottle, listening for the telltale rattle to thicken up and stop, unscrews the cap and pulls it with its densely coated brush. He takes her foot from his head with his free hand, supporting without clutching her warm sole in his long fingers so her toes extend up on his pulsing wrist. He bends forward in the gloaming and with great precision paints a broad red swath along the center of her great toe from just above the cuticle all the way to the nail's smooth edge. Two more careful strokes, one on either side of the first, and he holds the foot out so he can see his handiwork. He puts the brush away without screwing on the bottle cap, blows cautiously across her foot until he thinks the coat is tacky, takes up the brush again, squinting to see her next toe, trying to gauge his line. The dog's right hind leg twitches in her sleep and she mews, it sounds to him, plaintively, chasing rabbits. The pink is gone, the grey is gone, blue gone, lilac gone. Darkness finally settles in.

A Reflection in the Mirror

BY D. D. SMITH

She sat on the edge of the bed, filling cardboard boxes with gathered pieces of her past, clinging desperately to harvested bits of her life, things she couldn't let go.

Sarah carefully folded the tiny blue cotton dress with age-worn lace. It was her first dress, the dress she wore in the baby picture that hung on the wall. She studied the photo wondering what had been done to coax that huge dimpled smile. She recalled fragments of quiet nights with her mother in a rocking chair, wrapped in a soft blanket, a soothing lullaby that lulled her to sleep. It reminded her of happier times, quiet nights—warm, and peaceful. A time when she believed the world was simple with white puffy cloud animals, and the feeling that she was protected because they watched over her.

Her understanding of life began under white sheets . . . She remembered playing under crisp sun-dried linen, cool grass beneath her feet, an entertaining game of hide-and-seek with momma under a clothesline. Her mother was a woman that could make heaven appear before her eyes, bringing all the good smells that paradise offered when her world was a bigger place. Sarah was too naïve to notice the wicked ways of others. Her life was uncomplicated, and her daddy provided everything she needed. He was a man with calloused hands, and sometimes too many harsh words. He worked hard, struggled for a modest existence, and cried when he felt defeated. When he died the obituary defined him by occupation, and what he meant to her went unnoticed. He wasn't afraid to look in her eyes—he was her father, and she was his angel.

Sarah continued to scan the pages of the faded newsprint, reaching back for memories that she kept inside for years. She examined outdated articles about that awful place. The indistinct black and gray photos offered insight to what life had been like for her in that small town. It was a place that screamed two hundred years of deprivation and harsh living. A town where the only money to be had was inherited, and the disadvantaged would always be just that.

Her hometown was cruel and uncaring due to those that belittled her for being a part of it. She'd never be a proud daughter of the elite lineage. She'd never understand the well-known families of the community, and why it was so damned important for them to be recognized for their contributions and public handouts with well-deserved pats on the back from the town of who-really-gives-a-fuck. For years she walked by classmates unseen, disregarded because she'd never be one of them. To them she was less. She would always be less. She held her hopes and dreams in clenched fists, and swallowed her pride.

She noticed when others stopped looking into her eyes. Women gossiped in conservative dresses, and held their breath as she passed them on the street. They were too busy looking down at the dirt-filled cracks in the sidewalk, even though she walked above that dirt in $6 sidewalk-sale shoes. The dirt was more significant to them than she would ever be. The women's lives were busy, full, and contented. They lived in denial. They were too occupied with dinner parties, the respected social gatherings of the season, school plays, and the worthy charitable events to notice her. They refused to believe that their husbands would fuck their best friend, their sister, or even an insignificant girl like Sarah.

The men were predictable, influential men with overriding duties. They noticed Sarah from the corner of their eye. They longed for her from the depths of their dark minds, and snarled hearts. They angrily paid the bills, spent too much time away from home, and ignored the growing stack of marital grievances. They defined the driveling whores of denial. Yes, whores, that's how Sarah saw them. These women traded their bodies, their souls, and their lives—trading all they could hope to be for the illusion of an ideal home and family. Everything about them was conventional and completely perfect on the outside, but underneath the surface they were resentful prisoners. She could see it in their eyes—they were embarrassed by their limitations, embarrassed for being women, surely covering their inhibitions with discouraging undergarments. For them sex was a chore, something to be withheld, a bargaining tool for marital negotiations.

Sarah was relaxed as she wandered down Main Street and into the bookstore. Her hips swayed boldly as she strolled past them in the hot afternoon. Her heart pounded, and loins tingled as a gentle breeze kissed her warm skin. The faded cotton print dress flipped around her legs; she felt free, even playful, exposing a lightly bronzed thigh as she turned quickly into the door.

She blushed under the hungry stares of men lining the aisle in the back of the store. She felt right in that hidden corner, an area reserved for those who craved something more than erotic books without pictures. She needed to surround herself with porn mags. It had to be hardcore sex to satisfy her. She yearned for glossy X-rated photos that were covered with plastic and brown paper strips. She didn't care about the correct spelling of cum (or was it come?), as long as the pages were filled with hard cocks and lustful hands groping for delicate lace and soft flesh.

Sarah pulled her fingertips through her wildly tossed hair, brushing it back from one eye as she made her selection. She ripped away the plastic and paper as she rocked steadily from side to side and flipped through the contents. They stared. She chewed bubblegum and blew large bubbles, sucking them slowly back into her mouth. She licked her lips seductively, and offered a clean-faced shameless grin. A wicked smile pulled at the corners of her lips as she loudly whispered the words from the page, "She lay squeezed between them. Filled with swelling pulsing cocks. Each hole of her body pounded and probed. She'd become the desired vessel of corruption. Cum-soaked she shook and soared to new heights . . ." She blew another bubble and hastily sucked it back between her lips.

Sarah glanced at the men standing beside her. Her lace thong panties were sticky and clinging to the lips of her cunt as she diligently continued to shift—each movement a reminder of her unreleased lust. They appreciated the scent of an uninhibited woman. They secretly desired her, wanted her for what she might do for them without passing judgment. She wanted to experience what the women in those pages were feeling, wanted to be them. Perhaps it was the sight of satin gliding across a well-defined thigh, a rope harness firmly tied and knotted biting into velvet skin, or yielding lace stretched tightly, and firmly drawn across an erect nipple. She couldn't decide if it was the clothes, or the lack of them, maybe it was a combination of material, lust, sweat, and pleasure. Sarah was only certain of one thing, she needed a lover with strong hands that understood her desires. Another whisper escaped her lips before thinking, "Mmmmmm, this is what I need."

"I'll take these," her voice purred to the store clerk as she slid the magazines and crumpled wrappings across the counter. The clerk was an elderly gentleman with a thick white mustache. His face quickly became a bright crimson under her direct gaze. It burned even brighter as she smiled and winked, taking the brown paper bag and turning to leave. Her voice was different this time—low and sultry, an erotic blend of sensuality and shy innocence.

She remembered that day, as if it were yesterday. That day she was a woman, one that knew within her heart what she wanted. It was too easy to gather what little she had and leave that place behind her. A borrowed suitcase and a one-way bus ticket out of there was her road to freedom, a road with no regrets.

She learned that the world was a wicked and sorrowful place, a place where evil things happened to good people. Sometimes even good people could do evil things, if given the right circumstances.

She thought about the books she read. Topics about the past being a key to the present, or perhaps it was the other way around. She couldn't remember. She thought about the college professor in starched shirts and new penny loafers—the way he'd walk between the rows of desks. He'd stop and put a heavy hand on her shoulder, peering down into the "V" of her cashmere sweater when he asked a question. He'd smile and give pats of approval if the answer was correct, and sigh shaking his head when she was clueless. What characteristics in her life might be a valuable contribution to the greatest good of the greatest number? How could her life, her past, or her future matter to anyone save herself? She struggled to find the answer, the words, the truth.

Closing her eyes, she lay across the brass bed feeling the heat of the sunlight on her weakened body. Ten hours of dancing and two hours on the highway had taken its toll. Her feet and knees ached as she counted the bruises, two long scratches on her thigh, and five cuts—a collection of fingernail marks on her upper arm, left by a too-drunk and too-excited patron that tried to force her to sit on his lap. She knew what he wanted; the bulge throbbing against her ass spoke volumes.

The phone rang twice before the machine clicked on, and as usual the person calling didn't leave a message. Maybe it was the same person that called other times at 2:00 A.M. with nothing to say. Perhaps they just needed to hear that silly message for the last time, it didn't matter anymore. She found an old tape—the one with his voice. Soon it would be packed away for good. Maybe she would find it by mistake years later. Why couldn't she muster the courage to throw it away?

She looked inside the opened closet doors . . . Bright colors of electric blue, day-glo orange, and fuck-me red took her back to hot summer nights and Harley riders. They were tough guys with warm hearts, trying to hide it under worn leather jackets. The born-to-be-wild-boys had lost their rough and rowdy edges on a lonesome stretch of highway. Somewhere they lost it—out there where it belonged, in that place where hell freezes over in the long forgotten

Wild West. They were thundering gods of the freeway, riding the roads most traveled with their eyes closed until one day they chose a blind alley and found her. She looked right through them, touched them with tender words, and found a cuddly bear. They reminded her not to take life so seriously. They stood solid in boots, protected her, laughed with her, and made her feel safe.

Teasing teal, and haunting black, were reserved for quiet nights. She'd find herself dancing slow for businessmen in the fall. They'd give her compliments, and give her their card. They walked too proud and cocky on the soles of $500 shoes. Gentlemen that called her hun or baby. Desperate men that needed a break from the daily grind. Tired of work, tired of the wife. Men that needed a blow-job, candy for a nose-job, and a new life with the woman that fucked them good when they were twenty-one. She kept her mouth shut and listened. Impressed them with patience and care. They shared fond memories of the glory days, back when they collected women like the trophies that gathered dust on the shelves in the corner of their office. They stroked her thigh, touched her arm, her face, looked in her eyes, knew she understood their confessions, and they loved her for it.

Pleasing plum and mystical magenta were for cold winter nights and long-haul truckers. Truck-stop cowboys, poppin' pills, riding the white line at the head of a heavy steel horse, going through the gears without fear. Push it hard, get it there, get it done, and move on to the next. Restless good 'ole boys that wanted to hunt, fish, and fuck— occasionally they'd talk about their dawg. They were usually content with a handful of ass and a mug of draft beer. Sometimes they needed more—a horny girlfriend to make them feel young, a dutiful woman that would keep them warm and satisfied. They didn't care how she danced, as long as she pushed it hard, got them there, got it done, and moved on to the next.

Cold chrome, glittering gold, and rhinestones reminded her of college boys and spring break. Educated shiny new faces were on a road trip to make waves at white beaches. They were headed south. They offered empty invitations and were always asking why she was there. Her answer was the same, "Baby, it ain't Broadway, but it pays the rent." Immature optimistic opportunists were wanna-be-lawyers, wanna-be-millionaires, wanna-be-something, anything as long as it was more than what they were. Some were wannabe-gynecologists after they met her. She liked to watch their lips while they sucked on cigarettes. They were young—they'd live forever. She'd watch their eyes twinkle when they shared dirty jokes. She'd humor them with tricks, picking up bills with her butt cheeks, and balancing beer bottles. They smelled like bubblegum, popcorn, and basketball games that went into overtime. They smelled like the future. Sweet boys, excited know-it-alls that liked to play games. What they'd give for one night with her . . . one would give his right nut. She smiled and held out her hand wearing six-inch heels and no regrets.

The colors, the men, her memories were too much for morning bight. Too loud, everything was too loud from the costumes to the shouts and applause from onlookers, to the music that blasted from the speakers, and vibrated her flesh. The thunderous sounds forced her to move across the stage. She could no longer hear herself think, stand still, and feel herself be. The noisy mixture of hues sickened her.

Long gone was the faded cotton-print dress. It was replaced by torrid shades that shocked her into realizing what she'd become—a dancing whore, a whore of denial. No, she wasn't a prostitute. She did

everything but fuck for money. Whorish mannerisms always produced a payoff. It didn't matter if the compensation was attention
gained, or dirty tips callously shoved in her panties. She was a sex
worker. There it was, the crude truth slapping her in the face as she
stared at the lurid garments that transformed her into a HO-BOT,
that's what she'd become. A mechanical dancing, air-humping strip-
per, a fuckin' HO-BOT! Her temperament was altered, nothing playful or peaceful about it these days. Methodical insanity, calculated
chaos, a submissive slave to perverse beauty. A vision that was clearly
distorted behind cartoon make-up . . . NO, fucked-up was more
like it.

Sarah glanced at the large collection of boots and pumps with
spiked stiletto heels. Intimidating boots with heavy chains and
pointy metal thorns, thigh high, shielding her knees, great for kicking nasty-ass patrons that couldn't restrain their hands. Dancing
shoes that made her appear larger than life, carefully chosen footwear
that doubled as weapons of defense, guarding her from insidious
hands that grabbed and scratched trying to pull her from the stage.

Lewd comments echoed in her mind—obscene advice from the
occasional psycho that dared to cross the boundary. They informed
her that she was sitting on a million dollars. They offered large sums
of cash for vulgar acts, picking and choosing their passion . . . FLESH
FOR SALE! She rejected them, frustrated them to the point of offen-
sive stabbing words. To them she was "Only a fuckin' whore—act like
one or find yourself living in a trailer park eating cat food when your
beauty fades." They barked negative predictions and terrorizing
threats, heaping curses on her. She wouldn't give in to their whims.
Some were just nuts with overactive imaginations and totally
screwed notions of the person *they thought* she should be, or what

they wanted her to be. Some were just plain cuckoo—like the guy that told her he could take his dog apart and put it back together. He was a creepy son-of-a-bitch who picked his nose, and then picked his fingernails with a pocketknife. Others were just slightly fucked in the head with too much energy and nowhere to go.

There were times that she decided she couldn't take one more night of it. Then there was the night that she lost her best friend. She saw Missy's momma crying because she came home in a body bag wearing six-inch heels and ripped skin. Missy took a ride in a limo and paid for it with her life. It was front-page news and nobody cared.

Sarah screamed and cried in the car on the way home, "Fuck them and fuck that! I can't—I won't do this one more night! I have to get away from this shit! Evil assholes, ALL OF THEM are wicked fuckin' assholes!" Then morning came and she realized that she was wrong, leaving wouldn't change a thing. Most men were decent, not all were assholes, not all were psychotic killers. She stayed for the ones that weren't. She stayed for the men that in spite of everything had hopes and dreams for something better. They just needed an entertaining distraction, someone to listen while they found their way. Like them, she was finding her way. She too wanted something more, needed it, and no one would stop her.

She touched the white lace and silk costume adorned with Austrian crystals—it was for him. Why white? It didn't represent anything ceremonial or virginal, it epitomized a white-hot passion she felt for him. A pure cleansing fiery emotion that burned uncontrollable, hotter than hell below the surface, much deeper than a smoldering crimson blaze. Sarah often fantasized that he would surprise her by coming to the club—and that would be the dress she'd select for his amusement. Night after night she carefully packed it into the carryall hoping and wishing on every star. Thinking of him gave her the power to get through it, but the dream never came true. All of those nights without him were cold and dark.

On hands and knees she'd crawl to the edge of the runway, moving slow while gazing into their eyes, thinking of her lover, never leaving him. Two barge candles burned brightly, placed in brass candelabra. She waited for the right moment, waited for the music to move her closer to him. Facing the audience she folded her hands, placed them under her chin, elbows bent, and back arched. A chest stand, her legs with toes pointed went up, up, up—behind her, then forward, past her shoulders, gripping and lifting the candles at the same time. She balanced, holding them steady. She lifted them high over her back. The flames touched, teased, licked, kissed, and came together as radiant light. She could feel him. She poured the wax, dripping it down the center of her back. Hot wax pooled along her spine and spilled over the sides. Sarah clutched the brass tip rail anchored to the edge of the stage, raised her chest off the floor, intense agony, then pleasure, tears trickled down her cheeks. She listened to the gasps and muted comments; the audience approved. Her heart was with him. He made it real. She wished he could feel what she was feeling. Could he taste her tears, share her pain, feel her pleasure? The music faded and applause filled the smoky air.

She recalled the morning in Vegas, sleeping naked between satin sheets. She could feel him beside her, covering her, caressing her, his hands exploring. She stirred in her sleep, tangled in the sheets, reached for him and woke from the dream. Sarah looked around the room, arranged the sheet around her body and walked toward the grand window. She stood silently watching the sunrise. Deep shades of red-violet changed to lavender, faded to azure, and lighter to pale blue. She thought about the color of his eyes. The mountains reminded her of his arms folded around her. The brilliant hues of burnt-orange, deep-yellows, amber, and pastel pink faded to subtle whispers of peach. She thought about his tender kisses on her neck. The temperate tones filled her heart with hope. The distance between them didn't matter. She realized there were no stars left to wish on— only the promise of a new day.

Sarah gazed into the mirror beside the bed. She remembered the night they met. He was older, much older. He was anxious, and for some reason seemed a bit intimidated by her. She thought he was attractive, even handsome, but what did she want with a guy in his forties? She'd never been with a man that wasn't close to her age, or younger. She studied his hands, strong but gentle—he's probably good with his hands. She watched his mouth and listened while he spoke, his lips—how would they feel pressed to hers? His words drifted into her fantasy. She could feel his mouth on hers, speaking softly, breathing him in between each hungry kiss. Sarah looked into his eyes—she tingled, heat stirring, wet with the thought of being face to face with his cock inside her.

She tried to look intent as she wiggled in her chair, remembering that she didn't wear panties underneath those too-tight jeans that felt really good at the moment. She could feel the thick inside seam rubbing against her clit. She pressed her thighs together, pulled her feet back leaning forward, and nodded. She studied the width of his shoulders, the sharp angles of his face, and finally she glanced down at the crotch of his pants—hmmmmmm, nice package. She was certain he could see her roused nipples through the champagne silk blouse. What would he do if she pulled him closer, and asked if he could make her cum? Would it shock him to know that she'd give him his heart's desire at that moment, if he'd ask? She'd love to touch him, hold him close, and cover his cock, grip it tightly, pump it slowly, watch it expand and swell. Finally, he touched her hand and asked for the first dance. It stoked the blaze. He held her tightly, pressed his body against hers, and she was lost in teasing flames. The first kiss lured her to the center of the inferno, pulled her in deeper. It was too late to turn back. The connection was there, and she wanted him desperately.

The reflection haunted her now, taunting her with whispers and moans, images they shared, things he said. She closed her eyes and thought of nights with candlelight and wine, the touch of his hands, the smell of his skin. He'd please her for hours, teasing and releasing her relentlessly. She knew quite well the pleasure he took watching her cum. It was amazing, the length of her climaxes—how he needed to feel and control the intensity of each wave as it washed over her. Seductive kisses on quivering lips entered her mind, and joined her soul. Did he know he would always be inside her?

Sarah came back to that place where she had every right to be, back to the tranquil silence where she could feel him, feel the serenity of her spirit when she was with him. He made her real, loved her, and lulled her to sleep. She found a comfortable place inside that reflection, always safe within his arms and wouldn't get up until she was ready.

Sarah thought about the night she stunned him—the night he came over to find her wearing a skin-tight transparent pink latex cat suit and matching stilettos. Her body tickly under the smoothly stretched fabric, her skin an immeasurable inferno mixed with lust and oil, aching for the slightest touch of his fingers. It was slippery and soft as the folds of her cunt, a second skin that would allow her to feel everything, feel him struggle to hold her, to break through.

She knew what she was doing when she pulled the constricting fabric past her calves, stretching it tighter, higher over her thighs, and finally stepping into those pink acrylic shoes, fuck-me-shoes. One zipper was deliberately placed in the crotch area, allowing entry to her ass and cunt. The other zipper was in the front, starting at the neckline plunging to the navel. She knew how he'd react, the pleasure he'd get moving his fingertips over the fine metal teeth. It would only take a moment for him to throw his clothes in a heap beside the door. His mouth on hers, soft kisses, passionate wet kisses, strong hands squeezing her ass, fingers moving between her thighs.

He made her stand in front of the mirror, "Look at you! What are you doing to me? Do you know how hard it is to resist you? You're soft and warm . . . I have to touch you, rub my cock against you. Tease you, make love to you . . . No, fuck you hard! I have to make you feel it because what I feel is stronger than love. It's bigger than that—I don't know how to stop. I lose it! I always lose it when I'm with you. One more step, and I have to go higher, take you higher over the edge with me." He sighed and rested his lips against her shoulder, "I'm trying to be good these days, trying to free my mind of naughty thoughts, trying to stay out of trouble. I thought you were trying— trying to be a good girl."

"I am a good girl . . ." She placed her hand over his fingers that were firmly wrapped around his cock, guiding him, pressing the head against the sleek polished fabric. A mischievous grin played across her lips. "I'm good for you. Admit it. You need this, need me when I'm naughty." She knew it was the tease that pushed him past limits. She needed it, needed to be with him—realized how good it was to feel and fuck for the sake of it. It was never enough once it began. Her blue eyes were drawn to his in the mirror—she waited for an answer.

"You need to be marked, and reminded . . ." He pressed against her harder, gliding his right hand over her ass, moving fingers along her spine until his hand reached the back of her neck. He forced her to the floor. "Kneel in front of the mirror!" She fell to her knees, worshipping him. "Tell Me," he pushed her, "Tell ME! I HAVE TO HEAR YOU SAY IT."

What did he want to hear her say? She was marked the night his seed passed her lips and filled the depths of her body. She was marked the night she offered him her breast and said, *Bite me . . . make it hurt . . . I don't care how hard.* She was marked the night he spanked her, and massaged the pain away. There were only two words she could think of—she whispered, "Your whore."

"That's right. Forget about those men at the club. They don't know you, not like I know you. To them you are nothing but a decoration. They don't see you. You're a doll in bold costumes. You're just a dream they wish for. They only buy your time. They'll never have you, not like I have you." He knelt behind her, rubbing his stiff cock over the cheeks of her ass. He pulled her back, wrapped his arms around her, and met her gaze in the mirror as he put one hand on her throat and the other between her thighs. His fingers impatiently pressed against the lips of her cunt. "They only wish they could fuck you. I'd like to watch them fuck you. It'd take more than one to make you cum like I do." He bit into her shoulder through the stretchy fabric, admired his mark, and struggled to hold her firm against his cock. "You'll never feel them like you feel me. I can get past this barrier. I know how it feels to get under your skin. I know what you think, and what you feel when I'm inside you. I'm with you. I'll always be with you."

In the mirror she saw the truth of the reflection. This day would be the beginning of a new life. She realized she'd always love him, her heart could never forget him, her body would still remember and surrender to the way he touched her. She covered the mirror, closed the door with regret, and realized she'd never be the same.

Bethany's Game

BY BRYN COLVIN

Squeezing my breasts hard against my chest, I begin the difficult binding process. It has taken years of practice to get the hang of it—how to sculpt my flesh with pressure and fabric. Initially there is some discomfort as my nipples are slightly erect and chafing against the cloth. It takes yards and yards of meticulously hemmed cotton to do the job, and nearly a quarter of an hour patiently wrapping, tightening, smoothing. When it is done I pause to look at myself in the mirror. I look like the result of some partial mummification. With a loose shirt over the top however, I am slightly plump in appearance, but there is no hint of a curve. I wear my jeans tight, with the shirt down over them. I put a rolled-up pair of socks into the front of the borrowed boxer shorts. The large boots are my own—an advantage of slightly bigger-than-average feet. Being tall and solidly built sometimes has its uses. I clear my throat, draw a breath and I feel different now. No more the girl, tonight I am Mark Orsiono and I go to face the world. I blame Shakespeare myself—I grew up with his cross-dressing heroines, wanting to be Rosalind in the forest or Viola guised as a boy and in the service of a certain Duke. Boys pretending to be girls pretending to be boys. It always had a certain allure.

I brush my hair flat, making a tidy center parting, keeping everything close to my scalp. Then I take an eyeliner pencil and thicken my dark eyebrows, making them full and more dramatic. I slap after-shave on my cheeks, put a wallet in my back pocket and study the effect again. A little boyish perhaps but not female, not any more. I've toyed with the idea of having one of those spiky bloke styles that seem to be in, but am afraid I would end up doing something far too girly. It seems better not to risk it. I pull my shoulders back, and mentally I shift gears. I feel powerful now, more solid and substantial. Borrowed clothes and suppressed gender—tonight I am someone else, something other. I can do or be anything. I am a handsome enough boy, not too pretty or delicate, a little on the rounded side, but possessed of soulful eyes. It isn't as simple as just finding this arousing or titillating. It runs deeper in me, sparking some hidden part of who I am, but yes, this self-knowledge is sexy in its own way.

"Ready?" she asks.

I turn to see Bethany framed by the doorway. As ever, she is splendid—long legs sheathed in shiny black stockings, a lacy black skirt that leaves the larger part of her thighs exposed. She has the kind of legs that make it hard to look anywhere else. Tonight she is in a dramatic pair of knee boots. They make her taller than me but I don't mind that. The little top is new and shows off the pale curve of her stomach.

"What do you think?" she does a little twirl.

"Do we have to go out?" I ask.

She pouts. "You promised."

She gazes at me from beneath long lashes, and I fight to quell my desire. The new top she has on is stretch velveteen, shimmering and alluring. The soft texture of the fabric calls to me, inviting me to slide fingers over the sensual surface. I chose it myself and it suits her well. The firm curve of her breasts is beautifully accentuated by the tight material hiding Bethany's secrets. The flash of stomach is inviting, the pale perfection of her flesh set off by the smooth darkness of skirt and top.

She pats her stomach "You sure it doesn't make me look fat?"

I growl at her. She knows full well that there is nothing wrong with her figure.

"What about the makeup?"

She has done something different with her eyes; they look more green than usual. She has something of a skill and I envy her that— I've never managed much beyond some basic lipstick and a bit of eyeshadow.

"Looks good." I tell her reassuringly.

I can tell from the way she is fidgeting and stalling that she is nervous. She always is when we go out, but it's addictive, exhilarating, and she cannot resist.

Arm in arm we wander through the streets, enjoying the warm air of a late spring evening. More than one man turns to look at my beautiful companion. I see the desire in their eyes and I smile, knowing what they cannot have. We go to a bar, and I have to remember that I am the one buying the drinks. The girl serving looks twice at me and for a moment I wonder if she's going to ask for some proof of age. I do look boyish tonight. She glances at Bethany, then back at me, and I can see the slow grinding of her brain. Bethany looks like she's about in her mid-twenties, and the barmaid does not ask.

We sit by the window, watching people going up and down the street—girls in their bight summer dresses, lads in open-necked shirts and baggy trousers. Most of them are eminently forgettable, but we watch anyway. From across the small table she flashes me her radiant smile, and rubs the toe of her boot against my shin.

When she makes a trip to the toilets, I turn to watch her glide through the crowd, graceful and predatory like a cat. A guy accosts her, his hand on her arm, his intentions clear even at this distance. I watch the delicate skin on her neck flush with color. He smiles. She glances in my direction, and I see him looking over. The conversation continues, and Bethany seems angry when she strides away. In my mind, I imagine him commenting that she could get a better bloke than me; I hardly look old enough to be out on my own. Part of me laughs. Part of me is enraged and would like to wipe the smile off his face with a well-placed fist. She returns to me without further incident.

"Did you see?" she asks in a conspiratorial whisper.

I nod, leaning forward so we can talk quietly. Her hair, spiky and sculpted in the current fashion, brushes against my face and for a heartbeat I think of nothing else.

"He asked me to go to a club with him, said he'd been watching me ever since I turned up," she says triumphantly.

"Way to go." I tell her. I am of course jealous, but I do not mention that. There is a light in her eyes and I do not want to steal it away with an ill-considered word.

"So what did you tell him?" I ask.

"I said I was flattered, but that I already had a date."

She sips her drink and gazes out of the window.

"Now that's just to die for."

There's a woman walking past outside, she's older than us, and her hair falls to her waist. It is her coat that has drawn my Bethany's eye, sleek black velvet. It must be hot in this weather but I share her pang of envy.

"If we find one like that, you'll have to share it with me."

"Done." She smiles.

We share a lot of clothes one way or another. There is something deliciously intimate about having someone else's garments against your skin. .

"I'm bored here," she says suddenly.

I finish my drink in a single swig.

"Where next?" I ask her.

"Let's just wander," she says. "It is such a nice night after all."

By now the tables outside are full. Bethany basks in the attention as we wander through the small throng of people and out into the thoroughfare. She moves easily in the heeled boots, covering the ground in long relaxed strides. It is a pleasure to watch her move. Arm-in-arm, we wander between the cafés and bars, watching the people and allowing them to watch us. Bethany's long and shapely legs draw numerous eyes, but I hardly seem to get a second glance. I am glad of this; I do not like being noticed, but she thrives upon it. Failure to attract attention usually marks success on my part.

We sit on a bench beneath the trees, largely obscured in shadows. It is cooler here and she snuggles against me, her body warm against mine. I ruffle her hair with my hand.

"You'll mess it up," she admonishes.

I sigh.

"Good evening?" I ask her.

I have stopped trying to keep my voice low—I can do it, but I have lost the inclination to keep making the effort.

"I enjoyed it. You?"

"I just wish I didn't look so young. Maybe I could get some facial hair or something."

"Ugh."

"But I look like I haven't even started shaving yet." I lament.

She slips her fingers between the buttons of my shirt, but I cannot feel them through the binding.

"We could get you a chest wig," she suggests playfully.

"Oh thanks."

"And my hips are too big. I'm not going to be able to get away with this much longer."

"You look fine, quit moaning."

She kisses me on the cheek, then on the lips. I find the taste of lipstick strange, but that is soon forgotten. I find the patch of bare back between top and skirt. Her skin is cool to the touch, smooth as silk and very sensitive. I feel her shiver in my arms.

"Maybe we should go home?" she asks.

"You don't like this bench?"

"It's not very private, is it?"

"True."

We get a taxi. Sitting together on the backseat I am acutely aware of her closeness, the warmth of her body, and the smell of her skin. She strokes my hand in hers, little circles that threaten to drive me mad. We manage to get safely inside and shut the door before we start kissing again—standing in the hall with my back pressed against the wall.

It takes a good while to get back out of my bindings. She unravels them slowly, her arms moving around me. At last my breasts are free again, the weight of them a surprise after the hours of having them held so tightly in place. I rub them slightly.

"Let me do that," she says, running her hands over my skin. Her touch makes me forget the ache. Her touch is pleasure, her kisses ecstasy. When I finally summon up enough willpower to pull away from her, I cast off the jeans and boots. She watches me with hungry eyes. Then I kneel before her, gazing up into her face. Her high cheekbones are framed exquisitely by her hair. I drink in the last vestiges of the beautiful illusion, the last moments of the game. I am partly reluctant to break the spell, but the desire to caress is more powerful in the end. I unlace her long boots, sliding them from her legs. She stretches her toes and I run my fingers over the smooth surface of the stockings. The legs beneath will be just as soft, shaved carefully only this afternoon while I was shopping.

I unbutton her skirt and pull it down, revealing her stocking belt and lacy knickers. Then I lift the tight top, helping her slip her arms free, revealing the generous bra stuffed carefully with rolls of fabric. I squeeze one of the fake breasts affectionately.

"Did I look pretty?" she asks, he asks. It is that in-between stage, that time of changing back and sliding out of assumed character.

"You looked really good. Very pretty. Better than I do in that stuff."

"Cheers." He has dropped the assumed voice now, and returned to the lower cadences of everyday life. His voice is rich and low, even when he pretends. I pull out the padding, but leave the bra to cover the small patch of chest hair around his nipples. I remember the socks in the boxer shorts I am wearing, and discard those too. He smiles at me.

"Well," I say "It seemed like a good idea at the time. Just as well I didn't have to go to the loo though."

That's something I've not yet managed. Bethany goes to the ladies with confidence, but in the ladies there are cubicles and so long as you remember not to leave the seat up, everything is fine. It is quite another thing to stand at a urinal, visible and exposed with a rolled-up pair of socks in your pants in lieu of a penis. So I don't drink much when we go out.

He goes to undo the stocking belt.

"Leave it, lover."

He raises an eyebrow. "As you wish."

There is something very attractive to my mind, about a good-looking man dressed in lace and satins. Better still that those flimsy garments are mine; I have worn them myself often enough.

He rolls me back onto the bed, kissing my neck and pulling my hair loose.

"You make a pretty good bloke," he says, smiling.

"You think? I'm a bit on the short side."

"You know what they say about small packages."

"That was quite a big pair of socks, in case you hadn't noticed."

He laughs playfully.

"Would you still want me if I was a girl?" He is serious suddenly, and fragile, a last wisp of Bethany in his eyes.

I think about this for a moment. I've never been much interested in women, but . . .

"Yes. It wouldn't matter who you were or how you looked. I would know you anywhere. I would love you."

Soul mate.

I wriggle out of the boxer shorts, a final encumbrance easily discarded. I am female again, my usual self. It feels peculiar for a moment, but his hands are on my body, my Peter, my guide reminding me of my own flesh and taking me back to myself. His stockinged legs slide smoothly over my skin. I slide my fingers over his stomach, reaching down through the tangle of hair into the hidden recesses of the knickers.

Carefully, I liberate his disguised manhood—I do not know what possessed him to try the trick, but he bends his member back between his legs, hiding the bulge and making his illusion of femininity more complete. It always makes me wince, but he tells me it does not hurt. Perhaps not so very different from me crushing my breasts into a more manly shape. It is a way of briefly denying the bodies we were born with.

I remember our first cautious forays into the game; all bedroom play and dressing up. I'd never so much as hinted to anyone before that I had a fascination with cross-dressing, and I think the same was true for him. It isn't the sort of thing you expect from a hetero bloke, and modern women don't seem to do it at all—perhaps because it's considered normal to wear trousers these days, and so the game is nigh-on impossible. The first time we went out, Peter guised himself as Bethany and we did the girly thing. It was a very long time before I worked up the nerve to try it myself. I'm never entirely sure if I pass, or if people just assume I'm an eccentric dyke. It doesn't matter so much—I do it for me. Bethany is utterly convincing, but there's still a certain thrill to the possibility of getting caught out. At least going out as a couple affords us some protection.

Then, after the game, still filled with playful enthusiasm and turned on by our disguises, we fall into bed to work off an evening's worth of suppressed desire. Exchange of fabric, exchange of kisses, tongues, and touches, it all runs together. We make believe and we experiment. More often than not we keep our costumes on, taking the game as far as we can. There's something about having to work around clothing, feeling it rub and chafe against your body as you move, something about the slight inhibition of movement it creates, about not fully revealing yourself to your playmate.

Peter runs his tongue slowly over my left nipple and I gasp, dragged into the moment by the pressure of his mouth on my body. The lace of his pants is soft against my inner thigh as he presses close against me.

"One of these days" he says softly, "We're going to run into someone we know."

I've thought about this often enough and wondered quite what will happen when we do.

"Just hope it isn't anyone from work," I murmur, not really wanting to think about it now.

I know what he's thinking. I know he wants to try it and see if anyone recognizes us. I don't know if I have the nerve to go that far yet, but he will persuade me in time; he always does. He rubs against me, teasing me with the press of his lace-enwrapped erection. I pull him close against me, feeling the underwiring on the bra dig into my own breasts slightly.

"What do you want?" he asks me.

"You." I tell him. He grins, and with deft fingers he undoes one stocking. He slides it off, and before I know what he is about, he ties my hands with it. Another game, for it would be easy enough to escape such a flimsy binding. In mock submission, I lift my hands above my head, resting them on the pillow.

"You have me at your mercy." I tell him.

With the other stocking, he binds my ankles, then drags me to the edge of the bed, lifting my feet so that they are over my head and I cannot see him.

As he moves himself into me, I can still feel the lace against my skin, rubbing softly on my clitoris with his slow, deliberate thrusts. It is almost too much.

Urban Noir

BY TARA ALTON

Her favorite place in the mall was Urban Noir. It was a hip, punk type of mall-based chain store with loud music, fake red brick walls, black clothes, rude stickers, and Hello Kitty accessories. She always felt like a bit of an imposter, though, when she went there. Getting married right out of high school and getting divorced before she was twenty-two had left her out of the trendy phase. Instead of night clubbing, she had been dealing with Ray, her alcoholic husband, who wanted her barefoot and pregnant, and who said no man would touch her if she ever left him.

She always came here on her breaks when her job at The Smoothie King got to be too much. After the end of her marriage, the only thing she could really do was cook and bake, so she'd tried to get a job in food service. But with no actual work experience, the best she could do was this place. At first, she loved all that swishing together of the frozen bananas, mangos, and pineapple juice. It seemed almost sexual, but then the boredom started to set in. The blandness felt like it was suffocating her. The only place she felt like she could breathe was Urban Noir.

What she really liked were the clothes along the black wall. Street wear. Retro lounge. Club. Gothic. Anything rubbery fascinated her. How she wished she had the balls to wear a Bettie Page baby T-shirt and a pair of bow rider black vinyl pants.

No one had ever known she hankered for the raunchier side of love. Not even Ray. He had thought she was a quiet, self-conscious girl. All through high school, she had been a wallflower, cute, but overlooked. She kept her trim little body covered up with baggy T-shirts and loose jeans. Only her diary knew of her dark fantasies about what would be more exciting, putting it on or taking it off.

The closest she had ever gotten to acting out her fantasy was when she was fifteen and realized every time she put on a pair of yellow rubber cleaning gloves, she got tingly between her legs. No wonder she always volunteered to clean. Her grandmother was always asking her why she was cleaning the bathroom when it was already spotless.

She would give anything to be back in her grandmother's kitchen, drinking her fresh brewed coffee and eating her mincemeat cookies. If only she could go back in time, see her grandmother, and erase the Ray years. She'd met him after her grandmother died. He was ten years older than she, good-looking with a fantastic body and a winning smile. Who knew there was some great character flaw lurking beneath the attractive package? It was like buying an expensive sports car, and then finding out the engine needed a complete overhaul.

Ray never wanted to have sex unless he was drunk and when he was drunk, he couldn't keep it up. She invested in a new pair of yellow gloves. She couldn't even begin to have sex with him unless she threw in a fantasy about wearing something like a wet-look PVC mini skirt she'd seen in a magazine.

Today had been a bad day, and she needed a dose of Urban Noir more than ever. An anal-retentive customer had noticed she hadn't followed the exact ingredients in a Blue Hawaii and complained to her manager. Of course, the smoothies were blended at the time of order so the customer was actually getting a smoothie and not an iced drink. Heaven forbid if she used too many blueberries and too much raw sugar.

After checking out the tall boots, studded chokers, and thongs, she lingered along the back wall, gently sliding her hand inside the sleeves. Burying her face in a black gown with thin shoulder straps and vinyl buckles on the front, she inhaled, pressing against it, her fingers straying between her legs. She'd thought about it before, blowing all her rent money on an outfit like this, then going to a wild club to get the shit fucked out of her in the back room by a tall, strapping, imposing German man.

Suddenly, she realized she was rubbing herself. She blushed furiously and stopped. Had anyone seen her? She glanced around the store. There was only Nick, the cute sales clerk with the dyed black hair, and a customer who looked like he should work in a used-car lot with his white dress shirt, his tan pants, his loud, tacky tie, and ponytail.

Composing herself, she moved onto a corset with red stitching. It was so fascinating what you could make out of PVC. She knew it was cheaper and more generic than the sleek, sexy sophisticated look of rubber, but she had read that it was more breathable and versatile. If only she knew for real.

"Hey, I notice you come in here every day, but you never try anything on," someone said behind her.

Christie jumped and looked over her shoulder. It was Nick. He was looking very good today in a casino-style, leopard panel shirt over a Bettie Page tank top and black cargo pants.

"I'm just killing time until I have to go to Smoothie King," she said.

"So why don't you try anything on?" he asked.

"I can't afford it. Not with what they pay me," she said.

The Bettie Page on his T-shirt seemed to be smiling at her. Christie smiled back.

"So you like Bettie Page?" she asked him.

"Yeah."

"My grandmother said my grandpa used to hide pictures of her in his sock drawer," she said.

"She's that old?" Nick asked. "I thought she was someone new."

"She's a pin up from the 1950s. I love that whole bad-girl/good-girl era."

"I have a tattoo of her on my chest."

"Really?" she asked.

He smiled at her. Boy, did he have the twinkling blue eyes and dimples.

"Why don't you try something on?" he said. "It can't hurt."

He pulled a black fishnet top and a black twill skirt with red argyle printed inserts off the wall, and he nudged her toward the dressing room. Christie hesitated, but relented. He looked so expectant, as if he really wanted to see her in the clothes.

With the dressing-room door shut behind her, she looked at herself in the mirror. She looked so boring in her work clothes, a pair of white jeans, and a white T-shirt. Thank goodness, her apron was back at Smoothie King hanging safely behind the employee's door, or she would look like a real geek in this store. Quickly, she undressed and inched on the skirt. It was tight and short, showing way more thigh than what she was used to. Over her white cotton bra, she pulled on the fishnet top, carefully not to get her fingers caught.

Opening the dressing room door, she found Nick waiting. His face lit up at the sight of her as if she was his prom date or something, but then he frowned.

"The bra doesn't look right with it," he said.

She looked down. The white cotton was ruining the effect. Momentarily closing the door, she removed the offending item. That was better. Now she looked really hip, but you could see her nipples. Wasn't that the point? To look sexy. She took a deep breath and opened the door.

Nick nodded in approval.

"Now that looks totally hot," he said.

"Really?"

He nodded.

"You look amazing," he said.

"It's not too tight?" she asked.

"It's fine."

Stepping back inside the dressing room, she looked at herself in the mirror, smoothing a lock of hair behind her ear. She looked so different. Was this her? She'd always felt like there was a mismatch between her inside and her outside. Was this the proof she needed? She stood up taller, feeling powerful.

Nick took a step inside the dressing room. He was almost behind her. Turning, she looked up at him. He was so cute, and he did seem to like her. Suddenly, she wanted to see his tattoo.

"May I?" she asked.

Before he could answer, she lifted his Betty Page T-shirt to look at his chest. He had baby-soft skin, hardly any muscle definition, and not a hair in sight, but there she was, Bettie Page on his skin, brightly colored and clear as day. Feeling aroused by the sight of his bare skin and a little brazen in the new clothes, she touched his chest with her palm. He recoiled and fled the dressing room as if her hand was made of battery acid.

Stunned, she watched after him. What was all that about? Hadn't he just been flirting like crazy with her? Then it dawned. He had been doing it to get her to buy something. Talk about being stupid. It had to be the oldest game in the mall. With that same winning smile, she saw him approach a new female customer in the store.

Disgusted, she went to close the dressing-room door when she noticed a display rack near the counter. Why did the Bettie Page on his chest seem to be winking at her?

Because she was a temporary tattoo. Nick was wearing a fake Bettie Page tattoo and passing it off as a real one.

Now really disgusted, she turned to put back on her work clothes when the used-car sales guy barged by her into her dressing room.

"Excuse me," she said. "Get your own dressing room. This one is taken."

"I like this one," he said.

Before she could shove him out, he took off his loud print tie and unbuttoned his white shirt. The sight of his bare chest stopped her cold. This guy made Nick look like an immature little weasel. He didn't have an ounce of fat on him and his abs looked like they could grate cheese. His shirt hit the floor. His entire arm was tattooed with eight balls, dragons, and crazy clowns. This was the real thing. She could see it now, the way the lines looked smooth, like gauzy light had settled over his skin.

She could barely pull her gaze away. Was it warm in here?

He tried on a navy cotton work shirt with a screen print of pin-up girls on the back.

"That's quite the shirt," she said.

"Isn't it?" he asked.

"Those are quite the tattoos, too," she said.

"Thanks. I got most of them in Venice," he said. "But I'm back here for good now."

She wondered if he was talking about Italy or California.

"I'm Kyle," he said and offered his hand.

Shyly, she took it. Touching his hand was fantastic. She blushed. She'd never felt this zing between herself and another person before.

"Christie," she said.

"I know. I bought a peach smoothie from you the other day. I kept hoping we might bump into each other again."

"I don't remember. I get in such a zone sometimes. Most of our customers seem to be either retirees walking the boredom out of their lives or mothers with strollers escaping from home."

"I know what you mean."

"You work here?"

"At the Spine-O-Matic kiosk."

Christie shook her head. After Urban Noir, the kiosks seemed boring with their cell phones, stuffed animals, and rice jewelry.

"I know you come in here a lot," he said.

Had he been watching her? Suddenly feeling self-conscious, she brushed her hand on her skirt and became aware of what she was wearing. She had been so caught off guard by Nick's behavior and Kyle barging in here, she had forgotten that he could clearly see her nipples through the fishnet. Why did they feel like they were getting hard? She crossed her arms over her chest.

"You've been watching me," she asked.

"Look, I'm not a stalker, but I know you work mostly days," he said. "And for lunch you have a pretzel with cheese, but once a week you treat yourself to chili cheese fries from the Coney Island."

"You are stalking me," she said.

"Just a fan."

She blushed, not sure if she should be afraid or not. He seemed harmless enough, and when was the last time a man had noticed her in a good way.

"Do you live around here?" she asked.

"At one of those weekly rental places on Michigan Avenue, but only until I get something more permanent. What about you?"

"That trailer park off Michigan near the Ford plant," she confessed.

Glancing at her watch, she noticed her break was nearly over. She had to get back before she got into trouble.

"I should change and go," she said.

"Wait. I know what would look fantastic on you," he said.

Ducking out of the dressing room, he brought back a corset. It was black matte PVC with boning, a metal back zipper, and an adjustable front lace-up with a matching miniskirt. Her nipples seemed to salute as gooseflesh broke out on her skin.

"I can't try that on," she said.

"Why not?"

"It's too sexy for someone like me," she said.

"Bullshit. I'm not leaving until you try it on."

Judging by his expression, he meant it.

"At least turn around," she said.

Closing the dressing-room door, she made him face the wall before she tried it on. She always thought this stuff would go on smoothly because it was rubber, but she had to be sweating bullets. Then she couldn't get the corset zipped up.

"Can you help me?" she asked.

He turned around and zipped her up. She knew the corset would be tight and nowhere near what a true lace-up would feel like, but still she felt a little flutter inside from being compressed, and she had to admit that, even for her, it gave her great cleavage.

His fingers were lingering on her shoulders far longer than the assistance of a zip-up dictated. Unbelievably, he started massaging her neck. At first, she wanted to tell him to get the fuck off her, but it felt so amazing. This guy really knew what he was going. All these knots of tension from The Smoothie King were melting.

"You have a lovely back," he said.

She stiffened. He was trying to sell her something. A visit to the Spine-O-Matic kiosk. How could she be so stupid?

He leaned in close to her and breathed in her ear. It was so intimate. Would a Spine-O-Matic salesman get this close to her ear?

"I can't believe how unbelievably hot you look in this," he said.

"I do?"

"You probably don't have any idea what you're doing to me right now."

She wanted to know. A boner meant he meant it. Lack of boner meant a sales pitch. She took a step backward against him and felt him against her. He was rock hard.

She exhaled, that brazen feeling coming back over her. Taking his hands, she guided them over her corset and skirt, taking pleasure in her own body and sharing that pleasure with him because she knew she was his fetish object as well.

"I know we don't know each other at all, but I really want to fuck you," he said. "In this. Right now."

Hesitating, she looked up from his hands around her waist to his eyes in the mirror. She'd never had impulsive sex with a stranger before. Would she even be considering it if she didn't have on the PVC? On the other hand, was it him? If Nick had flirted with her because he wanted her instead of a commission, would he be in here with her now?

Something deep inside her stomach told her it was Kyle. Without his geeky clothes on, he was incredibly sexy and he had this energy about him that was so damn attractive. Thinking about having sex with him was crazy and impulsive, but Kyle knew what she wanted, and he wanted her right back. Sure he could be a guy trying to get his rocks off in a dressing room at a mall, but she'd never felt like this from someone just touching her. She never wanted someone so badly in her life.

Trying to lock the door was her answer, but the stupid thing wouldn't latch. His hands started yanking up her skirt from behind, the PVC grazing her skin. She let him, frozen against the wall, her underwear being yanked to the floor, her bare ass exposed, the PVC being gloriously bunched up in front by her crotch.

Her fingers buried deep inside it, searching out her clit, when he entered her from behind. Opening her legs more and angling her butt up and out slightly, she felt him go in deeper. God he was huge. Did he have on a rubber? She caught a glimpse of a wrapper on the floor, called herself an idiot for not saying something first, but the thought was knocked out of her as he started fucking her.

So overcome at being so thoroughly fucked, she felt like a rag doll, bending to his will. He stretched her arms overhead as if she was in a line-up and ran his hands up and down her corset as he pounded into her.

Pulling her off the wall, he bent her over as if she was touching her toes. The corset cut into her stomach. She felt like she couldn't breathe, but this was different. This was good. He was hitting so deep inside her. This feeling was bubbling up inside her. It felt so good she was going to laugh.

Turning her head, she caught a glimpse of herself in the mirror. At first, she was so startled by what she saw she nearly stumbled. Could this be her? She looked like she was something out of a hot rubber porn mag. This hot slut in the PVC being fucked by this amazing guy who was staring at her ass like it was the last chocolate pudding sundae on the earth was her.

Suddenly, someone knocked on the dressing-room door. She saw the handle turning and grabbed it.

"Go away," she cried out.

"What's going on in there?" Nick demanded.

The door jerked open a sliver. She yanked it back. Kyle slid his hand around to her clit. She buckled with the shock.

"Go away," she shouted.

Nick yanked at the door again. She slammed it shut.

Jerking at the door handle like a serial killer was coming after him, Nick went ballistic. Suddenly, Kyle whipped open the door. Nick's face froze in horror at what he saw.

"Stop banging the door," he yelled and slammed it shut.

It worked. They heard him retreat. Turning her around and pressing her up against the wall, Kyle hiked up her leg and entered her from the front, kissing her as deeply as he was penetrating her. She felt so filled-up inside. The laughter was gone. Her whole body chilled, and she felt like she was being turned inside out. Her breath was so forced and frenzied as her hips gyrated against him. She was completely undone. A cry escaped her as she came.

As he climaxed a second later, he looked in her eyes. It was so intense and intimate. She started crying because no one had ever done that before.

The moment she broke apart from him, she wiped away her tears and realized she heard voices outside the dressing room. There were male voices other than Nick's. The voices sounded like security guards and employers. Peeling off the PVC corset, she felt a huge rush of air fill her lungs. It felt like she was taking off her own skin. Feeling oddly unsettled, she put her work clothes back on as Kyle changed back into his white shirt and loud print tie.

In the mirror, she saw Smoothie Girl with a very flushed face, or probably soon-to-be-fired Smoothie Girl. Panic flooded her, not at the thought of losing her job, but at her image in the mirror. She was back to being boring self-conscious Christie, or was she? Meeting Kyle's gaze in the mirror, she realized he knew differently and so did she.

She opened the dressing-room door.

Twentieth Century

BY LISABET SARAI

I don't belong here. The thought crossed Beth's mind as she stood in the chill November dusk, gazing into the shop window. Warm light glinted off the glittering treasures from another age and reflected in her face. The jewels were mostly fake, colored glass and rhinestones. Still, their whispers of the past drew Beth like magnets, made her heart beat a little faster, her eyes shine.

The awning offered some protection from the sleet that was the weather's latest unpleasant phase, but the slush had already seeped under the soles of her boots. At home there would be snow, pure glistening white blanketing the fields as far as the horizon. Here the days were dank and soot-gray, the dampness streaking the old buildings like tears.

A dark figure bundled in wool pushed past her, nearly impaling her with his umbrella. He didn't stop to apologize. She heard the shrill cry of his cell phone as he hurried off down the sidewalk and sighed.

A different place. A different time. Her novel, the one she had come here to write, was set in medieval Provence. Perhaps she should have gone to France instead, but Greenwich Village was quite far enough away from home.

Her English teacher had raved about New York, told her that anyone serious about becoming an author just had to be there. He had kindled her imagination with his tales of Art Deco towers and stately brownstone mansions. A far cry from her dingy one-room apartment, with its cracked washbasin and stained ceiling.

Beth turned her attention back to the window. She passed this little shop on Morton Street every day on her way home from the cafe. "Twentieth Century" read the awning. "Vintage and costume jewelry." The store itself was tucked away below street bevel in a time-worn nineteenth-century townhouse. She had never been inside, but she often paused to admire the arrangements behind the plate glass.

The displays changed every week. Whoever was responsible for them had an exquisite sense of taste. In someone else's hands, the merchandise, miscellaneous in the extreme, might have looked like a collection of junk. Instead, each window arrangement was a work of art. Beads, broaches, bracelets, jewel-encrusted hatpins and earrings dripping with pearls, heavy plastic bangles from the fifties and delicate Edwardian filigree, all mingled harmoniously, arrayed on crumpled velvet or spread against a backdrop of chiffon.

To offset the jewels, the designer might add a hat, a satin cloche or fur pillbox or wide-brimmed felt with an ostrich feather. There might be a pair of elbow-length kid gloves, carelessly draped over a beaded evening bag, as if in preparation for an evening on the town. Or a silver brush and hand mirror, the tarnished monogram unreadable but suggesting long-vanished luxury.

Each window arrangement used a different range of colors. Last week, Beth remembered, roses and purples had dominated, amethyst and garnet and perhaps even some rubies. This week the display was in shades of green, from citrine to emerald.

All at once Beth noticed the necklace. The chain flowed like liquid light over its black velour background. The rectangular pendant had a simple geometric design, brushed silver inlaid with some intricately patterned, green-veined stone. Inside her gloves, her palms tingled. She had an almost overwhelming urge to touch the lovely piece, to hold it in her hands.

It would make a perfect Christmas gift for Mom, she thought, making her way down the steps to the basement level. She knew that this did not explain her excitement. Her hand trembled a bit as she pulled open the heavy wooden door. A bell jingled, seemingly far away. She closed the door behind her, shutting out the wind and the damp.

Inside, it was dim, warm, very still. There was a faint, comforting odor: lavender, rose petals, old leather. Beth looked around her. The crowded, low-ceilinged room appeared to be empty.

A couple of sconces with etched-glass shades bit the interior of the shop. The golden light flickered on the cases lining the walls, shelf after shelf of outmoded finery.

Beth wandered from one display to the next, aching to touch the beauty locked inside them. Her cheeks were flushed; she shrugged off her bulky parka and laid it over the ladder-back of a chair piled with old fur pieces. Lost in admiration of a many-stranded choker of creamy pearl, she didn't realize that she was not alone.

"Lovely piece, isn't it?" The softness of the voice did not hide its intensity. Beth whirled around, startled. "It's from the fifties, a copy of a necklace worn by Bette Davis in *All About Eve*."

Beth found herself looking into a pair of pale blue eyes behind wire-framed spectacles. Something flickered briefly in those eyes, some passion incongruous with the narrow face, the thinning, sandy hair, the old-fashioned black suit and bow tie. She blushed, as though she had been caught gazing at something forbidden.

The man had a fleshy mouth, partly hidden under a dandified little moustache. He smiled at her, politeness masking the strangeness she had glimpsed in those sapphire eyes.

"I'm sorry, I didn't mean to startle you. That's one of my favorite items; I'm afraid I sometimes allow myself to get carried away."

"It's beautiful," Beth managed to say. "Actually, though, I was interested in the geometric pendant in the window."

"The malachite and silver? An Art Deco masterpiece. Fashioned some time in late 'teens, probably for the daughter of some baron of industry. Let me get it for you."

No, never mind, Beth wanted to tell him, I'm sure it's too expensive. Somehow she couldn't get the words out. Some odd nervousness gripped her. Her heart slammed against her ribs. She was hot and cold simultaneously, sweat trickling down between her breasts while chills ran up her spine.

She watched his slight figure as he reached into the window and retrieved the necklace. He could have been anywhere between forty and sixty. He moved with a kind of grace that men didn't seem to have anymore. She could imagine him waltzing, bowing from the waist, kissing a woman's hand. Her cheeks were burning, her earlobes swollen with blood. Perhaps she was coming down with a fever.

"Here you are, my dear." She extended her hand, open, and he draped the chain across her fingers. The pendant nestled in her palm, gleaming, perfect. A pang of longing shot through her.

"Would you like to try it on?" the shopkeeper asked softly. "I'm sure that it would suit you."

She met his eyes again for a moment, then looked away embarrassed. Her nod was almost imperceptible.

"Come with me into the back room. There's a mirror there, and more—privacy." When he took the necklace from her and led the way through dusty brocade curtains, she couldn't help but follow.

The back room was even more crowded than the front. There was an old chaise upholstered in blue velvet that had seen better days, an upright piano, a grandfather clock. Against the back wall was a full-length oval pier glass in a carved mahogany frame. Beth stared at her reflection, amazed at how flushed she looked. Her brown eyes were so dilated that she could hardly see the iris. A brief wave of dizziness took her. Must be the flu, she thought. I should get home.

The proprietor was standing behind her, watching her watch herself. Now he reached forward, positioning the chain around her neck. Just as he was about to fasten the clasp, he stopped.

"You know," he said, "your neck and shoulders should really be bare. To get the full effect. The girl for whom this was made would have been wearing spaghetti straps."

He took the necklace away, and Beth ached with loss. She was wearing a black turtleneck and black jeans, the neobohemian uniform of Moretti's Cafe where she spent her afternoons dispensing espresso and pastries. The jeweler's eyes locked with hers in the mirror. He smiled, encouraging her, a kind, cultured smile completely at odds with the danger she saw flickering in his eyes. He raised the necklace so that she could see it in the mirror, dangling it so that it caught the light. Tempting her.

Beth pulled her jersey up over her head and tossed it onto the chaise. She felt reckless and giddy. Beneath her shirt, she wore a plain white cotton bra.

The air stirred as the shopkeeper came closer, once again arranging the necklace at her throat. The silver was cool and heavy against her bare skin. His fingers were cool and delicate as he fastened the clasp behind her. Her body flared in response to the coolness, a heat that began between her thighs and traveled to her modestly hidden breasts. Her nipples tightened into rigid beads of aching flesh. She could see it happen, even through the cotton, and the shameless fact of it made her hotter still.

"Exquisite," the man murmured, close enough that his breath stirred the strands of hair that had strayed from her barrette. His hands hovered above her shoulders, tracing their shape without touching her. The silver chain gleamed against her paleness; the malachite winked like a green eye in the hollow of her throat.

"Too lovely for words." His palms drifted down along her bare arms, a fraction of an inch from her skin. Beth stood transfixed, holding her breath. If she moved, those long, graceful fingers might brush against her. Now he shaped his hands around her breasts, modeling their shape. She felt his presence, the ghost of a caress, in the pressure of the air, in some vibration of energy that seemed to flow from his fingers to her flesh across that brief gap.

She wanted more, wanted his skin on hers, wanted to experience the fire he hid behind those glasses. But he was very careful, and she did not dare make the first move herself.

This was so different from anything she had known. At the café, Carlos the cook flirted with her, patting her behind, letting his arm brush against her chest when they passed in the narrow kitchen doorway. He made her nervous and angry. When she objected, he just grinned at her, arrogantly assuming that she'd give in to him eventually. He even teased her about being a virgin.

Carlos had no grace, no finesse. He was a product of his time.

This man was a different story. Yes, that was it; Beth was sure that there were some rich tales this man could tell, stories of passion and tragedy and heartbreaking beauty.

All at once he took his hands away. Her form still vibrated with memories of his non-touch. Mortified, she realized that there was a damp stain visible in the crotch of her jeans. The shopkeeper, though, was still looking into her eyes.

"I believe that I have some earrings that match the necklace. Shall I go get them?" Beth did not move, hardly breathed, but he saw her answer in her eyes. He disappeared between the curtains. Beth was immobile. It was as if he had bound her there, enchanted, with some glamour compounded of nostalgia and desire.

I should be getting home, Beth thought shakily, just as the shopkeeper returned, holding two silver and green rectangles suspended on short silver chains. She wanted them immediately, wanted to reach for them, but his voice held her still.

"Allow me, my dear." Now his sensitive fingers were on her earlobe, the wire probing the hole there, a sliver of pain transformed into shimmering arousal as he slightly misjudged the angle. He was generally skillful, though. In a few moments, the earrings swung from her ears like sparks of green fire.

She looked gorgeous, glamorous, someone other than her everyday, practical Midwestern self. If I saw this woman, she thought, I would want her. Her nipples throbbed, painfully constrained by the fabric of her brassiere, and she realized that the mundane garment really spoiled the effect.

Almost as if he had read her thoughts, she felt the shopkeeper working at the hooks behind her back. "With your permission . . ." he murmured. But he did not wait for her agreement. In the space of a half-dozen heartbeats, her breasts were naked to her eyes, and to his.

He licked those full lips of his. She silently prayed for his hands again, for him to bring those elegant fingers closer to her flesh, even if he would not touch her. Instead, he stood there gazing at her, hands clenched into fists as though he was fighting with himself.

"Something is lacking, I think," he finally whispered. Rummaging in an armoire against one wall, he came up with a headband of beaded black satin. Gently, he slipped it onto Beth's forehead. He allowed himself to stroke her hair briefly, before pulling himself away.

A scarlet feather hovered rakishly above her brow. It changed her look from elegant to mischievously seductive. Beth suddenly felt brave. She turned to face him, her bare breasts swelling inches from his chest. "What do you think?" she asked. He was silent.

She raised her arms above her head, offering him her achingly hard nipples. Do you want me? she longed to say. Will you take me? But even now, she didn't dare.

He leaned toward her, and for a moment she thought he would give her what she desired. Instead, he brushed his lips against her cheek. They were as cool as his fingers. "I think that it's time for you to go home, miss. It's late, and I have to close the shop."

Crushed, Beth searched his eyes, trying to understand why he didn't want her. He wouldn't meet her gaze, though. He turned and handed her back her bra, then made his way back to the front of the store. Beth dressed slowly, aroused and confused, trying to understand what had happened.

When she emerged into the front room, all the lights but one were out. He was wearing a rusty black wool topcoat. He held the door for her, still the consummate gentleman, then locked up the shop behind them. "Have a good evening, miss," he murmured. Then he turned and strode off toward MacDougall Street, leaving Beth marooned on the sidewalk, aching and alone.

She stayed awake until four A.M. that night, writing. Her heroine, a nobleman's daughter who flees her home dressed as a boy in order to avoid being sent to a convent, seemed to have a mind of her own. When she finally slept, her dreams were laced with jazz, shimmering fringe, and pale bare skin.

For the ten days, she took a different route home, avoiding Morton Street. However, she thought about the shopkeeper constantly. Carlos kidded her about her distracted state, asking her if she had fallen in love. There was an edge in his voice, though, that made her wonder if he was jealous.

Thanksgiving came and went. Beth didn't have nearly enough money to go home for the holiday. I'll see the family at Christmas, she told herself. She realized that she had never asked the cost of the Art Deco pendant, then tried to put the thought out of her mind. More than I can afford, she assured herself. At least until my book is published and I'm rich and famous. That reminded her of Twentieth Century, too, the repository of the glories of other gilded ages. She dreamed of faceless men in black suits and white gloves. She dreamed she waltzed at a grand ball, naked but for the diamonds at her throat, in her ears, bound into her hair.

Finally, she could stand it no longer. On a Tuesday night, she headed down the slippery sidewalk toward Morton Street. It had snowed that afternoon, a dusting that was already hardening into gray, gritty ice.

The window was blue: sapphire and lapis, aquamarine glass and powder-blue porcelain. A Wedgwood cameo and matching earrings held the center of the display, replicas, most likely, of Victorian pieces. Beth caught her breath at the sight. Yes, she thought, those will do nicely. Her heart pounding, she pulled open the door and stepped into the dim, welcoming interior.

The proprietor appeared almost immediately, summoned by the bell. His eyes flickered with recognition, but he spoke formally, pretending not to know her. "Good afternoon, miss," he said. His low, nuanced voice sent a delicious chill through her body. "How can I help you?"

Beth smiled at him, trying to be encouraging. "In the window. There's a lovely cameo set. Necklace and earrings."

"Ah yes." He smiled back, unable to disguise his enthusiasm. "Turn of the century. Last century," he added with a little laugh. "A wonderful find. It would suit you perfectly."

"May I try them on?" Beth asked. She could scarcely breathe from nervousness. A part of her was aghast at her audacity. Without waiting for answer, she sauntered toward the curtained archway.

The shopkeeper's expression was impossible to read. He nodded. "I'll bring them in."

Alone in the back room, Beth stripped out of her black skirt and blouse, panties and bra. Wearing only her boots, she stood facing the mirror, watching the reflection of the draped doorway behind her.

He made her wait. Or perhaps he was reluctant to take up her challenge. The sound of her own heart drowned out any noise she might have heard from the front of the shop. As the minutes passed, her confidence ebbed away. She gazed at her naked form, all gentle curves and creamy flesh, and wondered vaguely what she was doing here.

Her body knew, though. The swollen nubs tipping her breasts, the rapid pulse beating in her neck, the trace of dampness in the warm brown curls below her belly—the truth was obvious. Then there was the ache between her thighs, which she tried unsuccessfully to ignore. Desire and fear fought within her, the balance swinging from one to the other and back as the grandfather clock ticked off the seconds.

Finally, she saw the brocade curtains stir. The shopkeeper entered, the earrings cupped in one palm, the necklace in the other. His eyes flared when he caught sight of her, but the rest of his face remained bland and controlled as he came up beside her.

"Here you are, miss." He held out the jewels.

"Would you put them on for me, please?" Beth was shaking with excitement.

The man hesitated for several breaths. Then he nodded, an odd half-smile ghosting across his lips. "Of course, miss. It would be my pleasure." He handed her the cameo and its chain. "Hold this for me, if you would." Then he reached up to insert the first earring.

Without thinking, Beth closed her eyes. Once again she felt his delicate fingers on her earlobe. The bulb of flesh felt huge, taut, gorged with blood. His touch sent delicious chills down her spine to her sex, which was now more than just slightly damp. She kept her eyes shut as he addressed her other ear, overwhelmed by sensation, too embarrassed and aroused to meet his eyes.

"The necklace, if you please?" Beth ventured a glance at his face as she returned the pendant to him. He appeared composed, but glancing down at his trousers, she thought she detected signs that her state of deshabille was having some effect on him.

The jeweler circled behind her, draped the necklace around her neck and fastened it. Beth thought that he was especially careful not to touch her, and that thought drove her mad. She was almost ready to beg, to fall on her knees before him and offer—what? Anything. Whatever he might desire, if only he would lay those cool hands on her fevered flesh again.

"Look," he whispered in her ear. "See how lovely you are." And she was. The cameo nestled between her breasts, blue as the Madonna's robe. The matching silhouettes in her ears swayed as she turned her head from side to side to evaluate the effect. She looked aristocratic, refined, despite her nudity.

Beth turned her gaze from her own form to her companion's eyes, reflected in the glass. That blue fire was burning there, unrestrained. "It is unfortunate that I do not currently have a Victorian corset in stock," he murmured. "That would be so appropriate with these jewels. However, I do have something else that you might appreciate." From a wooden chest in the corner, he extracted a folded piece of fabric, intricately patterned in jewel-like colors.

He unfurled it behind Beth's back. It was a triangular silk shawl bordered with long fringe. Complicated designs flowed across it, ruby, emerald, lapis, asymmetrical and compelling. "This is an original William Morris piece," he said softly as he let the silk settle over her shoulders. The edges draped down over her breasts, sheathing them in gorgeous swirls of color. Beth noticed that her erect nipples poked brazenly through the shawl. She was suddenly dizzy as a wave of desire swept through her.

His hands hovered above her shoulders again, as if he would smooth the silk over her body, but he did not move. "Do you like it?" he asked softly. There was another, more intimate question in his eyes.

Beth was silent. She reached up, grasped his hands, and brought them down to cup her silk-swathed fullness. She expected him to pull away, and so she held him there as she held his eyes in the mirror, bold and shy at once.

He did not resist her, though. Instead he squeezed her breasts, kneaded them gently, rolled the swollen tips between his slender fingers until Beth moaned aloud. The silk slithered over her skin, teasing and sensual.

She closed her eyes again and leaned against him, letting the wonderful sensations wash over her. Slight as he was, he had no trouble supporting her weight. She felt the rough wool of his trousers against her buttocks, and sensed the hardness beneath.

Fear stabbed briefly through her. She knew so little of men. Would it be painful? Would she disappoint him? Then her doubts dissolved into new moans as he slid his arms around her waist and brushed his fingertips across her pubic fur.

The lightest of pressures, the briefest of touches, but it sent tremors through her sex. Instinctively, Beth parted her legs and rocked her pelvis forward, seeking more solid contact. The shopkeeper obliged, slipping one slender finger into the mass of moist curls to her center. Sparks leapt from that finger, raced through her leaving her weak and breathless.

"Please . . ." she tried to say, not really knowing what she was asking for but wanting it more than anything. She had no voice, though, no will. She could barely stand.

The proprietor smiled at her reflection, kind, encouraging. "Come here, my dear." He led her to the velvet chaise. "Lie back. Relax."

Beth's mind flailed wildly, even as her body obeyed the man's suggestions. She searched his mild, middle-aged face, seeking reassurance. In response, he knelt in front of her, gently but firmly pushing her thighs apart. Then he removed his glasses, and his eyes were unveiled. Beth thought of the ocean, of the sky, then of a gas flame, azure bright, almost transparent. And then of a star sapphire, ever-changing light sparkling in blue depths.

Then he bent his mouth to her sex, and Beth forgot to think.

Sensation and emotion, velvet wetness and diamond sharpness, his tongue a feather and a sword. She writhed and shook, keening like a madwoman. The shawl slipped from her. The velour upholstery grew damp beneath her. Beth did not notice. He licked, nibbled, probed her depths, breathed her, drank her, buried himself in her, swallowed her whole. She did not know what he did, only that it brought near-unbearable ecstasy. The world shattered and fell away as pleasure drowned her.

When she floated back to consciousness, she was lying on the chaise, the gorgeous silk draped over her. The shopkeeper perched on a chair beside her. The fire in his eyes was banked. Instead, Beth read concern in his expression, and some kind of sadness.

"I should not have done that," he said softly. "But I could not resist."

Beth reached for his hand. It lay coldly in her own. "No, that was right. That was good. It was what I wanted. Thank you." She was about to bring it to her lips, but he shook his head.

"No, I took advantage. I'm not the one for you."

"But you want me," Beth said. She glanced down at the telltale bulge in his lap. She had a wild desire to touch it, but he seemed so skittish now that she didn't dare.

"Of course I want you. But I can't have you."

"Why not?" Beth asked. "Are you married?"

There was a trace of bitterness in his laugh. "No, I never did manage to marry."

"Well then. There's nothing to come between us."

"If you only knew . . ." A distant look crossed the man's face, and his strange eyes sparked again, briefly. "You remind me so much of her. The one who should have been my wife."

Beth sat silent, full of excitement. She knew that he had stories to tell. He did not continue, however.

"What happened to her?" Beth asked finally. Still he was silent, lost in some reverie.

Finally he spoke. "Would you like to see her picture?" Without waiting for Beth's nod, he made his way through the arch. In a moment he returned, with a miniature in an intricate silver frame. He handed it to Beth. "This is Lucy Foster, my betrothed."

Beth examined the painted likeness. The resemblance was indeed uncanny. Lucy had the same deep brown eyes, the same slightly up-turned nose, the same dimple. Her hair was cropped into a shoulder-length bob, while Beth wore hers long, usually pinned back or piled atop her head, but the chestnut color was identical. Beth looked at the portrait for a long time before giving it back to the jeweler.

"Astonishing," she said. She was desperate to know what had become of this woman who was practically her twin. It was clear, though, that her companion did not want to speak further on the subject.

"You should go now," he said, offering Beth her discarded clothing. "It's late."

"I'd rather stay," Beth murmured, but he shook his head.

"That's just not possible, my dear."

"May I come tomorrow?" she asked. Suddenly playful, she grabbed a mink boa from the coatrack in the corner and twisted it around her neck. "I could wear this. And perhaps I could try on that rhinestone tiara in the window . . . ?"

The shopkeeper smiled despite himself. "Perhaps."

Beth came close to him, then, and brushed her lips against his. He did not resist, but he did not kiss her back either. The hint of ocean flavor on his mouth made her heart beat suddenly faster. Deliberately, she laid her hand over the bulk of his erection. The lust in his eyes mingled with pain.

"And perhaps," she whispered, "perhaps you'll make me a woman?"

"You are already a woman, my dear. A delicious, desirable woman. Now get dressed, please, and go home."

They did not speak again until she stood beside him in dusk, watching him lock the shop. "Till tomorrow," she said.

"Tomorrow," he nodded. "Farewell until then."

Beth slept deep and dreamlessly that night. The next day was slow, delicious torture. She would be waiting on a customer and suddenly remember—his eyes, his hands, his mouth. She was in a state of constant arousal, her panties damp and bunched between her thighs, her nipples hard and sensitive under her jersey.

Everyone she met seemed to be aroused, too. She would lock eyes for a moment with a customer in the café, and feel that he was undressing her in his mind. Somehow, this did not bother her. Carlos caught her in the corridor that led to the unisex bathroom, daydreaming and idly strumming her thumb over her nipple. He pulled her to him and kissed her deeply. Beth allowed him to continue, opened her mouth and returned the kiss. She needed the stimulation, to keep her from exploding. To help her survive until that evening.

Promptly at five *p.m.*, she fled the café, racing down the few blocks to Morton Street. Her pulse and her sex were pounding in time. Turning the corner, she looked ahead for the glow lighting the shop window. Strangely, the street was dark.

She stopped in front of the townhouse that housed Twentieth Century, confused. The awning was gone. The window was covered from the inside with newsprint, and sealed outside with a can-tilevered steel security gate. The stairwell leading down to the door was littered with soda cans and other trash.

Beth pushed her way through the refuse and tried the door. It was locked. She knocked, then pounded on its wooden surface. No one answered. More and more desperate, she considered breaking the glass in order to get inside. She searched the sidewalk for a rock or a brick, something that she could use as a tool but found nothing except a withered tree branch that cracked in her hand when she swung it.

Tears streamed down her face. "Please," she pleaded, knowing that there was no one to hear. "Please, let me in . . ." She leaned against the door, clutching herself, rocking back and forth and sobbing.

A passing policeman noticed her. "Are you alright, miss?"

Beth looked up, startled. The young man had startling blue eyes, so similar . . . She fought down her sobs. "Yes, I'm fine, thank you. I recently lost someone I love, but I'll be okay."

"Do you want me to take you home?"

"No, thank you, I'll be fine, it's just a few blocks away."

"Alright, if you're sure. Good evening, then. And Merry Christmas."

"The same to you, officer."

Christmas? As she trudged back to her apartment, Beth realized that the holiday was only a week away. She planned to take the bus home to see her family. Now she wasn't sure that she really wanted to leave New York. Something held her here, even though it appeared that her lover was gone.

Her studio apartment was strangely welcoming, a sanctuary of privacy and silence. Beth shrugged off her coat and threw herself on the bed. She was going to cry again. At the same time, her body was strangely alive, still burning with desire and anticipation. "He's gone," she whispered to herself. "Gone."

She drifted into uneasy sleep, only to waken at the sound of a knock on her door. Startled, she tiptoed over and peered through the peephole. There did not appear to be anyone there. Puzzled, she unlocked it and opened it cautiously, leaving on the chain.

The hallway was empty. There was something on the threshold, though, a silver-colored box tied with a purple ribbon. Her heart slammed against her ribs as she picked it up and brought it inside. The label on the box read "Twentieth Century."

She was a bit afraid to open it. When she did, she gasped in astonishment.

The box contained three items:

The miniature portrait of her doppelganger, Lucy.

A yellowed clipping from the 1912 *New York Times,* listing the casualties of the *Titanic* disaster. She knew even before she looked that the name Lucinda Foster would be among them.

The lapis and silver Art Deco pendant.

Beth raced back to the door and flung it open, ran down three flights of stairs to the street, and frantically gazed up and down the quiet block. No one was there. Somehow, that was what she expected.

A calm descended on her heart, quieting her fever. She stood on the sidewalk, shivering without her coat, looking around her as if seeing the place for the first time.

Thoughtfully, she returned to her room. She took the necklace from the box and strung it around her neck. Then she pulled out her laptop and began writing. Before long, she was lost among the woods and towns of ancient France.

Sometime around two A.M. she looked up from her work to find that it was snowing, luxurious fluffy flakes that looked, finally, as though they would stick.

Skirting Pleasure

BY SAGE VIVANT

She shifted in her seat, suddenly apprehensive about getting up. She'd never gone without panties for so long and now understood why. The flimsy gauze of her skirt clung insistently to her exposed labia. Since they'd left Wisconsin, the skirt behaved like a sponge dedicated to absorbing her most intimate emissions. She tried to sit with her pussy tucked neatly between her cheeks to keep it from touching the thirsty fabric.

Not only did she have to avoid sweating but she had to turn off her libido. Try as she might, however, she was unable to resist her urges whenever Nick leaned in close, took her hand, or slipped an arm around her waist. Her body would flush and she would feel the familiar warmth rush to her private parts.

And so, throughout the day, as the couple made their way from Wisconsin to Jamaica, she'd become fairly skilled at diverting her attention from the carnal to the cerebral (or at least the mundane). She couldn't possibly bear the thought of walking around with a telltale wet spot on the back of her skirt.

The irony of the situation would be funny if it weren't so pathetic. She'd gone without panties to excite Nick and now her own arousal threatened to ruin her plans. She fidgeted again and, to take her mind off her growing wetness, tried to think about the mistakes the caterer had made at the wedding.

"What's the matter with you?" He looked askance at her from his seat to her right. "You've been acting like there's a thumbtack on your seat," he joked.

She sighed and leaned her head against the back of her seat. "Not quite but it's nearly that ridiculous," she admitted, closing her eyes in surrender.

He caressed her thigh lightly. "What is it?"

"I'm not wearing panties," she said softly, angling her body towards him so he'd hear her.

His eyes sparkled. "And that's a problem?" He leaned toward her now.

"When your skirt develops an unnatural attachment to your crotch, it is."

"Well, who *wouldn't* be fond of your crotch?"

"Nick," she chided, laughing in spite of herself. "It's a problem because I have to stay dry, if you know what I mean."

"Hmmm, how interesting. You want me, a man with a vested interest in keeping you lubricated, to help you stay dry. Is that correct?"

"Yes, please."

"I see. But first I have a question. Why aren't you wearing panties?"

Her eyebrows came together as she said, "To turn you on."

He grinned in that magically lopsided way she adored. "You succeeded. I can now think only of your unprotected cunt."

"You're not helping me, honey."

"So, knowing that I could tap the flight attendant on the shoulder with my dick right now is making you wet?"

"Stop it!" She giggled, cradling her forehead in her hand.

He surveyed the aisle fore and aft before he whispered into her
ear. "Put your tray table down."

Her eyes never left his as she released the latch of her table. "Like
that?"

"Exactly like that." His hand dug under the billowy skirt folds
alongside her legs until it made contact with her skin. As he inched
up her thigh, she caught her breath. The tray blocked her access to
his hand, which would have been an issue only if she'd wanted to
stop him.

"What if that guy turns around and sees us?" She nodded toward
the middle-aged man with a newspaper one row in front of them,
across the aisle.

"He'll probably stop reading his newspaper."

The hand crept closer to her throbbing bush. She longed to part
her thighs to welcome him but the seat was too narrow.

His fingertips brushed the boundaries of her furry vortex as his
breath warmed her neck. Her pussy lips swelled with the anticipation
of his touch.

The plane jolted enough to bounce his hand into her mound
then up into the tray table. Seconds later, the pilot's voice announced
turbulence ahead and the need for seat-belts. An efficient and in-
quiring flight attendant approached, checking passenger laps.

Rosalie slammed the tray table up as Nick whisked his hand out from under its steamy hideaway. Mortified, she caught a whiff of her own arousal, just as the attendant smiled vacuously at their row.

"Seat belts . . . seat belts . . ."

She barely heard the words over her reckless pulse.

"Damn," Nick cursed after the attendant had passed.

"This was such a bad idea," she lamented. "What was I thinking?"

He took her hand. "It was a great idea. See how hard you've made me?" He pressed her fingers to his bulging crotch. She imagined unzipping his jeans and sliding his hardness past her lips and down her throat. She squeezed her thighs together to erase the image, but he moved her hand over his restrained erection, stroking it slowly.

"If I'm going to be this hard, it's only right that you cream into your skirt," he said huskily.

His mouth touched hers tenderly but with the focused intent she'd come to recognize as can't-turn-back-now horniness. Her pussy ached for his fingers, his cock, his tongue—any part that might fit inside her.

As their tongues wrestled sensuously, he delicately encircled her breast with one hand and squeezed more than a little. Her juices spread over her engorged lips and seeped out toward the soft, white flesh of her inner thighs. Something about his touch always made her feel naked and liquid. Her nipple rose to push at his palm through her bra.

"Ladies and gentlemen, we are now beginning our approach into Montego Bay airport. Please be sure your seat belts are fastened and that your tray tables and seat backs are in their upright and locked position. We should be on the ground in approximately ten minutes."

The couple pulled apart, defeated yet again by the flight crew. They looked at each other and chuckled as the flight attendant trolled one final time. Rosalie and Nick busied themselves with the pilot's instructions so as to avoid eye contact with the attendant.

The skirt was surely drenched by now, Rosalie worried. It clung to the cleavage of her buttocks, tickling her as if to remind her that she'd lost the battle between pussy and fabric.

"Promise you'll stand behind me all the time so nobody will see the back of my skirt," she pleaded furtively to her new husband.

"Nobody'll notice a little wet stain."

"Promise me!" she insisted.

His expression changed as he understood her desperation. "Okay, babe. I'll keep the world from discovering your pussy actually does get wet." He kissed her forehead. "But how will I hide my woody?"

She smiled in relief. Holding his hand as the plane descended, she beamed inwardly. Her little seduction plan had worked, after all.

He trailed behind her dutifully from the plane to baggage claim. As he watched her full ass cheeks sway under her skirt as she walked, his pants got tight. She had no idea how much the sight of her voluptuous ass increased his blood flow. No matter what she wore, he pictured her naked, ripe, and juicy. He didn't stifle his smile when he noticed the saucer-sized wet spot precisely where she'd feared it.

"Can you see anything?" she muttered as they waited for their bags.

"It's tiny. I only saw it because I was looking for it," he assured her, wondering if she was still oozing juice.

The bustle of the airport relegated her stain and his erection to inconsequential concerns. Soon, they jostled with other tourists to determine the best route to their destination. Miss Ruby's in Treasure Island was their goal and Miss Ruby had advised them to take the number 17 bus. Nick found a bus schedule posted outside and the couple then waited with a stoic-looking Jamaican woman in her thirties for their 17 bus.

The heat permeated everything with an intense haze, as invisible as it was palpable. Humid restlessness settled into Nick immediately.

"Do you feel that?" he asked Rosalie.

"Feel what?"

"Something in the air. Something, I don't know, primal."

"Maybe you're just still horny," she teased, blushing and smiling simultaneously.

The rickety bus, long ago deferring any scheduled maintenance, barreled toward the stop, braking too late. The standing passengers, of which there were many, jolted forward and back without complaint. More than half the bus exited, balancing bags, knapsacks, and babies with cheerful dexterity.

The newlyweds clambered aboard after the native woman. Two seats remained, despite the ten or twelve standing passengers. Nick and Rosalie settled in, ready for adventure, at the rear of the bus.

The native woman stood nearby, never losing her quiet elegance, even when she politely declined Nick's offer of his seat. Diagonally behind her stood a Jamaican man roughly her age, engrossed in a folded newspaper.

All the windows were open, giving the bus all the ambience of a cattle car. Though the ride was somewhat smoother than Nick anticipated when the contraption had first pulled up, the bumpy Jamaican road and defunct shock absorbers kept things rattling. Rosalie stared out the window with a wide-eyed excitement. Nick watched as the Jamaican man with the newspaper squeezed the quiet woman's shapely butt cheek. Nick prepared himself for her outrage.

She didn't flinch. As she continued most serenely to take in the passing scenery, the man bunched her loose skirt slowly into his palm until he could slip his hand under it. Once he'd gained access, he let the fabric cascade over his wrist, his hand now hidden beneath her skirt.

Nick watched the woman's eyes close as her breathing changed. She remained immobile. He nudged Rosalie and nodded surreptitiously toward the couple. Rosalie's jaw dropped and she stared back at her husband incredulously.

No one seemed to notice the man's brazen exploration of this woman's snatch. Nobody seemed to care that he was fondling her wet folds, probably burrowing into them with experienced, agile fingers. In his mind, Nick became the man, pleasuring the surprised but juicy cunt, imagining the cunt to be Rosalie's, yielding to him in silent, slippery assent.

The bus screeched to a halt, dislodging some stored bags as well as the man's hand.

"Treasure Island!" announced the driver.

Nick scrambled to his feet, angry with himself for not paying attention to the previous stops in order to prepare for this one. Rosalie followed him, helping with the luggage.

As the bus pulled away, Nick wiped the start of perspiration from his brow. "That may just be the most incredible thing we see on this trip," he said.

"She didn't even move! Do you think that goes on all the time here?"

"I don't know but I can tell you that you won't be riding any buses here without me!"

They turned to see Miss Ruby's place just a few yards away. A dark, middle-aged, rotund woman with gleaming white teeth stood on the porch, smiling as she waved them over. The couple returned the greeting and headed toward the large, rambling house-turned-hotel.

"Welcome!" she boomed. As she ambled toward them, her enormous, unfettered breasts swayed in unison. "I am Miss Ruby and this is my house. You must be Nick and Rosalie, yes?" She extended a hand to Nick, who took it warmly, already enchanted with her eccentric, exotic demeanor—and her remarkable breasts.

"I know you are honeymooners so I won't waste no time showin' you to your room!" She laughed, leading them to the tiny reception area, which was an alcove just inside the front door. "Sign in and I'll take you where you want to go!" She laughed again.

As Nick signed in for himself and his wife, Miss Ruby instructed a young man she called Bobba to deliver the couple's bags to their room.

"You two just follow Bobba and we'll see you again when you're ready to come down. You hurry now, Bobba," she added kindly to the young man.

When they were halfway up the stairs, Miss Ruby called after them. "Chile, I can get that stain outta your pretty skirt if you just bring it by later!"

Bobba, quiet, strong, and pleasant, smiled broadly when Nick put a few coins in his hand. He exited quickly.

Rosalie immediately unlocked and opened her suitcase, searching wildly for the shorts she knew she packed. After extracting them from the neat assortment of clothing, she pulled down her skirt, letting it drop to the floor.

"What, no foreplay?" Nick teased, admiring her dark triangle as she donned her shorts.

She felt herself blush. "No, silly, I'm bringing Miss Ruby my skirt right now so she can take care of my little problem." With that, she headed down the stairs.

At the foot of the staircase, she stopped, suspended by the vision that greeted her. On the sofa in the living room, across from the reception alcove, sat Miss Ruby, abundant legs spread wide. The hem of her blouse had been stuffed into her underarms, exposing her formidable breasts. Kneeling between her legs with his head buried in her pussy was the compliant Bobba. He ate quietly as his hands kneaded the meaty titflesh of his employer. Miss Ruby's eyes were shut in mindful oblivion and she groaned periodically. Her skirt had been pushed up to her hips.

As Rosalie stood, mute and transfixed, a hand slipped between her own legs and began to caress her. She gave a start but instantly realized it was Nick behind her, taking in the same scene. With his other hand, he played with her breast, emulating the rhythm and motion executed by Bobba on the big woman.

Rosalie's pussy pulsed with need as it creamed for the umpteenth time that day. Neither she nor Nick spoke, so as not to be discovered. She knew they were both torn between watching the servant pleasure Miss Ruby and running upstairs to pleasure each other. In minutes, the latter option won out.

Once in their room, Nick said, "I'm beginning to see why skirts are so common here in Jamaica." He practicably tore her shorts off her.

"Do you wish my breasts were as big as Miss Ruby's?" Rosalie asked, removing her top shamelessly.

"To me, your breasts are perfect," he said, bringing his face to a nipple. "I dream about dying with my head between them." He licked at one nipple while he tweaked the other.

She reached between her legs to touch herself, coating her fingers with juice. Her own touch was not enough. She needed his—had needed it all day.

"Play with me. I'm so wet for you," she whispered. Once his fingers found her clit, she came in seconds.

Nick never imagined he could fuck one woman so soundly, so repeatedly, and yet have his hunger for her grow rather than subside. He and Rosalie retreated to Miss Ruby's two, sometimes three times a day, never running out of positions or enthusiasm.

They'd spent most of their time at the beach, so the hotel helped cool them off a bit, too. By the fourth day, Rosalie suggested they do some sightseeing. "Let's go to Rose Hall Great House. It's supposed to be a beautiful old house."

"I'll go on one condition."

"What's that?"

"You wear a skirt."

"Nick! Nothing can happen on a tour of an old house! I'm sure we'll be with other people, anyway!"

He would not be dissuaded. He'd been on the island long enough to know that anything was possible.

The next morning, they agreed not to begin their day with a sexual romp—they wanted tensions high when they took their tour. Rosalie continued to dismiss his dubious plan but her lack of faith only furthered his resolve.

At Rose Hall Great House, about twenty people milled about the base of the steps. The view of the deep blue Caribbean helped soften some of the home's ominous mood, but still it exuded a presence strangely at odds with the tranquility of its setting.

A cheerful Jamaican woman appeared from a portal beneath the house and greeted the group of sleepy tourists. At 9:00 A.M., many were still recovering from their evenings. Nick, on the other hand, had never been more alert and eager.

"Hello, everyone!" The guide spoke in that lovely patois that made Nick think of reggae and bright colors. Most everyone in Jamaica talked as she did, but her voice was clearer and her diction better than most.

"Welcome to Rose Hall Great House. We will soon be touring about seventy-five percent of this old mansion and as we go, I will tell you about its mysterious legend." Her eyes widened for dramatic effect. Rosalie looked at Nick and grinned indulgently. He winked, thinking her dark hair gave her a particularly sexy aura today. Her tank top clung to her curves in blatant invitation, to which his cock prepared an urgent RSVP for immediate delivery.

The guide led the trudging group up the majestic stairs toward the main entrance. As she turned to face the visitors, a subtle breeze slithered by and she paused until it passed.

"Do you feel the restlessness here? Legend has it that the owner's sexual appetite was insatiable, so insatiable that she murdered three husbands as a result of it."

Predictably, her audience gasped. Rosalie raised an eyebrow at Nick who nodded smugly.

"A woman named Annie was taught voodoo by her Haitian governess. By the time Annie was a young woman and ready to marry, she'd set her sights on John Palmer, then owner of this house. Because she knew how to make men fall in love with her through voodoo, it wasn't long before she became Annie Palmer and moved into this house. Let's go in and I'll tell you more."

Nick and Rosalie straggled behind the crowd. In the grand foyer, a male and female uniformed attendant flanked the incoming group, smiling as they counted heads. The man accepted a piece of paper from the guide and the woman walked to a small desk to write something down. The guide then continued her story.

"Within three years of the marriage, Mr. Palmer was stricken with a sudden and unidentifiable illness that killed him. Mrs. Palmer didn't take kindly to widowhood or celibacy so she found herself a new husband quickly. I guess that's easy to do when you know a little voodoo, eh?"

As the tourists chuckled, Nick whispered to his wife. "See? The house *inspires* sex!" Though Rosalie rolled her eyes, she also blushed. Nick could tell by the color in her cheeks that her excitement was building. He could picture the start of glistening moisture under her skirt.

But why just picture it?

As he'd seen the man on the bus do to the beautiful, silent woman, he grabbed a handful of skirt and slowly stuffed his palm with increasing amounts of fabric until her derriere was nearly exposed. Alarmed and beet red, Rosalie did not move as he let go of the skirt and slipped his hand between her thighs.

Oh, yes. She was wet, all right. Her juices coated his fingers immediately and the heat between her legs coaxed him deeper.

They both stared straight ahead at the guide, who regaled the group with the fates of Mrs. Palmer's next two husbands. Both had been murdered but not before Annie the nympho had exhausted their sexual usefulness.

The guide led her charges into the dining room where heels clicked around the wooden floor. Nick and Rosalie continued to straggle behind. Nick's hand remained in his wife's slippery folds, swollen now with mounting desire. He stroked her as they walked and when they stopped at the table, he pushed a finger up inside her. He heard her breathing, heavy and erratic.

They moved to the deep rose-colored bedroom, him frigging her clit with each step. If he unzipped his shorts now, his cock would slap him in the face.

"After her third husband, Annie took many lovers among her slaves. But her abuses finally caught up with her on the day her slaves revolted and strangled her in her bed. Though the furnishings here are all replicas of the originals, this is indeed the room where Annie seduced her lovers and the room where she died. Some say she died while a slave made love to her."

"So, she died happy, then!" A tourist commented, pleased with his droll insight. The group laughed politely.

The guide led the visitors out of the bedroom. Nick kept his busy hand in motion, whipping Rosalie's cream to a froth. With his free hand, he held her arm to keep her in the room. When the crowd had moved on, he guided her toward the white-canopied bed, nudging her from behind until she crawled up on it with her full, beautiful ass in the air.

The scent and sight of those spread, shapely cheeks, the sheen of her succulent center—it was too much. He dove face first into her pussy, tonguing, lapping, sucking at her sweetness.

As he ate her, he diddled her now engorged clit. Her muffled shouts poured into the aging coverlet. Grasping a bedpost, she tried to steady herself.

Her orgasm was so strong that she ejaculated into his face. Her pussy lips spasmed and she pushed her ass toward him, unconsciously grinding her cunt against his nose and mouth.

When she'd finished, she turned over, legs sprawled, her luscious hair disheveled around her face. She raised her head only slightly to meet his gaze.

"Fuck me," she pleaded. The whole room smelled like her.

He was a step ahead of her, yanking off his shorts, aiming his thick, needy cock at her drenched opening. When he thrust himself into her, she yelled. He put a hand over her mouth to keep the tour from returning.

He pumped her wildly, desperately. Her pussy sucked him inside her, squeezing and massaging him. Each time he banged her, her tits absorbed the force and bobbed in response. He leaned forward to free her breasts from her top. Once they were unencumbered, he took hold of them with both hands as he continued to fuck her. She bit her lip to keep from calling out.

Holding her tits pushed him past the point of restraint. He let go into her belly and the release reverberated throughout his body. The way her pussy clutched at him, he knew she was coming again. The knowledge kept him pumping, obsessed now with never stopping.

Finally, she pushed him away. He fell gently on top of her, kissing her face and hair, running his hands along her rounded hips and breasts. He thought he'd wait until he shrunk to pull out of her, but when it became clear he would be hard for quite a while, she spoke up.

"I think we should go, don't you?"

"I suppose."

They moved quickly, smiling and giggling throughout until they noticed the male and female guards at the doorway.

The woman stood in font of the man, with her skirt hiked up high enough to display her bush, where her hand was buried and busy. Behind her, the man grabbed both her breasts.

"Are you finished now?" The woman asked, breathless.

"Yeah, sure," Nick stammered.

"We want to do what you did. You've brought the voodoo back to Rose Hall!" the man whispered reverently. His gratitude and awe were almost comical.

Nick and Rosalie let them in and then slid past them before sprinting out of the mansion, laughing uncontrollably.

Author Biographies

TARA ALTON'S erotica has appeared in *Best Women's Erotica, Guilty Pleasures, Clean Sheets,* and *Scarlet Letters.* She lives in the Midwest, collects tattoos, worships Bettie Page, and writes erotica because that's what's in her head and it needs to come out. Check out her web site at www.taraalton.com.

TULSA BROWN is an award-winning Canadian author, who donned a hat and dark glasses and snuck over genre lines in the middle of the night. His agent believes he's just at the beach. Shh.

M. CHRISTIAN is the author of the critically acclaimed and best-selling collections *Dirty Words, Speaking Parts,* and *The Bachelor Machine.* He is the editor of *The Burning Pen,* the *Best S/M Erotica* series, *The Mammoth Book of Future Cops,* and *The Mammoth Book of Tales of the Road* (with Maxim Jakubowski), as well as *Confessions, Ama-*

zons, and *Garden of Perverse* (with Sage Vivant), and 18 other anthologies. His short fiction has appeared in over 200 books and magazines including *Best American Erotica, Best Gay Erotica, Best Lesbian Erotica, Best Transgendered Erotica, Best Fetish Erotica, Best Bondage Erotica,* and . . . well, you get the idea. He lives in San Francisco and is only some of what that implies.

ELIZABETH COLDWELL is the editor of the U.K. edition of *Forum* magazine. Her short stories have appeared in anthologies published by Black Lace and Circlet Press, among others.

BRYN COLVIN dabbles in a variety of writing forms (short fiction, reviews, pub quizzes, novels, songs) and some online publishing. She has previously had work published in magazines both online and in paper form, including *The Scarlet Letters*—her first foray into the world of erotica.

KATE DOMINIC'S stories have appeared in dozens of anthologies and magazines under a variety of pen names. In her first solo collection, *Any 2 People, Kissing* (Down There Press, 2003), she slides up and down the Kinsey scale in male and female voices. She once again reminds her mother that erotica is not necessarily autobiographical.

O. Z. EVANGELINE writes erotica, humor, and experimental fiction. "I'm a film lover. Characters and celebrities often find their way into my work. I enjoy playing with pop culture. I like to have fun." She lives in California where she casts rain-making spells. Visit her online at www.ozevangeline.com.

DEBRA HYDE'S fiction appears in N. T. Morley's *MASTER/slave* anthologies and in the past featured selections, *Desires* and *Strange Bedfellows*. Check out *Erotic Travel Tales 2*, *Best of the Best Meat Erotica*, and *Ripe Fruit: Erotica for Well-Seasoned Lovers* for more of Debra's fiction and visit her at www.pursedlips.com. Personally, Debra prefers leather to lace. Totally naked flesh, however, trumps everything.

MOLLY LASTER is a well-rounded writer based in Canada. She divides her time between doing the type of writing she likes (erotica) and the type of writing that pays her bills (you don't want to know). Her short stories have also appeared in *Girls On the Go* and *Gone Is the Shame* (both published by Masquerade Books), and in *Naughty Stories from A to Z* (Pretty Things Press).

CHRISTINE MORGAN is the author of the *MageLore* and *ElfLore* fantasy trilogies, an upcoming series of horror novels, and various short works including the Origins Award-nominated *Dawn of the Living Impaired*. She lives in the Pacific Northwest and welcomes readers to visit her at www.christine-morgan.net.

TOM PICCIRILLI is the author of ten novels, including *The Night Class*, *A Choir of Ill Children*, *A Lower Deep*, *Hexes*, *The Deceased*, and *Grave Men*. He's published more than 120 stories in the mystery, horror, erotica, and science fiction fields. Tom's been a final nominee for the World Fantasy Award and he's the winner of the first Bram Stoker Award given in the category of Outstanding Achievement in Poetry. Learn more about him at his official website www.mikeoliveri.com/piccirilli.

Author Biographies

STACY REED has contributed essays to *Diverse Words, Whores and Other Feminists,* and *First Person Sexual.* Her erotica has appeared in magazines such as *Peacockblue, Mind Caviar,* and *Dare,* and in collections including *The Oy of Sex* and the *Herotica* series. Since 2000, she has written at Custom Erotica Source (www.customerotica source.com).

M. J. RENNIE is a Pacific Northwest writer of many sports and civics books for middle school students. Since 1999, he has been producing a series of romantic, sensual novellas, usually with a dynamic, assertive woman as the main character.

THOMAS ROCHE'S short stories have appeared in more than two hundred anthologies, magazines, and websites. His books include *Dark Matter; Noirotica 1, 2,* and *3; His;* and *Hers* (both cowritten with Alison Tyler).

JASON RUBIS lives in Washington, D.C. His fiction has appeared in *Leg Show, Variations,* and several anthologies, including *Desires, Guilty Pleasures, Sacred Exchange,* and *Fetish Fantastic.* He is the author of several fetish novels from Pink Flamingo Publications (www.pinkflamingo.com) and MTJ Publishing (www.mtjpub.com).

LISABET SARAI has published three erotic novels, *Raw Silk, Incognito,* and *Ruby's Rules,* and is coeditor of the anthology *Sacred Exchange,* which explores the spiritual aspects of BDSM relationships. Her stories appear in a variety of anthologies including *Erotic Travel Tales II* (Cleis) and *Wicked Words 8* (Black Lace).

D. D. SMITH is a writer, voice actress, and painter. Her stories and articles have been published in various on- and offline publications. She enjoys recording erotic audio, and nothing (absolutely nothing) shocks her. A former exotic dancer, she admits the experience allowed her the opportunity to explore and broaden her sexual perspective. She is a freelance writer because it gives her freedom to go beyond the black and white, and delve deeper into the shades of gray.

KAREN TAYLOR has been writing erotica on and off for the past decade. Her most recent work can be seen in *Best Transgender Erotica, Best Bisexual Erotica 2, The Academy: Tales of the Marketplace, Friday the Rabbi Wore Lace,* and *First Person Sexual.* She is currently collaborating with her spouse, author Laura Antoniou, on a short story collection entitled *Slaves of the Marketplace.* Her story here was previously published in Antoniou's *Leatherwomen III* (now out of print) under the pseudonym Vivian Vincent Sinclair.

SAGE VIVANT operates Custom Erotica Source (www.customerotica source.com), the online resource for tailor-made erotic fiction. With M. Christian, she has edited *The Best of Both Worlds, Confessions,* and *Amazons.* She is the author of *Giving the Bride Away,* due out in 2006. Her stories have appeared in numerous anthologies, including *Best Women's Erotica* and *The Mammoth Book of Best New Erotica.*

JAMES WILLIAMS is the author of . . . *But I Know What You Want,* published in 2003 by Greenery Press. He is widely published in erotic anthologies and magazines, including several editions of *Best American Erotica.* He can be found at http://www.jaswilliams.com.

Credits

KILLING THE MARABOU SLIPPERS by Molly Laster © 2002 by Molly Laster. First appeared in NAUGHTY STORIES FROM A TO Z. Used by permission of the author.

WHEN CALLS ED WOOD by Tom Piccirilli © 2003 by Tom Piccirilli. Used by permission of the author.

UNDERNEATH YOUR CLOTHES by Elizabeth Coldwell © 2003 by Elizabeth Coldwell. Used by permission of the author.

CRUISING WITH VICKIE AND MARGE by M. J. Rennie © 2003 by M. J. Rennie. Used by permission of the author.

A NOVEL OF MANNERS, SET VAGUELY IN THE HEIAN ERA by Jason Rubis © 2003 by Jason Rubis. Used by permission of the author.

I AM . . . by Christine Morgan © 2003 by Christine Morgan. Used by permission of the author.

CONTENTED CLIENTS by Kate Dominic © 2000 by Kate Dominic. First appeared in BEST WOMEN'S EROTICA 2001. Used by permission of the author.

A LITTLE BIT LIKE A SLUT by Thomas Roche © 2003 by Thomas Roche. Used by permission of the author.

NACHT RUCK by Karen Taylor © 1998 by Karen Taylor. First appeared in LEATHERWOMEN III under the pseudonym Vivian Vincent Sinclair. Used by permission of the author.

DRESS PINKS by M. Christian © 2001 by M. Christian. First appeared in UNIFORM SEX. Used by permission of the author.